# THE ST LOUIS MASSACRE!

'Ladies and gentlemen, we must clear the arena immediately! There is a bomb in the building!' There were, perhaps, two seconds of dead and dread silence. Then panic. People ran, shoved, tripped, fell, trampled, were trampled. The parking lots surrounding the building became chaos. Police attempts to direct an orderly flow of traffic were ignored. The exits became jammed and cars stuck in the snow. The bombs went off simultaneously at 8.30 p.m. . . . The still-falling snow was discoloured on the ground by steaming water, gasoline, oil, brake fluid, and blood. Some people fled back into the building, and offices were ransacked, trophy cases broken, and mementos destroyed or stolen. In dark corners of the building and the parking lot four women were raped. The riot raged on . . .

# The Money War

**TERRENCE LORE SMITH**

Research and Cartography by
David A. Doman

SPHERE BOOKS LIMITED
30/32 Gray's Inn Road, London WC1X 8JL

First published in Great Britain by Hamish Hamilton Ltd, 1979
Copyright © 1978 by Terrence Lore Smith
Published by Sphere Books Ltd, 1980

Lines from 'The sun shines down on the ships at sea' reprinted
from *The English Auden: Poems, Essays and Dramatic Writings*,
edited by Edward Mendelson, by permission of Faber & Faber Ltd

TRADE
MARK

Printed in Great Britain by
William Collins Sons & Co Ltd
Glasgow

War consists largely of acts that would be criminal if performed in time of peace—killing, wounding, kidnapping, destroying or carrying off other peoples' property. Such conduct is not regarded as criminal if it takes place in the course of war, because the state of war lays a blanket of immunity over the warriors.

TELFORD TAYLOR,
quoted in
*The Law of War*

The poet reciting to Lady Diana
While the footmen whisper 'Have a banana,'
The judge enforcing the obsolete law
The banker making the loan for the war,

The expert designing the long-range gun
To exterminate everyone under the sun,
Would like to get out but can only mutter;—
'What can I do? It's my bread and butter.'

W H. AUDEN
"On This Island"

# CONTENTS

PROLOGUE: **FIRST BLOOD**                    1

BOOK I: **THE MONEY WAR**                   15

BOOK II: **WAR CRIMINALS**                 157

BOOK III: **LAST CASUALTIES**              179

EPILOGUE: **PEACE**                        235

# INVASION

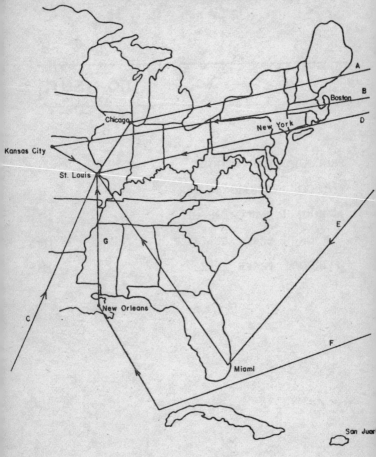

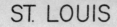

# ST. LOUIS

A. Donovan—London to Chicago* to
   St. Louis.
B. IWACs—Shannon to Boston* to
   Kansas City, via auto to St. Louis.
C. IWACs—Paris to Mexico City to
   Dallas* to St. Louis.
D. IWACs—Brussels to New York* to
   St. Louis.
E. IWACs—London to Miami* to
   St. Louis.
F. The Casablanca—Marseilles to
   New Orleans.
G. Armaments—New Orleans** to
   St. Louis via truck.

*Cleared Customs at designated city.
**Cleared Customs illegally at designated city

# PROLOGUE: **FIRST BLOOD**

Cry "Havoc!" and let slip the dogs of war!
*Shakespeare*, JULIUS CAESAR

From a hundred feet above, the surface of the Mississippi looked like choppy gray sludge. November air was hard, crisp. Sunday sun slanted off the Bell Ranger bubble as the helicopter fought a slight crosswind. Noah Peterson grinned at his passenger and jerked a thumb westward toward the city. Bucky Walters nodded. The blue and white Ranger began to climb slightly and banked left—west. The St. Louis Police Department helicopter was at nearly two hundred feet and still climbing as it sailed through Eero Saarinen's nine-hundred-sixty-foot golden Gateway Arch on a slightly northwest angle. It climbed over the Mansion House Center and hovered above Fourth Street and the downtown riverfront area of the river's queen city. Below was an odd-shaped, uneven-storied, Bedford stone and brick building which occupied an entire square block—the Federal Reserve Bank for the St. Louis District.

Noah was looking away to the south. He glanced over at his brother-in-law.

"What do you think, Bucky? Shall we buzz the football game?"

Bucky laughed. "You just want to rub it in because you think the Cards will beat the Skins again. Sure, one pass and then you better get me out to the airport."

The helicopter crossed to Broadway and slid south. Busch Memorial Stadium came up quickly. The St. Louis Cardinals were playing the Washington Redskins. Tiny figures in red and white and red and gold uniforms ran around the arsenical green field. As they hovered, one red and white figure detached itself from the pack and ran away. Another red and white figure in the middle of the pack threw a brown speck high into the air. The detached figure seemed to run under it, catch it. Red and gold figures chased it. A figure in a black and white striped shirt, holding its arms

3

aloft, followed the red and white figure off the end of the field. Noah laughed.

"Hart to Grey for six more big ones."

Bucky sighed, "I guess it's time we started singing 'Goodbye Jack' back in Washington."

"Again?" Noah turned the helicopter north toward Lambert Field.

"I think his number's probably up this time."

"That's what you said last year."

Crossing the city, the crosswind was not as strong and the Ranger moved smoothly. Noah loved flying. Although he was licensed for anything up to commercial and military jets, he was not supposed to fly the department's helicopter, and certainly not for private use. But he was a major and the third-ranking officer in the department, and it was very nearly the only perquisite he allowed himself.

Once inside the terminal, they walked toward the cocktail lounge. They had nearly an hour until Bucky's flight would be boarding. They looked something of a Mutt and Jeff team walking side by side. Bucky was six-four, one-ninety, rangy and had closely cut salt-and-pepper hair that made him look older than his forty-six years. Or perhaps it was the seams in his face or the tired lines around his green eyes. Noah was five-ten, one-sixty-five, lean but tightly knit with medium length blond hair and crystal-blue eyes in a clear, fair face. Perhaps it was his easygoing disposition that made him seem younger than his forty-three years.

Noah ordered Stingers for them and Bucky laughed; it was a joke of twenty-some years' standing, dating back to their days in Army Intelligence together. Noah shook his head ruefully.

"Poor old Rackly. Whatever happened to him?"

"He gave up drinking Stingers, for one thing." They laughed. "I'll never forget the look on his face when the Brigadier walked in." They laughed again. "Actually the Army cashiered him a few years ago. He never got higher than captain. He almost had apoplexy the day I made major.

4

And when I made light-colonel—well . . ." Bucky shrugged. The drinks came. They touched rims. "To the Baily girls. God bless them."

Noah nodded and sipped. "The best thing that ever happened to the likes of us. Speaking of which, Elizabeth gave me strict orders to bug you. You are to bring Margeret along the next trip. Liz would like to see her sister some time soon."

"I will. The very next time the 'Company' gives me some time off."

"Tsk-tsk, Colonel Walters, I shall have to report you to your superiors. Breaking cover like that." He gestured vaguely around at the dozen or so patrons of the bar. "Even laymen such as these might know that the 'Company' is the CIA. You're supposed to be a retired Army colonel."

"Lieutenant-Colonel. When you're a top executive like me, my boy, it doesn't much matter. The cover is strictly pro-forma. Half the intelligence services in the world have dossiers on me."

"That sounds like bragging."

Bucky grinned. "Would you believe a third of them? A fourth? Two or three? Actually, the cape-and-dirk stuff is highly overdone. Mostly it's boring paperwork." He glanced around the lounge. "I doubt if anyone in here—" He stopped and stared at a table in a far corner. There were three men at the table. They all wore cream-colored trench-coats and mirror-tint aviator sunglasses. One man was small, red-faced, fortyish; one was burly, red-bearded, fortyish; one was black, slender, mid-thirtyish. Bucky frowned as he picked up his drink and drained it.

Noah finished his and signaled the waitress to bring two more. "You know those men, Bucky?"

"I think so."

Noah shrugged. "Well, why don't we go over and see?"

Bucky's face was rigid. "No, we won't do that."

"Oh . . . you, uh, know them . . . in the way of business." Bucky nodded as the waitress set their drinks on the

5

table. They took tentative sips. Noah was puzzled. "Spies, Bucky? What would spies be doing in St. Louis?"

Bucky shook his head. "Not spies . . ." He was glancing out of the lounge and down a passenger walkway when his face froze again. This time all the color drained out of it. Noah followed his glance. Another man in a cream-colored trenchcoat and silver sunglasses was coming toward the lounge. This man was very tall, nearly as tall as Bucky. He was heavy-set and had graying black hair and a full beard and mustache, neatly trimmed. His skin was tanned, weathered deeply in a full, fleshy face, but he was not fat, not heavy-looking. It was the way he moved. Lightly, gracefully, very erect. He had the bearing of a man who demanded respect and was accustomed to receiving it. The brown leather safari-style bag seemed to weigh nothing in his large hand. Noah would never forget his first sight of Donovan. And what he would remember most clearly was the way the man carried himself.

Bucky buried his face in his drink as the man passed their table and crossed to the three men in the far corner. The other three stood to greet him, but they waited until he extended his hand before they offered theirs, and they waited until he was seated before they resumed theirs.

Bucky muttered, "What the fuck is he doing here?"

Noah frowned. "You know, Bucky, I wouldn't press you, but I *am* a member of the St. Louis Police Department. I have—I might have, what was the phrase . . . oh yes—a need to know." He lifted his brows quizzically.

Bucky smiled gently. "Major Peterson, I think I can assure you these men won't be a problem for you. I don't know what they're doing in St. Louis, or the United States for that matter, but I seriously doubt if it concerns you."

"They're not spies?"

"No. They're free-lance soldiers, mercenaries. The big man that just came in is Colonel Terrence Donovan, commander of the Irish West Africa Company, the best group of mercenaries in Africa in the last twenty years. The black

6

man was one of his captains. The burly man was his ranking non-com, I forget his name. I don't know the little red-faced man."

"Oh."

"That's right. Oh. I don't know what . . . no that's not right—maybe I do know. The last war they were in was the mess in Imbannailand. Donovan had some black Americans with him. I think a number of them were from St. Louis."

"So?"

Bucky shrugged. "Maybe he's here recruiting for another go-around in Africa. They took pretty heavy casualties at Simba Pass and then at Port Imbann when Ossungi double-crossed them. They had to fight their way out of the country. Didn't get paid either."

It was Noah's turn to shrug. "Recruiting mercenaries— well, that's out of my line. No law against it." He paid for their drinks and they began walking toward the gate for Bucky's flight.

Bucky was distracted as they walked. He muttered to himself and paused to think several times.

"I wonder . . . where he's going this time." Stride, stride, pause. "Angola again? . . . no, maybe Rhodesia . . . Zaire?"

Noah smiled bemusedly. He paid little attention to Bucky's ramblings. As soon as he had heard that the men were mercenaries, he had tuned out. That was Bucky's world, not his. He was just a cop.

The little red-faced man was Cpl. Patrick Joseph Hogan. He drove. As he always had, even in the IRA days. Terrence sat beside him. Sergeant-Major McGregor and Captain Jackson sat in back. The rental sedan moved easily through light traffic. In the weeks that he'd been in St. Louis, Hogan had learned the American driving patterns and the routes he needed to know. Still, he felt better now that Terrence had arrived.

He left the Mark Twain Expressway at Carr, turned immediately south on Broadway. It was a warehouse district near the river. At Cole he turned again and halfway down the block pulled in at an entry drive. He honked twice and a heavy door slid back. He eased into the building and the door closed behind the car.

The warehouse was jammed and active. There were four delivery-style vans, windowless, filled with radio equipment and gasoline generators. There were twenty-three rental sedans much like the one Hogan had driven from the airport. There were two giant tractor-trailer trucks filled with equipment—Swiss automatic rifles and ammunition, asbestos suits, white, wool-lined, hooded, heavy, winter jumpsuits, several twenty-pound cartons of plastique explosive, ropes and lines and pulleys, twenty-four large, Day-Glo-orange, molded fiberglass containers with fat rubber beltlike bands around them and what appeared to be canvas sacks on their lids, two heavy-duty air compressors, several hundred feet of hose, several dozen large gas canisters, and more. Nearly a hundred men, casually dressed, moved about working. Some were black, twenty or so, the rest were deeply tanned and burned from years of continual outdoor life. They were hard-looking men and they moved without waste motion, worked briskly with little chatter.

Motion ceased when Donovan got out of the car. Some, forgetting they were out of uniform, started salutes, then stopped. Donovan looked them over. His company. What was left of them. The Irish West Africa Company. Bloodied, but never beaten. He nodded.

"As you were."

The men went back to work. Donovan and McGregor went into a second large room. In it were five fifty-gallon drums; they appeared to be ordinary oil drums from the outside, but they were custom-made and definitely unique; the insides were completely lined with two-inch tempered safety glass. There were two glass-lined caps on each drum. Later in the evening, Donovan would return with only six men. The drums would be lined up with the compressors and the gas canisters. One cap would be removed from a drum and fitted quickly with a triple air-sealed nozzle and hose that would allow fumes to be pumped from the drum by a compressor into the cylindrical tanks. There was an electronic meter with a red warning light and a buzzer to warn them if any gas escaped.

The second cap would be removed and fitted with a triple-layered rubber seal that would reseal itself if punctured. A large glass bottle of acid would be mounted upside down on top of the drum. Its nose would be a long, narrow needle to penetrate the rubber seal six inches down into the drum. When the rubber fitting resealed, a valve on the bottle would be turned to allow a thin stream of acid to filter down the needle, into the drum, into the chemical powder within. The compressor would start pumping fumes into a canister.

The introduction of the acid to the powder would create Agent VX. Ethyl S-dimethylamineethylmethylphosphonothiolate. It is a fast-acting nerve gas that is both potent and stable in the atmosphere, persisting for several days to several weeks at a normal temperature. In a group of people who breathed ten milligrams per minute (an extremely small proportion of the ordinary intake of breath) half would die quickly. Agent VX also differs from most other nerve gases in that even if it is not breathed, it can kill through exposure to the skin. Six milligrams per minute percutaneously is a lethal dose. If these dosages were raised slightly in a confined space, the kill rate would be one hundred percent in minutes. Agent VX was developed but not perfected in England in the 1950s. The United States Army *says* it found the gas so dangerous that experimentation was halted and that it presently has no stocks or reserves of the gas. To date Romania is the only other country known to have replicated this gas and to have stocks.

By early the following morning the Irish West Africa

9

Company would have bottled enough nerve gas to kill a fourth of the population of St. Louis.

Donovan checked into a room at the Holiday Inn in Mansion House Center—nine blocks from the warehouse. Jackson, McGregor, Hogan, and a dozen other IWACs were also staying there. The rest were scattered through fourteen other city hotels.

They all had false identifications, passports, international driver's licenses, etc., but Donovan had wanted their entry to be still more discreet. The men were mostly in their thirties or forties and too distinctive in appearance to risk being seen in a large group together; they were all extremely fit, unusually so for men their age; they all had the deep, burned tans of perennial outdoorsmen; they were hard-looking, bore themselves in a stiff military manner, were habitually curt almost to the point of rudeness. Any customs or passport officer confronted with a group of eight or ten men such as these would become immediately curious, inquisitive. At the very least they would be clearly remembered. No more than three men took the same flight. Only one morning flight and one evening flight (so as to encounter different customs shifts) per city was allowed. In all, it took nearly ten days for the IWACs to invade the United States. And Donovan came last.

Jackson, McGregor, Hogan, and Lt. Arthur Adams, another American black, came to Donovan's room. With Major Turrman still in Zurich, these were his senior staff. He took a new bottle of Paddy's Irish whisky, product of his native County Cork, from his flight bag and uncapped it. He held the bottle up.

"Without glasses or ice 'tis not very elegant, but will serve. Gentlemen, I give you absent friends." He took a swallow and passed the bottle to Hogan. Each man repeated the toast, swallowed and passed the bottle.

Hogan wiped his mouth with the back of his hand. "Lovely stuff. And so is this." He unwrapped two modest-sized packages. They contained plastique explosive fitted with detonators and timers. "So small they are for making such a rare fine bang. Ah, Terrence, I'm telling you, it'd been much better if we'd had this stuff in the old days instead of mucking about with gelignite."

"So it would've, Patjo, so it would've." They checked the times and the maps again. Hogan set the timers and activated them. He rewrapped them gently in the brown paper and banded them with several wide strips of industrial-strength, double-faced, nylon tape. He handed one to Adams and stuffed one in his coat pocket. Donovan looked at Adams.

"Right then, Lieutenant, you've the farthest to go so you'd best be off now." They gave Adams a twenty-minute start and then Hogan left. He took an elevator to the promenade level and walked out onto the terrace.

Mansion House Center has a Holiday Inn at the south end and luxury, high-rise apartments on the north. In between is the terrace or promenade level with a view of the Levee and the river and a small group of shops, a restaurant and a bar—the Spanish Door Lounge. It was to the latter that Hogan walked.

It was a small, leather-and-wood decorated lounge. Business was slow. The bartender was bored. There were only three other customers in the bar. Patjo ordered a shot of Jack Daniels and a Budweiser, carried them to an out-of-the-way booth toward the rear.

He drank slowly. The American whisky was nice. He didn't much care for the beer. Hogan was an expert, a connoisseur. His burgundy-colored nose and cheeks had been honestly earned during more than thirty years of hard drinking. He was a cheerful, simple soul with only four things in life he loved. Whisky. Beer. Blowing things up. And his boyhood friend, Terrence Donovan.

After about fifteen minutes, he slipped the package from his coat pocket, palmed it, pressed it flat against the underside of the table. He ran his hand back and forth across it to

11

insure that it was firmly stuck. He finished his drink and left.

Minutes earlier, Lieutenant Adams had left his package in Blueberry Hill, a dart pub in University City to the north-west. At 7:15 p.m., five minutes after Hogan left the bar, Captain Jackson entered a pay telephone booth and dialed 4th District headquarters of the St. Louis Police Department. When a desk officer answered, Jackson spoke rapidly.

"Listen up, motherfucker, because I'm only going to say this once. I'm speaking on behalf of the Afrikaners. We've put bombs in the Spanish Door Lounge in Mansion House Center and in Blueberry Hill in University City. You've got five minutes to clear them." He cut the connection as the desk man started to ask questions.

Patrolmen Larry Davis and Willie Brown were unfortunate enough to be cruising along Fourth Street when the radio messages came to clear the bars. Before Brown had fully stopped the blue-and-white at the foot of the steps leading up to the terrace, Davis was out and sprinting. Brown was seconds behind him. Davis was reaching for the door to the lounge when the bomb went off. A horizontal fault midway up the large oak door gave under the pressure of the blast so that while the bottom portion merely jumped out and fell away, the top section exploded outward decapitating Patrolman Davis in midstride. Patrolman Brown, fifteen feet behind his partner, froze in horror. He was far enough back that he should not have been seriously injured, but as he saw the square of wood shear away his partner's head, he felt a stabbing pain in his chest. He had just enough time to glance down and note the end of a long spear of glass sticking several inches out from where he presumed his heart to be. He was dying as he fell.

The bomb obliterated the inside of the bar, killed the barman and the three customers, shattered the windows of all the nearby shops. Although Blueberry Hill had considerably more customers, the blast was much smaller and there were no fatalities; three people suffered serious injury and half a dozen minor bruises, cuts, wounds, concussions.

They watched the television news in Donovan's room. The police acknowledged receiving a warning call from a group claiming responsibility. For the time being, the name of the group was being withheld. There were films of police inspecting damage at the two bars. One of the officers looked vaguely familiar to Donovan; he couldn't think why. After the news spot, McGregor switched off the television. Donovan and Jackson exchanged looks.

"Ah, that's grand then, Captain. They've accepted it just as we thought."

"Looks like it, Colonel."

"Not very original, perhaps, but then I don't suppose we're after dealing with very original minds."

The night air was very cold as Donovan left to supervise the "bottling" of the nerve gas. He walked up Fourth Street. Lights were, of course, still on in the oddly shaped, Bedford stone and brick building across the way. He tried to recall the police officer again but couldn't make the jump from Noah in uniform to the casually dressed man he had barely glanced at in the airport cocktail lounge.

# BOOK I: **THE MONEY WAR**

"Why do you rob banks?"
"Because that's where the money is."
*Willie (The Actor) Sutton*

Bucky Walters had retired from the United States Army only five years before, despite the fact that he had actually been working directly for the CIA for seventeen years. His military rank had been maintained as cover for field operations—as when he was assigned as a military attaché at the Tel Aviv embassy, but had in fact been liaison between the "Company" and Israeli Intelligence. It had no longer been considered necessary when he joined the senior staff in Washington. His covert days were over.

He was Assistant to the Deputy Director of Plans and he was in charge of the African Division of Plans (the covert-action section of the CIA). During his tenure at the African Desk, the CIA had employed Donovan and the IWACs in Angola. It was why Bucky could recognize the men in the lounge even though he had never met any of them. He had worried the chance meeting on the flight home and late into the night. Clearly, the DDP had to be advised.

The DDP's outer office was brightly, almost harshly lit and the colors were vivid, perhaps even garish. The DDP habitually kept visitors waiting ten to fifteen minutes in the outer office. It was Bucky's theory that this was done to disorient visitors when they entered the inner office. The inner office was windowless and paneled in black oak. The carpet was deep brown. The furniture was all dark browns and blacks, wood, leather, slate. The DDP sat behind a massive desk and on it a single strong lamp provided the room's sole illumination. It was positioned so that a visitor's face would be well-lighted while the DDP's was shadowed.

He rose to shake hands. "Good morning, Colonel. Pleasant trip?"

"More or less. Puzzling incident, though."

"Something with the people in Seattle?" Bucky looked carefully at what he could see of the man. Late fifties, short, heavy, but with no sense of softness about him. Bucky knew that the man was dangerous. Phillbin Brooke was a bureaucrat, not a spy. Mild of manner and capable of all the social graces befitting an upper-echelon executive, he had, however, clawed his way up the ladder in the only manner possible—bare-knuckled.

"No. The Seattle conference went about as we expected. Those people aren't much good and I think we're wasting our money, but we've been over that before." The DDP nodded. He was not a word-waster. When social graces were not demanded, he was considered by those in a position to know the curtest bureaucrat in Washington—a not unprepossessing achievement. "It was in St. Louis. I was visiting my brother-in-law for a few days on the way home."

"Major Peterson of the St. Louis Police. Was with you in Army Intelligence for two years."

Bucky smiled. The man's memory was also legendary. "That's right. We were waiting for my flight in the cocktail lounge. There were some men there who . . . one wouldn't expect to be."

"Who?"

"A few years ago we employed some free-lance mercenaries in Angola. The best of the lot was an Irishman named Donovan."

"Colonel Terrence Donovan and the Irish West Africa Company. They just pushed General Ossungi to power in Imbannailand. Took bad losses. Kadafii was supposed to be paying them, but Ossungi double-crossed them. They had to fight their way out and didn't get paid at all."

"That's the man. He came into the lounge and was met by some of his men. An American black, Captain Jackson; his ranking non-com—I don't remember his name; and another man I didn't recognize."

18

"McGregor. Sergeant-Major Andrew McGregor. Donovan's ranking non-com."

"Yes, that's the name."

Brooke took a cigarette from a silver box on his desk. He pushed the box across to Bucky and carefully fit his cigarette into a black jade holder. Bucky leaned across the desk to light his cigarette; Brooke's dark eyes were angry; Bucky was surprised. The DDP rarely displayed emotion. He leaned back and lit his own cigarette.

"We have a rather difficult situation here, Colonel." Bucky said nothing. "I had a phone conversation with Donovan early last week. He called on one of the secure lines." Brooke's laugh was unpleasant. "Secure!" He waved his cigarette. "No matter. That's being looked into." Bucky was too stunned to speak. The DDP looked at him, nodded. "That's right, Colonel. Something of a shocker. It gets somewhat worse. You've heard some rumbles about a treaty tentatively labeled the Damascus Agreement?"

Bucky was alerted, cautious. "Vaguely. No details."

"Briefly, it is a final solution to the Mideast problems. A Palestinian state, recognition of Israel by the Arabs, some oil concessions for us. I'm not pleased with everything in it, although it does pretty much destroy Russian influence in the area. But the President and the Secretary of State must have that treaty for the elections next year. Without it they're gone. Donovan threatens to blow it apart, which wouldn't be difficult to do at this delicate stage of final drafting."

"What does he want?"

"He doesn't say." The DDP dropped his butt into a gray ceramic ashtray and ground it out with a spiky piece of black metal. "Or to be more precise, he doesn't say precisely what he wants. He says they, presumably his mercenaries, are going to do something."

"Do something?"

"That's correct. He says it will become apparent after

19

they have done it. He offers to assure the security of the Damascus Agreement in return for our protection against the possible consequences of this something they are going to do."

"The implication is that the something would be rather public."

"Exactly, Colonel. And with your information, we can assume something in St. Louis or the midcontinent region. Frankly, the President and the Secretary of State are livid. I've had four briefings with the National Security Council. All highly distasteful. And the Forty Committee are going positively berserk. We are being put in the middle."

"The Company?"

"Yes. Of course, Presidential interests and Company interests are not always parallel. Unfortunately, *this* President is all too aware of that. He is putting us on the spot. And, of course, Donovan is. Cheeky bastard."

"But competent."

"Oh, there's no doubt of that, Colonel. What it comes down to is this. The blowing of the Damascus Agreement would do irreparable harm to this administration. Instead of being called heroes for creating a lasting peace in the Middle East, they would be made out as bungling incompetents for blowing the best chance in that area in thirty years."

"And the Company?"

"The bottom line is that it cannot be allowed to happen. No matter what the cost. The blowing of the agreement—from the Company standpoint—would be unfortunate, but not tragic. What would be tragic would be to have a former CIA employee—Donovan—involved in what we can safely assume will be some sort of public outrage, to have the same man blow a major foreign treaty that the public will perceive as vital to the national interest, to have his past and ours scrutinized. We've been low profile for several years. Watergate nonsense, the Busch and Helms revelations, all that has been dying down. We do not want to go public again—scandal, rehash of our roles in Africa. No,

20

thank you." The DDP shuddered. Bucky was impressed. The DDP was not a shudderer.

"So what are our orders?"

"Orders?"

Bucky squirmed. "Surely the President does not expect us to sit and wait."

The DDP smiled cruelly. "The President does not want to know. He wishes us to solve this problem by any means available and he does not want to know. The National Security Council do not wish to know. The Forty Committee do not want to know. They all want it handled discreetly. And they all wish to maintain their virginity."

Bucky shook his head. "Irresponsible."

The DDP nodded. He fit a fresh cigarette into the jade holder and lit it. The smoke drifted toward the light.

"Of course it is. That is precisely the point. They don't want to be responsible. And they are correct. They cannot be responsible. The government cannot be responsible for the kind of shifty hocus-pocus we are about to enter into."

"Why?"

"You're a Catholic, aren't you, Colonel?"

Bucky smiled, nodded. "Yes."

"Then you should understand. If you are a traditional Catholic, is not one of your fundamental moral imperatives obedience to authority, the authority of the Church?"

"Yes."

"And that is why the authority of the Church must never be shown to be wrong. Disobedience brings disintegration. To society as well as to religion. In order for a government to have moral authority it must not be shown to be wrong. Not on a major moral question."

"Then . . ."

"Someone must be willing to do these things in the national interest without sanction from higher authority. If things go wrong, the government must have someone—in this case, me—to point to as a culprit. You're too young to have worked with Bill Stevenson, or Intrepid, as he was

21

called." Bucky did not respond. It was not a question. "My first years in the intelligence field were with him. As a liaison. He taught me that the highest form of patriotism is to do the dirty work, expecting neither shield nor thanks from your government. Of course, one tries not to be caught out, but that's fair enough."

"Then we wait and see what happens, and patch over any mess Donovan might leave in his wake."

"Yes."

"And try not to get caught."

"Precisely."

## ST. LOUIS, MISSOURI/12:00 NOON, CST/MAJOR NOAH PETERSON

Noah awoke thinking about politics, just as he had gone to sleep thinking about them. Not the elective party politics of ordinary times, but the insane terrorist politics in vogue in a bewildering and hostile world. The bar bombings had gone down about midway through his shift as second watch commander. He had had to call in the Chief, the Chairman of the Police Commissioner's Board, and the Mayor. They were all petrified that a wave of political bombings might be starting. St. Louis had not had to cope with terrorist bombings before. The only incident of that sort to date had been the fire at the U.S. Army Records Center. And they only *suspected* arson had been committed, could not prove it.

Noah was afraid of the possibility of a terrorist bombing campaign, too. The random nature of that kind of attack made it almost impossible for the police to deal with. Anticipation was the problem. You could not anticipate what a fanatic would do next. It took the problem out of the orderly, the rational. But Noah was more than worried. He was bothered as well. Something—he couldn't think what— did not fit his notion of the way these things went. Some "feel" to last night's incident did not seem "right." He had thought of the men Bucky recognized at the airport, but

22

dismissed the idea. The Afrikaners had claimed the bombs. The department had heard of the group, though their files were hopelessly inadequate. But something was wrong. He shook his head. Whatever it was, it would not come.

He got out of bed and went into the large blue-tiled bathroom off the master bedroom. He could hear Elizabeth in the kitchen downstairs making breakfast for him. He began to shave.

At forty-three, Noah was the youngest major in the St. Louis Police Department. He was one of the new breed of career officers who were slowly beginning to make their presence felt in departments all across the United States. He was graduated from St. Louis University at twenty and drafted immediately. He had done two years in Army Intelligence, taken his law degree at Yale, and married shortly afterward. He had worked for the District Attorney's office for a little over a year and then joined the force.

His rise had been rapid. He served a nominal nineteen months as a patrolman to gain street experience and then jumped to detective sergeant on the vice squad. After fourteen months, he had been transferred to homicide. In three years, he compiled the best arrest and conviction record in the department's history and, after solving the spectacular Grunemann murder case, he was made the youngest lieutenant in department history shortly before his thirty-third birthday. He broke the age records again by making captain at thirty-seven and major at forty-one. There was some grumbling about "college boy cops," but Noah had a facility for getting along with the old-line officers who had worked torturously up the seniority list and he was very popular with the rank and file. No one doubted he would break the final age record by becoming the department's youngest Chief in two or three years, unless he decided to take an early pension and go into politics.

He stepped into the shower stall and adjusted the water. He sighed as the hot water streamed over him, began to lather his body with soap. Life was good. To him and to his.

The Petersons lived in a large two-story Tudor home in one of the best areas of Webster Groves. Elizabeth and her sister Margaret Walters had split a several-hundred-thousand-dollar inheritance from their father four years before that had eased all their economic worries. They had a negligible mortgage on the house which was valued at ninety-three thousand dollars. Noah III had pre-senior-year college acceptance, would be a freshman at Yale next fall. The twins, Cheryl and Charles, sophomores at Webster Groves High School, would be able to go to any college or university of their choosing. They had no debts, owned two late-model automobiles, dressed and ate well, traveled. They were a happy family and Noah and Elizabeth were still lovers. They led a well-ordered, privileged life.

Occasionally it bothered Noah's Catholic conscience. His mind despised randomness, ached for order, yet he knew it to be a random thing that he and his family lived so well when others lived so poorly.

In some ways he was not a good Catholic. He knew this. The parish priest of his boyhood had despaired over Noah at times.

"It's God's will, my son," the priest would say.

"Why?" Noah would reply.

He wanted a personal revelation. He did not want to be told that it was a mystery, an ordered purpose of such scope that mortals could not see the pattern for the details. At times it was as if Noah was asking God to justify his works to Noah so that Noah might judge God—a heretical reversal of such staggering proportions that Noah's priest feared for Noah's immortal soul.

But Noah submitted. He "accepted" things as they are with the chronic uneasiness of a knife-thrower's "target"—always dependent on the accuracy of another for one's safety.

Perhaps he had joined the force because of his ache for order. To some it had seemed a whimsical, nonsensical decision to leave a promising career in the District Attorney's

24

office to become a policeman. Elizabeth understood. She had said, "Noah wants people to be safe. He wants order. He wants the good guys to win and the bad guys to lose." Then she had laughed, "And he wants to take the responsibility himself—he's afraid to leave people to their own devices and he's a little afraid that God's not paying strict attention."

Noah smiled at his memories, thoughts, at himself. Perhaps one should not blink in the face of good fortune. It was just that . . . well, one should deserve things. Earned grace was a very real concept to him. He did not feel comfortable with opulent and easy gifts. For himself or others.

He came downstairs in his bathrobe and sat at the large, padded breakfast booth in the kitchen. His eyes followed Elizabeth as she moved about the room. She felt his eyes, knew they were on her. She smiled the content of being loved. And how many husbands and wives are still lovers after years of marriage? Not nearly enough. She set a plate of scrambled eggs, broiled Boone County ham, and English muffins before him. She poured coffee for both of them and sat with him. She was thoroughly Irish. Short-waisted, dark, leggy, and slim, with perennially amused brown eyes.

"How were the kids this morning?"

"Let's see—Charles was cranky because he doesn't think the coach is going to start him at halfback this week. He's been having bad practices lately he says. Cheryl is elated because she thinks the Hamlin boy is going to ask her to the dance this weekend. Noah, well, who can tell with that son of yours—he doesn't speak at breakfast. Just works on chess problems. Oh, and he wants to go to the Blues game tonight."

"Okay with me. The season tickets are in my top desk drawer."

"Jack Foltz called for you."

"The county Democratic Chairman?"

"That's right. He said Senator Eagleton wanted to talk to you in a month or so about next year's elections."

25

"Goody."

"They'll want you to run for something."

"Probably." He took her hand and squeezed it gently. "Don't worry, Liz. If they want me to run for President I might give it some consideration, otherwise, no."

She laughed. "I don't suppose that's what they have in mind."

"No, and I told them last time I wasn't interested in being a state assemblyman." He pushed his empty plate away. "Wonderful breakfast, Liz. Thank you."

"You're welcome. When do you have to leave?"

"Two, I guess. Why?" He sipped his coffee.

She put her hand on his knee and the warmth in his loins reminded him he had worn nothing under his robe. She licked her lips. Her voice was husky.

"I have been enjoying one aspect of this second shift, Major Peterson. It's so nice to have you home in the afternoon when the house is empty."

"I suppose I could leave at quarter after."

"Make it two-thirty."

Upstairs, he entered her quickly, galloped them the first time. Later he mounted her dog-style and they rocked leisurely.

"It's sooo . . . NICE . . . soooo NICE . . . to have you . . . ho-ME IN . . . the after-NOON!"

ST. LOUIS, MISSOURI/4:30 p.m., CST/
CAPT. ALBERT LEROY JACKSON

Jackson stepped out the glass double doors at the promenade level. He took one brief look at the roped-off wreckage of the lounge, then stood by an iron railing. He was waiting for Pete. Every afternoon, when Pete's shift ended, they met here and took the elevator up to the Blue Island Lounge for a couple of drinks while Pete passed him the day's tally.

It made the whole transaction seem civilized, a smooth and pleasant business deal. Today, of course, was different. Donovan was waiting for them in the bar. Nothing would ever be quite the same after today.

It was like the first time he ever ate a genuine beefsteak. He was a senior in high school. He'd scored twenty-four points in a basketball game and his team had won the league championship. The coach took all the players to Stan Musial's restaurant. He had had a ten-ounce filet smothered in onions and mushrooms. It had changed his life. It had been the motivator. He promised himself that night he would get into a world where you could eat like that.

He shivered. It was particularly cold for the first week of November in St. Louis and, even as he stood there, the lowering gray sky turned noticeably darker and a few fat flakes of snow began to slide past his face. It was a break they'd hardly dared hope for. Snow would keep people off the streets tonight.

He saw Pete hurrying across Fourth Street, bareheaded and without a topcoat. He frowned. Suddenly he felt as if his entrails were in the icy grip of dead spirits, as if his bowels would turn to water any moment. He had the sick nausea of fear in his stomach. It was just like the summer past when he came back to recruit Pete. A life-or-death decision hanging over the head of his best friend. Today Donovan would make the judgment. This summer it had been up to Jackson. Whether or not to kill his best friend.

Pierre Laclede (Pete) Jones and he had boosted cars together as teenagers, gone to St. Louis University on basketball scholarships, worked at the Federal Reserve Bank together as part-time mail boys while in college. They'd gotten drunk, gotten laid, been in fights—sometimes getting whupped, sometimes kicking ass, played ball together so long they were like one player with two bodies on the court; they both had been lost middle children of poor families, had become each other's family; they'd been cut buddies for twenty-eight years, since they were six years old.

27

After college, they had both worked at the Fed Bank for a while; Pete stayed when Jackson joined the Air Force, went to Nam, wandered Europe, became a mercenary; Pete had married, had three children, a forty-eight-thousand-dollar home in University City, had become director of data operations at the bank, with a good income and heavy debt—the upwardly mobile American dream. And a few months ago Jackson had dropped back into Pete's life. The ghost of a ghetto boyhood friend come back. With an offer of money. And the implication of death.

The proposition was simple. In the fall, for a period of thirty or forty days, Pete would supply Jackson with the daily totals of cash on hand and the daily totals of certain selected bearer bonds on hand. Each day that he did this one thousand dollars' worth of Swiss Francs would be deposited in a Zurich account for him. Later there would be a bonus. He would not have to do anything else. He would not have to know anything else.

Jackson took him to a Cardinal–Cub game to make the proposition. He layed it out in the third inning. It was in the fifth inning when Jackson knew Pete was seeing the implications. If he refused, Jackson would have to kill him.

Donovan had asked him about this when the possibility had been discussed. It had been easy, in London, six thousand miles away and not having seen Pete for three years, to say yes. Yes, he could kill him if he had to. Donovan had pointed out when they had chosen the little four-inch Cedibra .32 (because it was small and easy to smuggle, powerful and not noisy for close work) that he would have to stick the barrel in Pete's ear, see his face, his eyes, smell his fear and hear his pleas, watch his head explode like a melon. Donovan had known how hard it would be, had ridden him about the details, had tried to make him feel it. You had to respect Donovan. He didn't bullshit *at all*.

The sun had been high and the day hot; the colors profuse; the beer cold and delicious. Watching a Cub relief pitcher warm up to try to stem a Cardinal rally, Jackson had

28

experienced a sweet melancholy. What he supposed was the saddest moment of his thirty-four years. He realized he *could* kill his friend. He *was* ready to murder Pete. He looked at Pete and saw he knew too. They didn't speak for an inning. Then Pete looked at him again and grinned lamely.

"How big a bonus?" They had both laughed then.

"Six figures for sure." They had laughed some more then and during the game and later, but it was not the same any more, couldn't be, would never be again.

He shivered again as Pete came up the steps to him. They hurried inside. Jackson pressed the elevator button.

"Why no coat, Pete? You turning Eskimo?"

"No. I have to go back to the bank. I thought I wouldn't bother with my coat and hat." The elevator came and they entered. "Bad mistake on my part. I didn't know it had started to snow."

"Why do you have to go back to the bank?"

The elevator stopped at a floor and another passenger got on. They rode in silence up to the bar. A waitress took them to a back, somewhat secluded booth. Donovan was waiting. He did not rise or remove the silver sunglasses.

"Pete, this is an, uh, associate of mine. Colonel Donovan. Colonel Donovan, Pete Jones."

As they sat, Pete said, "Colonel, a pleasure to meet you."

Donovan nodded. "Mr. Jones."

The waitress leaned over the table as she took their order to give them a shot of her breasts in a low-cut uniform. Nice, thought Jackson, say thirty-seven-Cs; he could almost see her nipples as the uniform leaned away from the soft hanging mounds; he resisted an impulse to shoot his hand into the exposed cleavage. The impulse told him he was nervous. Tension always brought on mild antisocial whims.

"Double Jack Daniels on the rocks." Jackson pointed at Donovan.

"Grand."

"How about you, Pete? The same?"

"Better make mine a single. I can't stay too long." The waitress walked away toward the bar. "That girl sure gives you a nice shot of her cakes. Nice cakes, too."

"Sure, it's good for tips and keeps the customers drinking. You got to keep ordering to get another peek. A fifty-buck lay any night of the week and not worth the price. What's this back to the bank stuff, Pete?"

Pete shrugged. "A special study we've been running on check flow. The big boys want it tomorrow and I can't trust my assistant to run the printout in proper sequence. Guy's an idiot. Dumb shit's got a degree from M.I.T. and he can't find his ass with both hands. And just because he's a fucking egghead honky he'll be regional director of data operations in five years. I'll still be farting around with flow studies."

The waitress returned with their drinks, leaned low to set them down and smirked when three pairs of eyes fastened on her breasts. Pete glanced from Donovan to Jackson, shrugged.

"You want it now?" Jackson nodded and Pete fished a three-by-five file card from his jacket pocket, palmed it, and slid it across to Jackson. He looked at only the totals, not the breakdowns, before he slipped it across to Donovan: CASH/$233,888,400.00 SELECTED BONDS/ $319,108,000.00.

Donovan smiled and put the card in his pocket. "Now that *is* grand, boyos." They all took quick swallows of their drinks. Donovan looked at Jackson. "I think we'll chance it, Captain. He'll do." Relief flooded Jackson so profoundly he thought tears might well up. He was pleasantly surprised to find that he cared more than he had thought was possible.

His voice was husky. "The thing is, Pete, I wouldn't go back to the bank tonight if I was you. Develop a stomach ache or a pressing appointment you'd forgotten or tell the kid you've decided to give him his big chance to solo on this printout. Whatever. I just wouldn't go back to work tonight

30

if I was you." Pete stared at him a few seconds, shot Donovan a quick look, then looked out the window at the skyline. Occasional flakes stuck to the glass, melted, ran down.

"Tonight, huh?"

"Tonight."

"Okay. I can think of something. He took a swallow of bourbon and sighed. He spoke softly, almost wistfully. "You know it's been going along so nicely, I began to hope maybe you would decide it wasn't feasible after all. Just give up the idea and I'd get to keep the money anyway."

Jackson frowned and shook his head. "Jesus, Pete, you sure you're really a nigger? You haven't been fooling me all these years with burnt cork and jive talk? Any nigger lives to be as old as you just got to know there isn't anything good comes free and like as not they'll charge you double for the bad."

"I know."

"It's going to be a little rough in the morning, Pete. Don't lose your nerve. It would be fatal."

Pete nodded. "I know that too." He shivered. "Where's that waitress? I think I'll have another drink."

**ST. LOUIS, MISSOURI/4:41 p.m., CST/COL. TERRENCE DONOVAN**

Donovan left them in the bar and went to the elevator. He ascended to the top floor, unlocked the door to the rooftop pool area and went out. In this season it was not used. He crossed to the wall overlooking Fourth Street and pulled a RK89 transmitter from his coat pocket. He selected a frequency.

"Unit One, this is Gold Leader. Proceed as scheduled."

"We copy, Gold Leader."

As if conjured, a Union Electric van turned off Market onto Fourth Street, cruised past the Holiday Inn, and stopped at the Federal Reserve Bank. Donovan took field glasses from inside his coat and focused on the van. Corporals Spain and Felton, American black IWACs, dressed in Union Electric repairmen's coveralls, got out of the van. They took tool chests from the back. Ostensibly there to check the bank's auxiliary power generators, they would plant small plastique charges timed to go off later in the evening. This was the first critical moment. They entered the building.

Donovan lit a cigarette and paced. He mused on Jones and Jackson. He was not a man who liked avoidable risks. It would have been safer to kill Jones. All that would have been required was to let him return to the bank. Donovan knew he was a hard man. He could kill or order killing. He was not afraid of the decision—life or death. He suspected he let Jones live because he respected Jackson's self-knowledge. Jackson wanted money. Badly enough to be willing to kill his friend. And he was human enough not to want to kill his friend. That, of course, amused Donovan. It was another reason. But in the end it all came down to judgment. Donovan was dispassionate, a good judge of character, a quick study. He knew Jones's nerve would hold. He had the ability to tell. It was one reason he was a leader.

He checked his watch. Twenty-two minutes. Was that long for a routine check? He lit a cigarette and paced. At 5:19 he lifted the field glasses to his face again. They were coming out. He stiffened. There was a guard with them. He seemed to be holding them by the arm. It was hard to see in the dimming light. Were they? . . . No—they were laughing, joking with the guard. It was all right.

The van pulled away from the bank. Static crackled momentarily on his RK89, then cleared.

"Gold Leader, this is Unit One. It's a go."

"I copy, boyos."

Donovan smiled as he went back down to the elevator. On schedule. The warehouse next. The power plant teams had to be gotten off.

32

Twenty-two men stood lined up in front of Corporal Hogan. At their feet were identical small bundles of equipment. False passport, one-way airline ticket out of the country, three thousand dollars cash, one SIG 510–4 automatic rifle, disassembled, in opaque oilskin carrying case, twenty clips of twenty rounds of .30 caliber ammunition, appropriate road maps. The men wore nondescript casual clothes to be disposed of at the sites if necessary. Each had two changes of clothes in a small airline carry-on flight bag. None of the clothes had any labels or other identifying marks. Each man had a toilet kit with grooming items of standard brand and no personal possessions. The only singular items of clothing or jewelry were their watches. Four-hundred-dollar Rollex Swiss watches, but these had been purchased on the black market in Libya and were virtually untraceable. The plastique explosive charges and detonating equipment had been placed in the trunks of the appropriate sedans and Hogan had checked them all thoroughly. He turned to Donovan.

"They're all ready, Colonel. Our watches have been synchronized."

"Right enough, Patjo." Donovan walked down the line shaking each man's hand and wishing him good luck. "We'll meet again in Cork, lads." The men took their bundles and got in their cars. Four with Hogan for Portage Des Sioux. Four with Private First Class Nordmann for Baldwin, four with Corporal Richardson for Meramec. Two each for the switching substations and the Bell Telephone Company batteries. The Bagnell Dam team, south of Jefferson City, had checked in, were already in position. The doors were rolled back and the sedans slipped out on their separate routes.

It was snowing fairly heavily now and some was sticking

to the streets, making them wet and slick. Hogan did not mind. He'd driven in worse weather on worse roads. It might make the Baldwin team hurry it a bit, but he'd plenty of time. He pulled onto the Mark Twain Expressway heading north. He liked the big comfortable American car. Good heater, too.

They passed a building in an industrial area with the legend SLIGO STEEL on its side, white letters on a black background. He shook his head. Donovan and he had laughed when they saw that the first time they drove the route. The Sligo raid. That had been a bad day. He'd lost Terrence there for a while after the Sligo raid. And young Seamus was killed. He took the exit for Broadway north.

At a traffic light, he fished a pint of bourbon from his pocket and took a long pull. Lovely stuff, the American whisky. Hogan was happy. He liked to be doing again. An operation with Terrence running it. He liked driving in a good car and being warm with a good dose of spirits flooding through him. And he liked to blow things up. It was a thing he'd discovered early in the IRA days. He was good at it, workmanlike, proper, and he loved to see something go in a rare old bang. He wished he'd be at all the sites tonight, but at least he had the biggest and the best for himself.

He left Broadway at Hall's Ferry Road and soon picked up Route 367. They were in the gently rolling hills of the northern suburbs. At a stoplight, Hogan took another pull on the pint bottle.

"Ah, that's wonderful stuff." Private Perete, a large, nervous Belgian, frowned at him.

"Don't you think you'd better go easy, Corporal?"

Hogan smiled. "It'll be being a larger bottle than this'll greatly affect Patrick Joseph Hogan, lad. And it's not so much of an operation we've to do tonight, is it? Nip in and blow the place and off we go." Perete grunted. Hogan began looking for a diner. They had plenty of time, so they might as well eat something. They wouldn't want to stop afterward until they got to Chicago.

The other four Canadians had met in Sergeant Macklin's room and he had checked their equipment again. It was the same as the power station teams' except for the absence of the automatic rifles and ammunition. He went over the instructions for the last time. Then they waited for the call. They were staying in the Chase, one of the city's older hotels with a long tradition, as was the visiting hockey team, the Montreal Canadiens, who would play the Blues at the arena tonight. The phone rang and Macklin an-answered it.

"Hello."

"Unit Ten?"

"Right."

"Gold Leader here. It's a go. Good luck, lads."

"Right."

Macklin gave the thumbs up sign and the men picked up their equipment. He stopped by the door.

"Just remember, not too close and not too far once the punch-up starts."

"Give it a rest, Sarge. That's the hundredth time you've told us." They checked out and had their car brought around. They were all very large men and they were a little cramped, even in a full-size American sedan. They started for the arena.

Macklin wondered if the snow would hold the crowd down to such a small figure that their operation would be an exercise in futility. He was surprised when he arrived at the arena to find traffic backed up and the parking lots filling rapidly. It was one of those freak evenings in sports when all the fans have the idea that bad weather will hold the crowd down and it will actually be fairly easy and pleasant to attend the game despite bad traveling conditions. A capacity crowd of over seventeen thousand was building. It was well after seven when the five IWACs were able to make their way from their car to the outer arches and the series of double-glass entry doors beyond.

The arena is an old brick and wood structure that looks a little like a beached whale. Inside the building there is a high area of seating near where the wooden roof joins the rest of the structure. It was to these seats that the five Canadians made their way. Each carried a large transistor radio, ostensibly to listen to the radio play-by-play broadcast while observing the game—as many fans do. Closer inspection, however, would have shown that these five were all clock radios set to each other's time. And if anyone had opened the radio cases, they would have found a fair-sized plastique charge in each, wired to the clock mechanism. The men found their seats. They were placed nearly equidistant around the oval. Macklin checked his watch. 7:28 p.m. In two minutes the first operation would begin across the city. He glanced down. The players were warming up, skating in lazy arcs, fooling with pucks or snapping long slap shots at the unguarded nets. The Blues were on a short winning streak and the Montreal Canadiens had long been arch rivals; crowd anticipation and enthusiasm were building rapidly; Macklin found himself caught up in it. He had been a fair junior hockey defenseman in his youth in Winnipeg. Then he caught himself up. He almost laughed aloud at the ridiculous emotions he had been experiencing. There would be no hockey game at the arena tonight.

**7:07 p.m.: LT. ARTHUR ADAMS**

On Kingshighway Boulevard, Art Adams was worried as he maneuvered his lead car carefully through light traffic. He had eight men in his team, four to each car. He had charge of the team with the trickiest getaway—under full

36

fire—and he did not like the traffic conditions. He was having a hard time keeping his sedan from fishtailing at any speed above twenty-five. He had not cared for the vagueness of Donovan's instructions, either. Donovan, normally so precise, had left the time to break off action and retreat almost solely to his discretion. Adams was a native St. Louis black, as were all the men in his team. They had been recruited for the war in Imbannailand by Jackson (once Donovan recruited him, he had in turn recruited twenty-six other black ex-servicemen from the St. Louis area). He couldn't help wondering if Donovan's ambiguous orders weren't more of a pressure for him to keep his team in action dangerously overlong, rather than an expression of confidence in his command judgment.

Donovan was going to be disappointed if that was it. Art Adams had no intention whatsoever of getting his tail shot off in this raid. Unlike most of the rest of the men, the money was not an end in itself for him. It was a means toward a dream long frustrated. Adams was only twenty-four. Four years before, he had still been a promising tennis player, always on the verge of breaking into the select circle of world-class players. Money had always been the problem. He was poor and he had never been able to find a sponsor to keep him going on the tour until his winnings would begin to pay his way. Now he would have the money. He would go back into rigorous training, find a first-class teacher to help him polish his game again. He would finally get his chance at the international circuit. Hell, he'd always been able to take Connors when they were kids, and now Connors was top dog on the circuit. They'd see. He still thought he could make them forget the top American black player with the so-similar name—Arthur Ashe.

Across from the Rexall plant on Kingshighway is a nicely cared-for middle-class black neighborhood of sturdy brick family homes, many on a series of cul-de-sacs. The two cars pulled into one of these and parked, lights off, but motors running. It was too cold to sit in an unheated car.

# THE BATTLE OF 13th STREET

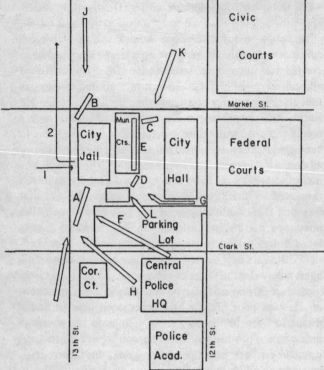

**Afrikaner Positions** (bars)

A. Held 7:30 p.m.—9:26 p.m.
B. Held 7:40 p.m.—9:41 p.m.
C. Held 7:42 p.m.—9:44 p.m.
D. Held 7:42 p.m.—9:55 p.m.
E. Held 7:58 p.m.—7:37 a.m.

**Police Thrusts** (arrows)

F. Two patrolmen repulsed—
   7:36 p.m.
G. Sergeant Vincente's patrol
   decimated—8:14 p.m.
H. Support patrol routed—
   8:19 p.m.
I. Took position A—9:26 p.m.
J. Took position B—9:41 p.m.
K. Took position C—9:44 p.m.
L. Took position D—9:55 p.m.

Position E assaulted in force with
helicopter support 7:24 a.m.—taken
7:37 a.m.

He crept past the entrance to the St. Louis jail in his sedan at less than ten mph. He was the head of an eleven-car caravan. Behind him were ten cars filled with Afrikaners all hopped up with the present of fifty automatic rifles and four hundred rounds of ammunition per rifle. Dumb shits. Recruiting them had been a contribution of his to the refinements of Donovan's plan. Of course the original idea had been his. Ever since he had gone to work at the Fed Bank as a teenager he'd dreamed about robbing it. All that fucking money. His idea. But Donovan's plan. Well, Donovan was the Colonel. And tough. You had to respect him, and men followed him. Jackson pulled over to the curb near the next intersection and glanced back. The other cars were pulling in and waiting. He lit his cigarette. Waited.

One thing, Jackson thought, the part with Pete had been hard—recruiting him and knowing he might have to kill him—that had been tough, but the Afrikaners, that was different. He didn't feel a thing about using them. And setting them up. Dumb shits. Sure they were black. So what? If a man was a dumb bastard that was more important to Jackson than the color of his skin. Of course Freddy was a dumb bastard and he did feel bad about him. But Freddy had been a friend.

It had been murderously hot when he parked on the east side of Fairgrounds Park and waited for Freddy to come along. The park is in the Grand Boulevard slum area between St. Louis University and the crossover to Grand Avenue. It is less well known than Harlem or Chicago's South Side or L.A.'s Watts, but it is every bit as ugly and soul-chilling as those other slums.

Jackson had come home after seventeen years to make contact with the Grand Boulevard Bad Asses, an extremely loose-knit organization drawing upon a variety of political and social orientations ranging from Black Muslims and Black Panthers to street gangs, pimps, pushers, and car thieves. There is, of course, some overlapping—it is possible, for instance, to be both a Black Panther and a pimp. The organization is what in English public school circles would be referred to as an "old boy network." Its main activities consist of exchanges of information and the occasional collaboration in ass-kicking when the interests of several member groups are threatened. Jackson had been a Bad Ass along with Pete. They had boosted cars, peddled a little dope and a little ass, and were the leaders of a street gang— the Bailey Street Raiders. So he had waited in the heat of August for his contact.

He had to look twice to make sure it was Freddy coming down the sidewalk. He had been a short, squat, muscular fireplug in their youth—an all-city halfback the two years he had managed to remain in high school. Now he was a short, very fat, black man in old canvas shoes, no socks, stained and baggy brown trousers, a soiled blue T-shirt. Jackson was shocked. Freddy was his age within a month, but looked an easy fifty or so. White and gray showed in what remained of his hair and his bristly several-day stubble. His eyes were caked and red-rimmed, he stank and the layers of fat around his no-neck jiggled when he drank from the bottle of Petrie Port that Jackson plied him with.

The group that sounded best was a bunch of young hotheads with armed separatist notions. They affected dashikis and the name, the Afrikaners. Jackson couldn't believe his ears when Freddy told him the name and made him repeat it and swear to it. He laughed until the tears came. A bunch of bastards so ignorant as to adopt the name of the white South Africans for a black separatist movement must surely be the perfect tools.

He arranged for a meeting that night at the park with the leader of the group—John 3X Brown. Freddy was to introduce them, identifying Jackson as Ed Wilson, then leave them alone. He gave Freddy a five and promised ten more and another bottle that night.

John 3X Brown was a large, stupid bull of a man, self-important in his leadership of a hundred or so other similarly simple-minded men. He was easily manipulated with the right mixture of political jingoism, flattery, and promises of power and wealth. The gift of several hundred dollars and the mention of a supply of automatic weapons were also helpful. Jackson elicited a series of phone numbers where he could contact or leave messages for Brown without letting Brown know how to contact him. They met several more times at Busch Stadium. The arrangements were set.

At the end of the week, the body of a short, fat, black wino was fished out of the river. The body was unidentified and taken to the morgue as a John Doe. He had been shot in the left ear with a medium caliber handgun, probably a .32.

No one in the Afrikaners knew who Jackson was. No one would ever be able to link him to the group, thus no clear connection could ever be made between the IWACs and the Afrikaners.

Poor Freddy. Jackson stubbed out his cigarette. Poor Freddy, hell! Others would die too. And he was responsible. It would be universally viewed as an ugly, sordid act done merely for the sake of money. Fuck that. He was able to view it as a logically and ultimately extended capitalistic business venture. He had seen the effects of napalm on the human body, but napalm manufacturers did not give a damn about that. Profit and loss. They would say this was different, but that was the old bullshit. If you made napalm and sold it to the Air Force knowing they were going to drop it on people, you had helped kill the people, no matter what PR lies you told. And you did it for money, no matter what PR lies you told. And you really didn't care, no matter what PR lies you told. You just didn't want business to fall off.

His RK89 crackled and Donovan's voice came on: "Red Leader, this is Gold Leader. Are you in position?"

41

"Affirmative."

"It's a go."

"Check." He honked his horn three long blasts. Figures began emerging from the parked cars. He could make out Brown in the lead at the jail door. He waited until he heard the first burst of automatic fire, pulled away muttering, "So long, suckers."

When you enter the St. Louis jail, you are in a narrow passageway with visitors' rooms and offices on either side. Farther along, up a very short set of stairs, is a guard desk and behind that a width-of-passage safety glass and a barred door leading to the interior of the jail and the prisoners' cells. The guard desk has a foot pedal which controls the door. The desk is manned by a single guard. Another guard post, also singly manned, is just behind the safety-glass door.

John 3X Brown came through the outer door running, followed quickly by his men. The guard at the desk looked up puzzled. He half rose instinctively as Brown took the steps in two bounds and then the guard reached for his revolver with his right hand and an alarm button with his left. Neither hand made it A short burst, perhaps seven or eight shots, from Brown's rifle at that range lifted him off his feet, up and backward, slammed him into the wall at waist level and he bounced, rolled over in mid-air, landed face first on the floor, bounced slightly again, and settled. Since the second shot had hit his heart and literally exploded it, he was dead before he hit the wall, his body temperature was beginning to drop by the time he settled on the floor. Brown and two of the Afrikaners knelt on one knee before the door while another went behind the desk and stepped on the foot pedal, rolling it back. The second guard, stationed behind the door, had drawn his revolver and begun to retreat toward the inner jail. He paused to fire three shots as the door rolled open. This gave him the dubious pleasure of seeing a large red spot open in the center of John 3X Brown's forehead just before he pitched violently backward and the back of his head tore open. The guard paid for this fleeting pleasure with his life, as eleven out of sixteen shots fired instantly by the other two Afrikaners ripped him apart. The Afrikaners flooded quickly into the heart of the jail, quickly killing the remaining guards and setting the prisoners loose.

The city jail in St. Louis has a semihumane capacity of less than two hundred prisoners and, like most inner-city jails, normally houses a little more than double capacity. That night, due to a particularly rough weekend, there were four hundred fourteen prisoners incarcerated. Most of them were black. Many were friends or relatives of the Afrikaners or were from the Grand Boulevard area. They greeted their liberators with glee and high spirits and some dozen of the true hard cases accepted shotguns or pistols and joined the Afrikaners for the night. Other prisoners were simply glad to be set free and fled quickly out the main door with little or no pause for comment or thanks. A few, mostly those whose terms were very near completion, did not want to leave and were prodded out at gunpoint. At 7:41 p.m., within eleven minutes of John 3X Brown's first shots, the jail had been cleared of all prisoners.

The city jail occupies part of a large city block bounded on the west by Thirteenth Street, on the east by Twelfth Street, the north by Market Street, and the south by Clark Street. It shares that block with the municipal court building east of it, the city hall farther east, a community center building southeast of it, a large parking lot southeast of it, and an open area directly south of the jail. Running north to south between the municipal court and city hall is a narrow parklike walkway with a large statue of the city's founder, Pierre Laclède, at the north end. It was in this passage between the buildings that most of the firefight took place. The press later dubbed it the "Battle of Thirteenth Street," certainly a misnomer since the area is nearly equidistant from Twelfth and Thirteenth and much closer to Market than either of those.

43

The building which houses central police headquarters and 4th District headquarters of the St. Louis Police Department is on the southwest corner of Clark and Twelfth streets, somewhat south and east of the jail. A guard in the second tier of cells, before he was killed, had managed to hit an alarm which was connected with 4th District headquarters. At 7:36 p.m., two patrolmen came hurrying out of the headquarters building onto Clark Street. They crossed the street and cut diagonally through the parking lot toward the jail in a kind of careful lope because the footing was treacherous in the drifting snow. Wind and snow made even normal night visibility very poor. They saw the flood of prisoners pouring out the door and fleeing north on Thirteenth Street at about the same time that two Afrikaners opened up on them with their 510–4s. One officer drew his pistol and returned fire, but the other grabbed his arm and quickly pulled him away. Neither was hurt and they, sensibly, retreated in the face of superior fire for reinforcements. Because of the poor visibility and the fact that only two Afrikaners opened fire on them—they grossly misjudged the force that they were facing. They assumed that a few armed men had assaulted the jail, a not wholly unwarranted conclusion, since anyone familiar with staffing and security at the jail knew that was all it would require to effect a major breakout.

Fourth District commander, Capt. Jack Harshman, decided to consult with Peterson, who already knew of the alarm from the jail. He called Peterson's office in the command post and relayed his patrolmen's report.

Peterson sighed. "Automatic weapons, that's just dandy. All right, I'll send you down six of my men and you take six of yours—give them the AR–15s. Send half of them across the parking lot to engage the gunmen and the other half up Twelfth Street. They can cut between the community center and city hall and the jail and the court building. That way they can come up behind the gunmen from the north corner of the jail. I'll have the dispatcher pull half a dozen blue-

and-whites to come down Thirteenth Street for support."
Peterson hung up and groaned. The first bad storm of the
season had produced a large number of sick calls and sufficient replacements hadn't yet been found. He was understaffed and could ill afford this crisis. And somehow he was
certain they would still hear from the bombers again tonight.

What he did not yet know was that he was facing a force
of over sixty armed men, fifty with automatic rifles, and the
jailbreak had merely been a lure for an ambush. The Afrikaners, with Jackson's guidance, had set a very neat trap.
When Peterson walked into the dispatch room to begin pulling patrol cars for the emergency it was 7:49 p.m.

The St. Louis Police Department is divided into nine districts, each with its own headquarters building, but radio
dispatch is completely centralized. Down an aisle of the
large, square-shaped room known as the Command Post is
an extensive L-shaped area which is glassed off from the
rest of the room and completely soundproofed. There are
eleven desks in the area. At ten are the communications
officers for individual districts, one of the districts using two
desks. They handle routine traffic for each district. The
eleventh desk is the central dispatch. Each car in use by the
department has a radio set that receives on the frequency of
its district desk, but the radios also have an override device
which allows central dispatch to broadcast on two frequency ranges which, when received by the car sets, will
shut out all other transmissions. In this manner, "all-car"
transmissions override district transmissions. When either
of these two frequencies is using sufficient wattage, the cars
cannot receive any other radio communications. It was this
facet of police communications, with its inherent and obvious vulnerability, which finally had convinced Donovan
that the operation was possible.

Peterson stopped to talk to Lieutenant Garrison, a sharp,
young, black officer who was a protégé of his. Garrison
nodded as Peterson explained the situation.

"Okay, Major, I'll pull two cars from each of the three

close districts and replace one each temporarily from three of the outer districts. That'll get the cars there faster."

"That's good, Bill. I think we're going to have to do a lot of juggling tonight. It may get pretty hairy." Garrison walked off to the dispatch room. As Peterson turned to go back to his office, a desk officer nearby held out his telephone receiver.

"Captain Harshman for you, skipper."

"What now, Jack?"

"The bomber called again."

"The same one?"

"For sure. DiAngelo took the call last night and tonight. He says it was the same voice both times."

"What's the bad news?"

"He said there is a bomb planted at the arena due to go off at 8:30."

"Jesus Christ!" Peterson glanced at his watch. 8:02. "Okay, Jack, I'll take care of it." He ran into the dispatch room and grabbed Garrison by the arm. "There's a bomb in the arena set to go off at 8:30. You get ahold of the detail chief out there and tell him what's going down and then start pulling as many blue-and-whites over there as possible. I'll call the arena management, tell them to start evacuating."

He sprinted to his desk and looked up the number, dialed. It took him four agonizing minutes to get ahold of the assistant manager. He drummed wildly with his fingers and pounded his desk with his fist. "Come on, come on!"

"Harold Wilby, assistant manager."

"Mr. Wilby, this is Major Noah Peterson of the St. Louis Police Department. There is a bomb in the arena due to explode at 8:30. You'll have to start evacuating the arena immediately."

"Is this some kind of joke? There are over seventeen thousand people here! The game has started—"

"LISTEN TO ME! This is not a joke! The same people that bombed the Spanish Door last night have planted a bomb in the arena. The chief of detail will come to you immediately and we're sending as many extra police as we can, but you must start evacuating now!" He glanced at a wall clock: 8:08. "You have less than twenty minutes to clear that building!"

The man's voice was shaky now. "All right, Major, we'll do it as quickly as possible."

Noah stabbed the cutoff button, released it, and began dialing the Chief's home number; he hated to call him; he had only finished his tour as watch commander five hours ago, but the night was shaping up badly and he had to be told. After a five-minute conversation, the Chief said he would come back in. As Noah hung up, Lieutenant Garrison came to his doorway. Suddenly Noah turned pale, sweaty, he almost vomited and his hands began to shake.

"Oh, my God!"

Garrison stared. "What's the matter, skipper?"

Noah's voice was choked. "My boy, my son . . . Noah was going to the hockey game tonight."

"Jesus, skipper!"

Noah looked at his phone. If he called Liz to find out if young Noah had gone to the game, he would have to tell her why he wanted to know. They did not lie to each other. At all. And that would put her through hours of agony. Perhaps unnecessarily. Or, perhaps, prematurely.

His internal debate did not last long. Trust won. Liz was just not a fool. She would not go to pieces. He dialed his home number. He squeezed the receiver hard as he listened to the rings. Just let young Noah answer. That would make it all right. The fifth ring was cut off and his son's voice came.

"Peterson residence."

Noah exhaled deeply, slumped back in his chair, looked up at Garrison and winked and smiled almost as one act.

"I thought you were going to the hockey game, son."

"Pop?"

"Yes."

47

"Not me, Dad. Noah went to the game."

Noah groaned and leaned forward over the desk. Sick again.

"Sorry, Charles, your voice sounds so much like your brother's . . . is your mother there?"

"Sure. Hang on."

Liz's voice: "Hi, honey. What's up?"

"I don't want you to get too upset, but . . . there's been a bomb threat at the arena."

"Is it . . . are they . . . the same ones? As last night?"

"We think so."

"But, Noah, that wasn't a threat—they did blow up those bars. People were killed!"

"Please don't panic, Liz."

He could hear her breathe deeply, slowly. "Okay. I'm sorry. What—"

"We had more lead time tonight. They're evacuating the arena right now. As soon as I hang up I'll patch through to the chief of detail and stay in contact with him. I called Chief Dieter and he's coming back in. As soon as he gets here I'll go out to the arena and find Noah."

"Okay, but I could go now—"

"Liz, you mustn't. There will be chaos out there and no one will pay any attention to you. When I get there I can cut through quickly. I'll call you as soon as I find Noah."

"But, honey, I want—"

"Liz, I could have not called. You wouldn't know. I told you because I trust you to do the right thing. Not to go to pieces. Please stay at home."

She sighed. "All right. But . . ."

"I know, Liz, I know."

As soon as he hung up, Noah leaped from his chair, brushed past Garrison and began moving quickly down an aisle toward the radio room. He shouted over his shoulder to Garrison who was following.

"Who's chief of detail out there tonight?"

"Sergeant John Whitaker."

"Good. He knows my boy. I want to get through to him. He's got to find Noah and hang on to him."

Ernie Vincente stopped his detail between the city hall and the community building. He was to wait for the first sounds of shooting from the other patrol on the south side of the jail. Then they would cross the courtyard, go between the jail and court building and flank the gunmen from the north. The snow continued to fall and visibility was so poor that Vincente could only see twenty feet or so ahead. It was very cold, but at least between the buildings they had some protection from the wind. He checked his AR–15 and glanced at his men. A fat desk sergeant, a fifty-year-old patrolman, and three rookies in their twenties. No one looked very happy about the job, no one was eager to move. Their faces were pinched with the cold and the fear. Vincente, thirty-eight, married, six children, fourteen years on the force, understood; he was afraid too; he knew what automatic weapons could do, but he was a dedicated policeman. He believed in his duty. He suppressed his fear as best he could.

Sounds of gunfire came from the south side of the jail. Vincente stood up, looked around at the detail again. "All right, let's go. Stay close to me and keep low." He led out in a crablike trot, bent slightly at the waist. The men followed. The sound of gunfire continued. They were halfway or a little more across the courtyard when Vincente saw dark shapes crouched between the jail and the court building. He tensed and began to slow, straining his eyes to see better. The Afrikaners opened up when they saw the detail begin to slow. There were a dozen between the two buildings, a dozen on the roof of the court building, which had parapets, like a medieval castle, ideal for mounting and firing automatic weapons, and a dozen at the north end of the

49

courtyard. The distances were a little long for the visibility so that the Afrikaners were essentially shooting at shadows, but thirty-six 510–4s arranged in an L-shaped pattern, slightly disjointed and with varying elevations, can lay down a terrible and overlapping field of fire.

Vincente went down first, both legs hit, fell heavily and lay stunned, unable to move. The others broke and ran—two back toward the passageway between buildings they had just left and three south toward the parking lot; they slipped and slid in the snow; flung their weapons away; cried out in fear and pain. Two rookies making for the building passageway went down quickly, hit badly, died quickly. One rookie and the fat desk sergeant went down one after the other as they ran south and bled to death rapidly—both having been hit in major blood vessels. The fifty-year-old patrolman was hit in the right shoulder, then the left wrist, but somehow managed to keep his feet. He fled across the parking lot toward headquarters. He met the three survivors of the other patrol, falling back under heavy fire from the south side of the jail where a dozen more Afrikaners were positioned. Sergeant Vincente's detail had been so badly surprised by such overwhelming force that they had not fired a single shot in return. It was a detail, later reconstructed, that seemed to enrage the public disproportionately.

When Vincente regained his senses he lay still, his face nearly buried in snow. An Afrikaner was walking around checking the bodies. As he passed Vincente, he kicked him, by chance in the legs. Vincente bit his tongue and somehow managed to keep from making a sound or moving. The man walked back toward the north end of the courtyard. Vincente began to say silent prayers in his head. If he tried to crawl, one of them would come and finish him off before he could get away. If he lay there too long without help, he knew he would bleed to death or freeze to death or die of shock. He began to wonder what it would feel like. The pain in his legs, especially the left knee, was like fire and stab-

50

bing. He wondered if it would be a relief when his legs started to go numb, or would he be so frightened he would have to try to crawl away, bringing almost certain death. He wondered if he would be so enraged that he would blaspheme in his dying moments or would he be able to make a good act of contrition, have a chance of dying in a state of grace. He knew if he could forgive these unknown killers, it would be a good act. He tried hard to think of love, disinterested, pure love like the love of God: *agape*. He concentrated on ridding himself of hatred, cleansing himself of rage at this senseless and ridiculous manner of dying. He could not. He was merely a man and knew it, and he hated these bastards, whoever they were. He was exhausted from the mental effort. Silent tears trickled down his face, wetting the snow. He said softly, "Let God forgive them. I can't." No one heard him.

### 8:12 p.m.: SGT. RONALD MACKLIN

The Canadien's center and left winger were streaking for the St. Louis goal on a breakaway. The crowd rose roaring. There was only one St. Louis defenseman between them and the goal. He came up on the center, who had the puck. The center fed a drop pass to the winger and lowered his shoulder. Skating at full speed, he laid a vicious body check on the defenseman and they both fell to the ice, sliding apart. The winger had streaked by them with the puck. As he rode in on the goalie at close range he deked left, snapped a ninety mph slap shot into the upper right hand corner of the goal net, just over the shoulder of the goalie who was moving left after having taken the fake. The red goal light went on and the crowd booed and showered the ice with paper airplanes, soft-drink cups, wadded pages from game programs. The defenseman and center had regained their feet and were shoving each other and shouting curses. The defenseman swung a roundhouse left that landed on the

51

center's ear. The center kicked one of the defenseman's skates and shoved him to the ice. The defenseman grabbed a fallen stick and hooked the center's skates, pulled hard, and brought the center down. He crawled over to the center on his knees and began beating his head and shoulders with the stick, which snapped in two. The benches emptied of players. Some surrounded and jumped on the downed defenseman and center, some began fights of their own. The crowd was frenzied. It was at this point that the public address system was taken over by the assistant manager.

"Ladies and gentlemen! Ladies and gentlemen! Ladies and gentlemen! This is the arena management speaking, please, ladies and gentlemen, this is the arena management! We have an emergency! We have an emergency!" His voice was cracking now and people began to listen. "We have an emergency! The arena must be cleared immediately! The arena—" The rest of the sentence was drowned in howls of outrage. Sergeant Macklin and his men had moved at the first sound of the public address system. They left their radios underneath their seats and moved quickly to exit aisles. They were all well on their way out by the time the screaming subsided. Afraid the crowd would not move, the assistant manager's nerve went and he said the one thing he should not have said. "Ladies and gentlemen, we must clear the arena immediately! There is a bomb in the building!" There were, perhaps, two seconds of dead and dread silence. Then panic. The rest of the manager's plea for a quick but orderly evacuation was unheard in the noise of seventeen thousand people trying to get out of the building at once. People ran, shoved, tripped, fell, trampled, were trampled. The parking lots surrounding the building became chaos. Police attempts to direct an orderly flow of traffic were ignored. The exits became jammed and cars stuck in the snow. The bombs went off simultaneously at 8:30 p.m. They were not large charges, but they were placed so that several seats splintered upward through the wooden roof and the pattern weakened the structure so that the wooden cupola atop the roof groaned, sagged, and collapsed inward. Most of the debris fell in on the vacant ice and empty core seats. Some showered out and down the sides of the building. Half the crowd was outside, half in. Some few people were knocked down by the concussion or fell down in fear. The noise and sight of the blast seemed to paralyze the crowd for a few seconds. It was then that Sergeant Macklin and his men moved out of the shadows on various sides of the parking lot where they had been waiting.

A hockey crowd is a particularly volatile group of sports fans. They are devotees of the second most violent sport in the world. Only professional boxing is more brutal than the particular brand of mayhem practiced in the National Hockey League and the World Hockey Association. In recent years, speed, skating, and skill have been replaced by bullyboy defense and street brawling. The newer hockey fan goes to see fighting and violence under the guise of an organized game. This particular crowd had been brought to a fevered outrage by the coincidence of the enemy (visiting team) goal, the players' brawl, and the announcement that they must leave the arena with the game less than a third completed after struggling through foul weather to attend. Fear had been mixed into them with the knowledge of the bomb and panic had seized them, to be followed by terror and shock at the explosion. They froze momentarily, but they were ready to be exploited.

Macklin and his men moved into pockets of hurrying fans and quickly jostled, shoved, elbowed, and slugged several men each. Five small fights began instantaneously. They were like five matches tossed into a large pool of gasoline—they exploded and the flames fled in all directions simultaneously. Pockets of brawling erupted into mass battery. When the police tried to move in, they were turned on and assaulted. Someone attacked a car that was attempting to move out an exit lane and this provoked a general assault on automobiles, especially those with passengers already inside. Cars were rocked and overturned, windshields and

53

windows shattered, doors torn off. One man, wielding a fallen police officer's billy club, shattered every window, both headlights, all the instruments, and then helped others tear all four doors off a new ten-thousand-dollar-plus Cadillac sedan without ever realizing during the entire twenty-two-minute orgy of destruction that it was the car he had purchased four days earlier.

Cars rammed each other in what was originally a frenzy to escape, but which quickly developed into a massive, free-style demolition derby with crippled hulks, radiators steaming, smashing anything in range. One man, turning away from the exit lane on the upper incline of the front parking lot, got something of a downhill start and rammed straight into a pillar of an outer archway of the building. The front end of his compact car crumpled hideously, he was hurled head first through the windshield into the pillar and died instantly of a broken neck and crushed skull.

The parking lot was littered with broken glass, torn metal, fallen bodies, pieces of clothing. The still-falling snow was discolored on the ground by steaming water, gasoline, oil, brake fluid, and blood. Some people fled back into the building, and offices were ransacked, trophy cases broken, and mementos destroyed or stolen. In dark corners of the building and the parking lot four women were raped. The riot raged on.

Macklin and his men, after igniting the riot, began to fight and edge their way to the outer edges of the parking lots, and within eight minutes they had all been able to flee on foot. It was not nearly so hard to do as it might seem, since they alone among the crowd were not engaged in purposeless hysteria.


**8:14 p.m.: LT. ARTHUR ADAMS**


The eight men got out of the two cars, automatic rifles slung over their shoulders, each carrying small metal boxes that contained incendiary devices. One man had heavy bolt-and-wire cutters. Their breath clouded around their faces as they walked. They did not talk. They crossed Kingshighway Boulevard and waited while one man cut away a large section of wire fencing. Five men walked through the opening and the remaining three, including the man with the cutters, walked down the sidewalk and crossed the street to the neighboring plant. He cut away another section of fence and the three went through it.

Art Adams led the five men up to the doors of the Rexall plant. He used the butt of his rifle to smash a window in a door. An alarm sounded. He opened the door and the men entered. They made their way quickly to a storage area containing several large vats of cough medicine with a high alcoholic content. They shot holes in the vats and then tossed several small aerosol canisters with impact detonators into the quickly flowing liquid on the floor. The detonators exploded, igniting a kind of jellylike petroleum inside which immediately touched off the pooling cough liquid. They ran through the ground floor, tossing several canisters into each room or office. Outside, they shot holes in several second-story windows and tossed the remaining canisters through them. The men at the neighboring plant were finishing up the same way. When all the canisters had been expended, they retreated outside the fencing to the island in the center of Kingshighway and stood in a semicircle between two large trees. From their position they had fire cover lanes onto all three vehicular approaches to the two plants. The Rexall plant was fully aflame and pouring smoke; the neighboring plant was beginning to show a strong red glow through its windows, but was not yet smoking as heavily; it was seven minutes from the moment they had entered the Rexall plant. Lights were on in houses across the street and faces appeared at windows. A door opened and a man stepped out onto his porch. He stared for a few seconds then shouted at the men on the island.

"What's going on?"

Adams shouted back. "There's a fire there, mister."

"I can see that. What're you fellows doing?"

"Watching. You'd better phone in to the fire department."

"Oh. Yeah. Sure, okay." The man disappeared back into his house. Adams spoke to his men.

"Won't be long now."

One of them said, "Yeah."

They all checked their rifles. Most replaced their spent or nearly spent clips. They spread out slightly to increase the angles on their field of fire. They waited.

A fire engine arrived first. They fired on it when it was half a block away on Kingshighway to the south. It skidded to a halt, half-turned across the street. The firemen leaped out of the cab and hid behind the truck. Adams's men took turns peppering it with short three-, four-, five-shot bursts at thirty-second intervals. Just enough to keep the firemen pinned down.

Two patrol cars approached from opposite directions. The officers tried to engage the IWACs, but their pistols were totally ineffective at long range and they had to keep down behind their cars because of the firepower of the automatic rifles. It was 8:34 p.m. Adams decided they would hold until 8:50 or until heavy police reinforcements came, whichever was sooner.

### 8:38 p.m.: MAJOR NOAH PETERSON

He sat at his desk making small tense circles on the arm of his chair with his left index finger. Chief of Police George Dieter sat in a chair across from him. Bill Garrison stood in the doorway.

"We've got to do it, George. We've got a full-scale fire-fight over at the jail with a large number of men with automatic weapons. We've got a riot and bombing at the arena and a major fire at the Rexall plant with snipers keeping the

56

firemen away. All in the middle of the worst snowstorm in years. You've seen the duty rosters and flow sheets. We're understaffed and more than half our men are either out of their districts or soon will be. If we don't call the Commissioner and advise him of the situation—we're going to leave ourselves out on the limb and the Mayor and the PC will have an axe handy."

Dieter was a large balding man in his late fifties. He was noted for being ponderous and slow-moving—slow to act. He stared at the far wall and pulled on his right earlobe. He was grumpy, having been pulled back five and a half hours after his own shift as watch commander had ended.

Finally, he spoke: "What do you think, Bill?"

Garrison straightened, spoke levelly. "I think Noah's right."

"They'll want to call in the Guard."

Garrison nodded. "Probably will."

Dieter sat and stared at the wall. He rubbed the tip of his nose with a sausagelike thumb. Peterson began drumming his fingers irritably on the desk top, noticed it, stopped.

Dieter sighed. "All right, Noah, let me use your phone. I'll talk to the Commissioner and he'll have to get ahold of the Mayor." He crossed to the chair that Peterson quickly vacated. He thought for a moment after he sat, then lifted the receiver and began to dial. Peterson and Garrison stepped out of the room and Peterson closed the door. They crossed to Garrison's desk and stood.

"God, it's hard to get George to do anything. We should have made this move twenty minutes ago."

Noah turned and started toward the radio room. He spoke to Garrison again as they walked.

"This fear of calling for help is lunatic. Anyone can see we're not equipped for this kind of crisis."

Garrison nodded. "We're going to have to undercut George without getting him mad. The Mayor and the PC have got to call the Governor and have him get the Guard mobilized."

Noah shook his head. "Wrong. Wrongo. You're going to have to do that job, Bill. I've got to get out to the arena." In the radio room he went to a district dispatch desk. "Get me the chief of detail again."

"No can do, Major. The riot is full-scale. No one out there has time to answer radio calls. I can't raise anyone. I have to wait until one of them has a chance to call in."

"When was the last time you talked to anybody?"

"About five or ten minutes ago. Whitaker was on the horn for maybe thirty seconds screaming for more men."

"Anything about my son?"

"Nothing, Major . . . sorry, but it sounds like nobody has any chance to do anything, but scramble."

Noah nodded, turned, and started for his office, fast. Dieter was still sitting at Noah's desk. He stared as Noah put on his uniform overcoat and hard-brimmed hat with the gold badge and braid.

"Noah?"

"I'm going, George. I should have left ten minutes ago as soon as you came in the door. There's a full-scale riot out there and I've got to find my boy."

"Noah, the Mayor and the PC will be here any minute. You're on top of the situation and I've just come in cold. I need you to talk to them."

"Dammit, George, my boy's out there!"

"Noah, give me twenty minutes."

"George, don't do this." Noah felt like a man being cleaved in half. He believed in duty, but what of love? Family? Blood? Don't some things run deeper than abstract morality?

"Noah, you're a cop and a damn fine one. The best I've known in thirty years, but this is the crunch. This is your job. You've got to give me fifteen minutes."

Noah looked at his watch: 8:54. "Ten minutes, George. Ten minutes and I'm out the door."

Dieter nodded. Noah paced reflexively. Garrison stood in the doorway and watched. The essence of the policeman's

58

mentality is an unwavering belief in Dynamic Man. Any disaster can be avoided if you know how. Planning, foresight, training, communication, discipline are his tools. His fundamental philosophical assertion is that any situation can be saved if you make the right moves. Noah had always been of that mental bent, perhaps it was why he became a policeman. Now he was being tortured. His city was plunging into chaos. His son was in danger. And he was helpless. He pounded one fist against the other. Dieter and Garrison looked away.

### 8:39 p.m.: CPL. PATRICK JOSEPH HOGAN

They turned into the winding road that ran up to and behind the power plant. A large sign greeted them:

UNION ELECTRIC EMPLOYEES ONLY
NO TRESPASSING

As he approached the speed bumps, Hogan slowed and turned off the headlights. They coasted forward slowly in the dark. The glow of the smokestacks was eerie through the snow. They took the bumps gently and then pulled off the road fifty feet farther on, still well short of the guardhouse.

The Portage Des Sioux power plant is on the west bank of the Mississippi, north of St. Louis and within two miles of the spot where Lewis and Clark left their boats and began their great exploratory expedition. It is also the spot where the great council of the thousand chieftains was held. The plant is formed by a series of oddly shaped geometric boxes and rectangles of varying heights, with twin smokestacks set just slightly apart, so that the whole thing has the look at a distance of some curious insect with giant leading antennae.

They got out of the car and trotted in a crouch toward the truck entrance to the plant. One man veered off to dispatch the guard. They barely heard the quick rifle shots in the wind.

Inside the plant, two men rounded up the security force and small night staff and locked them in a windowless inner office. Hogan and the other two made their way to the generator room and quickly planted substantial plastique charges inside the generators. It was quiet work with no words passed. The only sounds were mechanical. Dim light bounced off slick metal surfaces in odd reflections. The scene had a slick greenish cast as if from an old science fiction movie.

Perete grunted once. "Isn't this a lot of plastique for what we're to do?"

Hogan nodded; his grin was impish. "Ah well, whatever's worth the doing, lad, is worth doing well." Perete grunted. Hogan laughed. "You can go off people, you know." Perete shook his head in silence.

They trailed the wire after them as they scuttled out of the room. On the edge of the truck dock they crouched and waited as Hogan connected the wire to a battery. He glanced at his watch: 8:49. One minute. Two sets of headlights were coming up the road quickly. The guard had not died immediately, and a state patrolman and a sheriff's deputy had responded to his alarm.

Hogan shrugged. "All right, lads, we won't wait." He flipped the switch. The explosions knocked them all off the truck dock. A back wall gave way and within seconds the smokestacks tumbled backward onto the building. As it started to crumble, fire jumped crazily like a skipping stone.

Hogan and Perete had recovered their feet first and scrambled away up a slight incline. Looking back, they saw the other three men go down under the crumbling wall, debris, and fire.

Perete swore. "You stupid bastard. I told you it was too much." Hogan tapped his elbow and pointed through the snow. The two policemen had recovered from their shock at the explosion and were moving toward Hogan and Perete,

60

guns drawn. As they unslung rifles from their shoulders, the police opened fire. The range was close. The first pistol shot hit Perete in the mouth and he fell backward hard, without a sound. Hogan loosed a long steady burst that picked up the sheriff's deputy and threw him backward screaming. The state trooper knelt and emptied his pistol. The back of Hogan's head hurt as he stared up at the snow-filled night sky. He lay on the ground from a blow to his right side. He rolled over, saw the trooper reloading his pistol. He crawled the yard to his rifle and turned it as the trooper swung the cylinder of his revolver shut. He squeezed off the last eight shots in his clip and the trooper slammed backward. Snow was in his eyes. He fumbled in his pockets for a new clip and inserted it, threw the empty one away. No one moved. He realized he felt cold. He used the rifle for a brace, struggled to his feet. Perete was dead. The trooper was dead. The deputy was dead. He tossed the rifle away and staggered toward the car. He fell once.

Inside the car was warm once he got going, but after he had crossed the river and gotten to Route 66, he felt dizzy and his side hurt. He pulled off the road and examined his wound. The hole was ugly and rather broad. He was not bleeding heavily, but there was a steady seepage. He hoped that meant nothing major had been hit. He switched off the interior light and leaned back. Northbound traffic was not heavy. He drifted for a time, almost dozed. The snow and the cold made him think of Sligo again. The old days. The IRA days. And the running.

Donovan and Hogan had grown up on neighboring farms on the peninsula between Bantry and Dunmanus bays in southwest County Cork. Hogan had been a typical farm youth, but Donovan had always been different. He was brighter. More intense. Almost otherworldly. He had a vocation. The priest encouraged it and the family saved money for him, mortgaged the farm and with a partial scholarship had been able to send him to the university in Dublin. Hogan stayed home and worked his father's farm.

Donovan won a special scholarship to Oxford where he majored in foreign languages. While in seminary, he had his first doubts when his parents and five youngest siblings had died in the influenza epidemic. His emotions were tied, as from childhood, to the Mysteries of the Church and Faith even while his intellect struggled with rationality. As a teacher in a Jesuit secondary school in Limerick he sought the release of social action in local politics, but was reprimanded five times by his headmaster and twice by the Father General in two years. When an attempt to transfer him was made, he simply left and returned to the family farm, now his, and began to work it with his younger brother Seamus.

Patjo was involved in minor, local IRA activities. When they resumed their friendship, Donovan became involved. It was a radical, socialist branch of the Provisional wing. Donovan soon welded an ill-fitting yoke to the spiritual ethic of Ignatius Loyola, the economic teachings of Engels and Marx, the nationalistic fervor of the IRA, and the perversity of the Irish temperament, which seems to delight in the Job-like afflictions of the Irish people as if the nation would lose half its identity without the English and the weather to complain about. Donovan made this spiritual marriage for his own emotional and intellectual reasons, an uncomfortable union at best and more from desperate need than clear belief. As Donovan began to dominate the group, they became more reckless. After a bank robbery in Clonmel, they were warned by headquarters in Dublin to limit themselves to their assigned tasks and quit developing their own enterprises. A month later they blew up the office of a British shipping firm in Cork City. Three people were killed and nine injured. By now, Donovan was an extremist of maniacal proportions, a near-crazed young man, brilliant and tortured by his inability to reconcile the world around him with either his emotional faith or his intellectual beliefs. Even his men were frightened of him, save only Patjo Hogan and his younger brother Seamus, who foolishly idolized him.

Headquarters disowned them publicly and, in a traumatic rage, Donovan and Seamus shot and killed a Provo staff captain on O'Connell Street, Dublin, at midday with several hundred witnesses. They were complete outlaws now, with every man's hand turned against them. For thirty-nine months, Donovan and his brother and Hogan rampaged through the midlands and along the west coast, robbing banks and running. For all that time, they never slept three nights in the same place. Hogan was a stoic who drank from breakfast until bedtime, was never drunk and never complained. Seamus was frightened often, but would willingly do anything his brother said. Donovan deteriorated. The hopelessness and futility of what they were doing wore most heavily upon him because he thought the most about the rationale of acts. He began to long for death. His faith in either God or man had long since deserted him, but some emotional mix of childhood instruction and shame at what he thought cowardice prevented him from taking his own life. But he longed for death all the same, lusted after it as he had never desired a woman, sought it willfully in ever more daring and foolish raids. He died in Sligo, on the barren northwest coast, a few days before Christmas in the winter of 1955.

They spent the night in a barn outside Inishcrone overlooking Killala Bay. They had been driving the same stolen car, a white Morris-Mini, for ten days. Patjo wanted to steal another one in the morning as they customarily only drove a car for a few days, but Donovan paid him no mind, only muttered in reply, "After the raid."

The sky was dark gray and low. They could not see the peaks of the Ox Mountains as they drove. Sligo Bay was wild. A light, wet snow began to fall, reducing visibility to less than five meters. They parked on Stephen Street and began to walk through the town, tipping their heads to the few pedestrians they met. There were five banks in Sligo. They robbed them all, one after the other, calmly walking from one to another.

It was much the same as always. A few customers, a few employees; terrified eyes in those who comprehended, eyes that could not tear away from the pistols; blank gazes of some, shocked into an unresponsive terror. In the first bank, Patjo actually had to lead the manager to the tellers' cage and help him start emptying money into the bag. There was not much money in these banks. They would take all the notes and then pocket their pistols and stroll down the street to the next one.

The Guarda followed them from bank to bank. The Sergeant and his men would barely have begun their questioning when a call from barracks would relay the message that another bank had been robbed and they would march briskly over to it, only to have the sequence repeated. At the door of the fourth bank, the Sergeant stopped suddenly and two of his men bumped into him knocking him down. As they helped him to his feet, he frowned in furious concentration. He stood thinking hard for several minutes as his men shifted from foot to foot, anxious to get inside out of the cold. Finally, he spoke.

"We'll go on up to the Hyde Bridge bank."

"It hasn't been robbed."

"Sure and maybe it is being robbed." His four men stared at each other and shrugged at the imaginative excess of their superior, but they duly fell into line behind him when he began marching up the street.

At the entrance to the Hyde Bridge bank, they stood aside and nodded to Donovan, Patjo, and Seamus as they came walking out. As they stepped inside, the manager came running up to them. He addressed the Sergeant in frantic tones.

"Praise Jesus, you're here, Sergeant! Those men just robbed us."

"What men?"

"The three you just passed coming in."

The Sergeant frowned a moment, then smiled and turned to his men. "Sure and you see, 'tis just as I told you. 'Twas being robbed." Several of the men nodded appreciatively. "Now, about a description."

"Description! You just passed them! They're out there in that white mini!"

The car had stalled and would not start. When the Guarda came out of the bank and began walking toward them, they jumped out and began firing. Patjo was hit in the thigh by the first Guarda bullet and fell heavily to the pavement, striking his head. He lay unconscious. One of the Guarda was wounded and the other men took cover behind cars or in doorways. It was hard to see where to fire through the dim light and snow. The Sergeant began to walk across the street directly toward them, firing his pistol as he came. A bullet caught Seamus in the throat and he went down. Donovan sat down and held his brother's head in his lap. The money bag had been dropped and fell open. Some soft-pink ten-pound notes fluttered around. One fell on Seamus's throat and quickly turned a deep crimson, like litmus paper in a chemical reaction. Donovan sat quietly and watched his brother die. He died too, if the life of a man's spirit is the measure of his living. He did not utter a word to his captors. He answered no questions. He did not even speak when he had been remanded to the prison in Dublin to await trial. He did not speak for three months. He did not think either. He was a vegetable that had to be led from one place to another and physically directed to perform even the simplest task. He had to be fed like a baby. The jailors soon tired of this and allowed Patjo to care for him. Hogan was a simple enough soul and he could not fathom what had happened to his friend. He was more frightened by Donovan's condition than by their immediate external peril of trial and long imprisonment or death. They were twenty-eight years old.

Hogan's head cleared. He let the bad days fall away. He took a soothing swallow from his pint bottle. He would have to move soon. If he could just make it to Chicago. To the airport. Ah, well, the job was done. Bit botched, but done just the same. And nearly on schedule.

The Portage Des Sioux plant went up at 8:49. The teams at Bagnell Dam, Baldwin, and Meramec had little trouble with minimal night staff and set off their charges at precisely 9:00 p.m. The three switching stations which can borrow power from neighboring states went up at 9:01, as did the telephone emergency battery depot. The city of St. Louis was completely without electrical power and telephone communications.

He stood quietly, alone in the shadows of the upper-level terrace of Mansion House Center. When the power had gone, he had slipped out the promenade level door and walked quickly to this spot. He had a good view of the bank. Their lights had come back on almost immediately as their emergency power kicked in. He lit a cigar and waited. When the explosions came, in three minutes, they were not really audible to him, they were more like sudden strong vibrations against his ear. The charges had been quite small, just enough to disable the generators beyond quick repair. The bank was dark. He selected a frequency on his transmitter and spoke.

"Gold Leader to Main Force—it's a go." McGregor received the message in the warehouse. It was his signal to bring the trucks and the men.

He slipped the transmitter back into his overcoat pocket and puffed on his cigar. The snow was beginning to bother him. At first it had been good, making a bad night for the police worse. Now it was going to make their job harder and he worried about the planes. If they could not get into Alton tonight . . . well they had an alternate plan, but he did not much care for it. He waited. Patiently. Motionless.

In a few moments he heard the first sound of the trucks rumbling down Fourth Street. He waited until the first one pulled into view. He crossed to the stairwells and began to descend to meet Sergeant-Major McGregor.

The oversize van had been parked in the lot of the aged and nursing home of Our Lady of the Snows, for half an hour. It was a scenic spot on the Illinois bluffs, overlooking the river and the city, not far from East St. Louis. Hauptmann and Private Mundt sat quietly, finishing the last of six Reuben sandwiches they had brought with them. They were tall, heavily muscled, classic Aryan physical types. They conversed sporadically in soft Bavarian German. They had been boyhood friends, brought together by a common love of skiing, hiking, mountain climbing, and other physical fitness routines. They were in their late twenties and had been lovers for eleven years. Hauptmann opened a can of beer and passed it to Mundt, opened one for himself. They both took several swallows and belched at about the same time.

Mundt smiled. "Liebchen, we should not have had the sauerkraut sandwiches on top of the chili."

Hauptmann laughed and held up his can of beer. "And the beer. I have the feeling it's going to get very close in here soon." As if his body felt compelled to confirm his observation, he farted long and loud.

Mundt giggled. "Schweinhundt!" He rolled down his window for some fresh air.

When the lights went out in the city below them, first the northern third and then a minute later the southern and western two thirds, Hauptmann eased into the back of the van, followed closely by Mundt. There was only the narrowest of passageways between the two banks of electronic equipment which filled the back of the van. They began fiddling with dials and warming up the equipment which constituted a 50,000-watt mobile transmitter, run off the engine and a support gasoline generator. Another van was

parked alongside of them, and it was filled with extra gasoline and the second generator. An identical team was parked
farther north along the Illinois bluffs, near Edwardsville.
They checked their scanner and then turned it on. It was set
to monitor the lower frequency range of the two used by the
St. Louis Police Department for "all-car" transmissions. It
was set to home on transmissions within this narrow range
so that it would automatically find and lock on "all-car"
transmissions if this channel was being used. The Edwardsville van was set to home on the other frequency range used
by ST.L.P.D. central dispatch. When they were ready to
transmit they would lock the scanner into the transmission
system and whenever it "found" a police transmission it
would lock on that frequency and transmit a terrible, ear-
piercing, high-pitched blast of electronic static. Situated
here on the bluffs, high above the city and with the power
of 50,000 watts, they and the Edwardsville van would close
off radio communications between headquarters and their
cars. The locking override frequency would not let the cars
send or receive any other signals. They began to monitor
the frequency.

"Central, this is eighty-one in niner, what the hell is going
on! There's no power out here."

"Eighty-one, this is central. Affirmative. There's no
power anywhere in the city."

Mundt farted. "Ah, Christ, turn the thing on. Let's get
out of here, I can't stand my own gas."

Hauptmann glanced at his watch and nodded. "I guess
it's close enough to time." He flipped a series of switches
and the system became automatic. They crawled forward to
the truck seats.


**9:09 p.m.: MAJOR NOAH PETERSON**

The power had failed at headquarters as it had all over
the city, but emergency generators had kicked on automat-

68

ically within seconds, just as they had at the Federal Reserve Bank. Unlike the bank, headquarters' generators continued to function.

He stood behind the central dispatch desk and watched. The dispatcher continued the process that he had been trying for several moments. He flipped back and forth between the two frequency ranges. The results were always the same. A second or two of clear broadcast or reception, then a continuing stream of electronic static. The noise was piercing, irritating. Each time it came, Peterson flinched even though he was prepared for it. After a few more tries, the dispatcher swiveled around to Peterson.

"That's it, skipper. We're being jammed." Peterson nodded. Since the jamming transmission locked the patrol car sets into the override function, the district dispatchers could not reach the men either.

"All right, Harvey. Keep trying."

"Okay, skipper, but you know what the men are going to do."

"What?"

"That noise is too irritating. After a while, they're going to turn off their sets and only check them every ten minutes or so. No one can stand to listen to that static continuously."

Peterson nodded again. "You're probably right, Harvey, but you keep trying anyway. Let me know if you get through."

"Okay, skipper."

Peterson left the dispatch cubicle and walked toward the Chief's office. Most of the desk men were sitting in pairs and trios, talking in hushed tones. There really wasn't much for them to do except routine paperwork since communication was cut off from the outside. Peterson felt both angry and calm, almost opposite energy flow. It was as if the anger he had left was in his conscious mind while his subconscious and his body were submitting to a kind of inevitability. They were accepting what his conscious mind

69

could not—things had gotten away from them, him, the department, proper authority; control had been torn away and it seemed there was little anyone could do but continue what feeble motions were still available to them. Occasionally, men would report into headquarters physically and could be given face-to-face instructions. A few men were available in the building to run errands or carry messages to the different district headquarters, but the value of that was limited since the districts could not communicate with their men either, except when the men might occasionally report in. It was something they all knew, but normally took for granted—constant, instant communication is the key to modern police procedure. Communication was the heart of it. Peterson stopped. Of course it was. Of course it was.

A shiver, a chill, a premonition ran through him as the idea finally forced itself from his subconscious. He walked the last few steps to the Chief's office slowly, his heart like a great weight, a perpend lodged in his chest. Garrison, Dieter, Commissioner Resnick and Mayor Allen were sitting in the office waiting for him. He was still wearing his overcoat and he stood in the doorway of the office refusing to come in or sit down.

"I'll give you a wrap, gentlemen, and then I'm leaving for the arena. Our last communications with field units leave us with this picture: One—the firefight around the jail complex continues and we've already lost eleven officers, killed or wounded. We had pulled a total of thirty-six blue-and-whites from their normal routines, the majority from out of their districts, to the scene, plus called in the sniper teams from each district. Two—the bomb at the arena did substantial damage to the building, a panic and full-scale riot started and we have sent twenty-one extra patrol cars to that scene to restore order, clear the crowd, and get the injured to hospitals. We don't have any estimate of casualties. . . ." Noah's voice broke; he breathed deeply trying to summon control.

70

Mayor Allen, a florid-faced fiftyish man, wheezed. "Take your time, Major. We all know the personal strain you're under."

Fat bastard. Fat bastard. You don't really give a damn—you're just a fucking politician. Noah's mind screamed at him, but he wrestled control.

His voice was flat, but steady. "We don't have an estimate of casualties, but from the fragmentary reports we've had they will be high. Three—we have a major fire at the Rexall plant on Kingshighway and the firemen can't get to it because of snipers. We pulled eleven blue-and-whites to that scene. That's a total of sixty-eight cars, over a third of our *normal* strength and I emphasize normal because we had about a ten percent sick-out tonight. In addition, the jailbreak loosed about four hundred prisoners onto the streets, and a large number of street officers, I don't know the exact figure, but at least forty men—twenty more cars—are engaged away from their normal routine trying to track down the escapees. I did that earlier in the evening, before we knew we were going to have all these emergencies. It was a mistake, but we can't get them back now."

Police Commissioner Resnick shook his head. "No one will criticize that decision, Major Peterson. It was sound command procedure."

Noah flicked that consideration away with a nervous hand gesture. "Whatever. The point is that we have half or more of our men dislocated doing crisis tasks and even when they are done with them, they'll be unavailable to us because we can't communicate new orders to them. Some may go back to their district headquarters, some may come here, some may resume normal patrols, but we've lost complete control of our forces because we're being jammed. The electric power and telephone service for the entire city has been lost. There were two early reports of a large explosion up by Portage Des Sioux and we know at least one of the inner-city switching stations was bombed. I think we have to assume sabotage. What does it all add up to?"

71

There was a moment of silence. The men exchanged glances. Resnick leaned forward.

"What do you think it adds up to, Major?"

"Sabotage on the grand scale. Design. Some sort of plan of diversion to neutralize the police department." His voice was rising, but he couldn't stop it. "Somewhere out there, someone is doing something that is so big that it's worth all this!"

Mayor Allen wheezed patronizingly. "That seems a little far-fetched, Major. Who's behind this conspiracy—the Russians, perhaps?"

Dieter snapped, "There's no need for sarcasm, Mayor. Major Peterson is an able and dedicated officer. He does not make frivolous suggestions."

"Does that mean you agree with him, Chief?"

"I didn't say that, but I don't think you ought to indulge in press conference repartee or impugn the intelligence of the Major. He's earned his rank on the basis of extreme merit. Not all of us can say that of ourselves."

Allen sat up straight, reddening. "Just what do you mean by that remark, Chief Dieter?"

Noah listened, his anger and frustration mounting; he was sick of their pointless bickering; finally he shouted at them.

"Shut up!" They stared at him in shock. No one talked to them that way. "You are babbling like a bunch of idiot children while the city comes down around your ears. Allen—you're looking to hang the whole department with this disaster to protect your political ass. Resnick—you're looking to get rid of George, and maybe me, with this one— you've wanted him out for two years. And dammit, George—you're playing their shitty political games. They're pols, but you're supposed to be a cop. A pox on all your houses. I'm going after my son." He half walked, half ran out of the Command Post.

The first-floor entry hall was crowded with wounded men waiting to be taken to City Hospital, runners bringing situation reports, men getting fresh supplies of ammunition, and

72

a dozen reporters. One of the reporters recognized Noah, called to him, and he was quickly surrounded and besieged with questions.

"Anything new to report, Major?"

"What's the situation now?"

"Is it true that the Mayor, Police Commissioner, and the Chief are up in the Command Post?"

"Do you think there's any connection between these crisis events tonight or is it just a coincidence?"

"Anything new on the power failure?"

Noah forced himself to be calm. He raised his hands palms outward asking for quiet and waited for the reporters to be still. He did not resent the press as some policemen did. He had often had favorable coverage during his career and he respected the professionals, as he asked them to respect him, dismissed the hacks with contempt, as he disdained lazy or incompetent police officers. When the reporters were quiet, he forced a smile that he was certain was not very convincing.

"There is nothing really new to report. Naturally, the Chief, the PC, and the Mayor are in the Command Post conferring about the events of the evening. As of now we have no evidence to link these events." Noah gagged on that last answer, but department loyalty made him utter it. "I have no further comments at this time. You'll have to refer your questions to the department information officer." As Noah tried to move toward 4th District headquarters offices the reporters pressed around him, shouted fresh questions, tugged at him. His composure snapped and he shoved several reporters aside, snarled at them.

"No more questions! Get the hell out of my way!" He forced his way through a door where reporters were not allowed and yelled at a sergeant to have his driver bring a car around. 4th District commander, Capt. Jack Harshman, came to his office door and motioned Noah in. Cass Michaels, an incredibly obese armory sergeant, was standing next to Harshman's desk. On it lay an automatic rifle.

73

"Look at this fucking thing, Noah. This is what those bastards we're fighting over there are using. You ever see one before?"

Peterson bent over and examined the weapon. He picked it up and looked at it, hefted it, took the clip out and examined a shell: .30 caliber.

He shook his head. "No. It's a strange one to me, Jack. But I'm really not a weapons man."

"Neither am I, Noah. Michaels, tell the Major what you told me—what kind of weapon is this?"

Michaels wheezed as he drew on the cigarette hanging from the corner of his mouth. Ashes flickered gently from the tip with the passage of his breath and floated to the outward slope of uniform shirt that covered his massive belly. Flakes, bits and smudges of ash dotted his shoulders and chest so that his shirt appeared to be some randomly patterned, mod, blue-and-gray sports attire rather than the proper departmental apparel. He wheezed again.

"Sturmgewehr."

Noah said, "Gesundheit," reflexively.

Michaels shook his head and wheezed again. "Sturmgewehr. This is the 510–4 of the SIG 510 series of selective fire rifles. Uses the standard NATO .30 caliber round. Twenty-shot box magazine with ammunition-state indicator; folding bipod which snugs under the barrel when not in use; large winter trigger." Michaels's voice had assumed the firm, scholarly tone of the expert lecturing on his field to novices. "One thousand fifteen millimeters, or slightly over forty inches in length; fully loaded with bipod and sling, as we see here, four thousand seven hundred forty grams, a bit more than ten and a half pounds." Michaels turned the weapon lovingly in his hands, indicating features as he described their function. "Aperture rear sight with range markings adjustable between one hundred and six hundred meters in one hundred meter steps. Lateral and elevation range adjustment, plus or minus two percent. Rate of fire, depending upon type of ammunition, is between four hundred fifty and six hundred twenty rounds per minute, with a muzzle velocity of eight hundred meters per second. It can be fitted with a sniper telescope, but, as you see, this rifle is not." He looked up at Noah. Noah felt as if he ought to applaud politely.

"SIG?" he asked.

Michaels coughed, then spoke. "SIG—Swiss Industrial Company of Neuhausen Rhine Falls, Switzerland."

"You seem to know a lot about it, Sergeant."

Michaels turned a cold eye on him. "I'm a weapons man, Major. This is, in my opinion, the finest infantry rifle in the world today. Far better than the AK–47, which is itself infinitely superior to the Armelite M–16. I've never seen one before." He gazed at the rifle longingly. "I've been trying to buy one for years."

"For the department?"

Michaels looked puzzled. "The department? What would they do with it? For myself."

"If this is a Swiss rifle, where *would* you buy one?"

"That I *don't* know, sir. As I said, I've been trying to buy one for several years. The rifle is out of production, and a relatively small number of them were actually produced. The Swiss Army have them and a couple of African and South American countries have limited supplies, but to buy one I suppose you'd have to go to Europe and make contact with black market gun merchants. That's about the only way."

Harshman shook his head. "What the fuck? We've got about twenty of them off stiffs, and a dozen or so are still firing from the courthouse roof. Twenty or more were carried off in the night when some of these yahoos cut and ran. Now that is fifty, sixty rifles—a hell of a lot of units for such a scarce item."

Michaels nodded. "I know that's a lot of units. All I can tell you is *if* you *could* find the weapons, they'd be expensive. Even in a lot of fifty or sixty, it'd be bound to run four or five hundred dollars a rifle. Say twenty-five thousand for the lot. And all the ammunition they've fired—say another twenty thousand."

"You're saying that it cost somewhere between forty and fifty thousand dollars to arm those men?"

"Yes, sir, Major. That I am."

Harshman slumped in the chair behind his desk. "What is happening?" He looked gray and older than his fifty years. He looked at Noah with pain and a plea for an answer in his eyes. "What's going down, Noah?"

"I don't know." Noah shook his head. "Forty or fifty armed men at a cost of fifty thousand dollars? Everybody in the department knows a kid with a squirt gun and bad manners could stage a breakout at the jail, but the fatheads upstairs still want to play like this is amateur night."

Harshman snorted, "Pols." He waved them away. "Assholes." A sergeant came to the door and told Noah that his car was ready.

Noah looked at Harshman. "Why don't you trot Sergeant Michaels and his fascinating little lecture up to the Command Post and let the Mayor and PC chew on that?" Harshman nodded, but didn't move. He seemed tired to the point of defeat. Combat fatigue.

He muttered, "Pols. What can you expect from them? They don't know what it's like out on the street. If fucking Martians invaded, they'd send for the PR people and the goddamn ACLU to decide what spacemen's civil rights were before we could detain them."

The snow had almost stopped. Noah's car crawled up Twelfth Street, stopped behind a jam of blue-and-whites. He could see men crouched around the base of the statue of Pierre Laclede on the Market Street side. They were firing sporadically and Noah could hear automatic weapons fire returning. An officer approached the car. Noah rolled down his window. The man saluted when he saw Noah's face.

"Sergeant Rowser, sir."

"What's the situation now?"

"About a dozen on the roof. We can't get at them until

morning. Maybe twenty of them are down and the rest have run. All the guards at the jail were killed and one of them was cut down by a guard."

"Who are they?"

"Don't know, sir. They're all blacks, but no ID's on them so far."

"How many of ours are down?"

Rowser swallowed tightly. "Seventeen dead and sixteen wounded—four of the wounded probably won't make it."

Noah looked around at the scene. Dim figures amongst the drifts, flashes from gun barrels, blue-and-whites with lights spinning like small airport beacons, a long, double row of mounds. He started. Those were the corpses. He turned back to the Sergeant.

"Pull them back."

"Sir?"

"Pull your men, all the men, back to safer cover. Just keep the bastards pinned down until we can dig them out in the morning. There's no point in getting any more men killed like this."

"Yes, sir."

Noah rolled up his window and the driver maneuvered around the jam of blue-and-whites. They started for the arena.

### 9:10 p.m.: COL. TERRENCE DONOVAN

The trucks were halted on Fourth Street. McGregor dismounted from the cab of the lead truck and approached Donovan. He saluted. Donovan returned the salute.

"Set up your perimeter, Sergeant-Major."

The doors of the trailers were swung open. Twenty-four of the men came out of the lead truck and jogged off to their perimeter positions. McGregor walked behind, checking off the assignments as he came to them. His job would be to complete a tour of positions every ten minutes and report back to Donovan.

Since the Fourth Street side of the bank was considered the least vulnerable, and the working parties would be able to lend immediate assistance in an emergency, only five men were deployed there. Two each on the far corners of Fourth and Locust and Fourth and St. Charles, and one man to patrol the upper level of the Mansion House Center to watch for unwary tenants or guests at the Holiday Inn. Five men covered the doors of the bank temporarily. The remaining fourteen went up to the Broadway side of the bank. On the corner of Broadway and St. Charles Street, the bank maintains a parklike courtyard, perhaps seventy or eighty feet square with a waist-high or better stone wall topped with a short iron picket railing. Inside the wall are plantings and shrubs. Three men entered the courtyard and ranged themselves along the Broadway side. Diagonally across Broadway and St. Charles, on the northwest corner, is a used car lot. Three men concealed themselves in the rows of cars. On the corner of Broadway and Locust, two men went to each corner. The perimeter was designed so that anyone penetrating it would immediately be covered from behind and entrapped. When the other five men were released from guarding the doors, they would patrol farther out, north, south, and west, and would give advance warning of any approach. Most of the evening, they would merely stand and shiver, since the storm had effectively taken care of pedestrian and automobile traffic in the downtown area. The men were all garbed in heavy white jumpsuits with fur-lined hoods. They were very hard to see in the snow-dominated night.

The Federal Reserve Bank of St. Louis employs nearly two thousand people and operates twenty-four hours a day. The major night operation is the check-processing department; most of the rest of the night staff are guards. There were one hundred eighty-eight employees on duty that night, a somewhat smaller number than normal. When the city power shut off and the bank's auxiliary power kicked in, people went to the windows, saw that power was out in other surrounding buildings, and were mostly amused. When the generators exploded and power went off completely in the bank, there was much confusion and milling around. Al Cronin, the senior security officer, dispensed flashlights to his staff and sent some men to the various departments to calm the other employees and a couple of men down to check what had happened to the generators. He was more mystified than alarmed. He could not imagine what had happened to the generators and he had no idea what was happening to the city outside. Security at Federal Reserve banks is so superb that the idea of anyone actually attempting to rob one seems ridiculous to insiders. It did not occur to Cronin that they were virtually isolated from the city now, and he did not know that the city was in chaos and isolated from the rest of the country. And he did not know that the final steps were being taken to imprison the staff in a tomb. He waited impatiently for his men to return and tell him what had happened to the generators.

Four men had jumped down from the lead truck and had run around to the St. Charles Street entrance to the parking garage. They had located the night attendant, bound, gagged, blindfolded him, and locked him in his cubicle office. He was the only one of the one hundred eighty-eight person night staff who would survive the evening. The lead truck was slowly circling the bank, stopping by its doors. At each stop, a team of four men took down one of the large, strange-looking metal plates that Captain Jackson had had manufactured specially. The doors of the bank were set back into thin archways in the Bedford stone and brick of the buildings. The metal plates slipped into the archways and covered the doors. The backs of the plates had four arms with 180-degree play at the joints and hydraulic hinges. When turned outward and locked into position against the insides of the archways, they held the metal plates firmly in position. The hydraulic hinges could be adjusted so that it would take a large battering ram wielded by fifty men to jar the plates loose from inside the bank.

The plates were quite heavy and shifting them about in the snow was quite difficult. The team of men was sweating and cursing before it even had the first one in place. Once, the plate for the third door slipped and fell on the leg of one man, cutting it open from just below the knee to a few inches above the ankle. A replacement had to be brought from another working party. As the plates were placed, the door guards were freed to take up their scouting beyond the outer edge of the perimeter. It took twenty-seven minutes to place all the plates in position over the doors.

Donovan walked into the parking garage. Three men followed him with the M–47 Dragon—a medium anti-armor weapon—and three missiles. They walked down the ramp to the lower level and on around a corner to the back wall of the garage. Donovan studied the wall and then paced it off. He took a black grease pencil and made an X on the wall a foot above the concrete flooring.

"That, gentlemen, is where Captain Jackson tells us the side of the vault will be. You may make your preparations and I will return to supervise the firing."

He walked up the ramp and back outside. He walked down to the corner and around to the Fourth Street side of the garage. Men were handing down the containers and carrying them into the garage. They would be followed by a small forklift truck. Six men, with asbestos suits over their jumpsuits, were carrying a long extension ladder across the roof of the parking garage to the back wall of the original building. McGregor came up to him and saluted.

"The perimeter is established, all's quiet, sir."

"Thank you, Sergeant-Major. Are the door plates in place?"

"Two to go, sir."

"Tell them to move along, if you please, Sergeant-Major."

"Yes, sir."

The snow made Donovan think of Sligo again. Not like that at all. He shook his head. The men moved fairly quickly in the dim light and treacherous footing. They were mostly silent except for the occasional curse muttered into the wind.

From the roof of the parking garage to the roof of the original building is an extremely long six stories. The power extension ladder was laid against the side of the building and the motor started. It went up in four sections with jerky, erratic movements. The wind made it hard to hold in place. Cpl. Carlos Diaz, the only Spaniard in the company and a former second-story-style burglar from Madrid, slung a small knapsack across his back and a large coil of rope over either arm. He began to ascend rapidly. Atop the roof, he moved quickly to the first two metal ventilation shaft covers in a series of five. He took the ropes, which had metal clasps at either end, and looped them around the vent covers, fastened each with one clasp, pulled them taut, payed out the lines to the edge of the roof and dropped the free ends over the side to the men at the foot of the ladder. He took the pack from his back and removed a number of large metal caps with suction rims, which he fitted over the other vent covers, making an effective seal. He took a crowbarlike tool from the pack and prised the tops off the first two. He fitted them with metal sleeves with suction rims at the bottom and hose-nozzle threading at the top.

The first truck came down Fourth Street to Donovan. He and the driver walked to the back. Just inside lay the man with the cut leg, Private Schiller. At the back were the compressors, gas canisters, and two giant coils of asbestos-covered hose.

Donovan nodded at the driver. "You can start paying it out now. They're ready for you." He turned to Schiller. "How are you doing, Private?"

Not well, mein Colonel. The leg has no feeling."

81

Donovan nodded. "I'll send Wilson over with the first aid equipment. He'll patch you up for now and we'll send you off in one of the early departure cars."

"Thank you, mein Colonel."

Donovan patted his shoulder as he watched the lead ends of the hoses being handed up to the men on the roof. Then he walked back toward the second truck.

Donovan climbed into the cab. With the engine running, it was still warm. He lit a cigar and watched the snow. It was thinner now. Perhaps it would stop soon. That would be dead perfect. No trouble for them or the planes. An effective additional problem for the police most of the evening. Almost like a sign. The hand of God, perhaps. He laughed aloud. A curious thought for one engaged on an enterprise men would not condone, let alone God. That was all dead now for a long many years. God was as dead for him as the people inside the bank soon would be. He glanced over at the building. Poor sods. He shrugged. It's hard luck on them, and there's an end on it. He'd seen his share of bad times and he asked no one for sympathy. Anyone expecting it from him would get precious little. He'd come from a family of eleven and the others were all dead except Margeret Mary, who was a teaching nun in Liverpool, and Maureen, who married a butcher from Athlone. And there had been the final fiasco in Imbannailand. That had been a bitter dose. He'd never mucked a thing up so badly in his life. Except maybe the Sligo raid. In the winter. At Christmastime. When he'd died. Died and gone to prison.

He was reborn in his prison cell several months later. He vomited himself back to life. In his sleep, he'd gagged on an unswallowed chunk of bread and began vomiting viciously. He rolled off of his bunk and fell to the floor, emptied his stomach completely and continued to retch long after it was empty. When he was finally able to stop and crawl back upon the cot, he was consciously aware of his surroundings for the first time since his brother had died in his arms. He felt nothing. He was sweaty and chilled, the cell was narrow, damp, cold, and dark. It did not matter to him at all. In the morning, the first words he spoke to the jailor were to ask for a shower and that the vomit be cleaned from his cell. Patjo, whose own wound was nearly healed, was overjoyed at Donovan's recovery.

The next day it occurred to him that he would soon be going to trial. Further, he would, he assumed, undoubtedly be found guilty on several charges of murder, amongst other crimes, and would, no doubt, be duly executed. He was surprised to discover that he no longer desired death. He was not distressed by the prospect, did not fear dying—he merely found it interesting or curious that he did not lust after death as he had. When he contemplated it, he decided that he no longer lusted for death because he had already died and it meant nothing. From the moment his brother had died until the fit of vomiting, he had been in a near-catatonic state which no honest philosopher could represent as a living condition. For that was the point for man—the death of consciousness is the death that counts. He had died and there had been no pain in it, it was nothing, meant nothing. The world in general was not at all affected by his living or dying and in the specific particular was affected very little. He did not believe in the existence of God. He placed no moral or philosophical value on the existence of man. Death was the only absolute, and since it meant nothing, life—or, rather, civilized social life, the life of the mind—was the greatest hoax of all, albeit a self-induced joke. The only thing that mattered was what mattered to you and, freed from the tyranny of morality and philosophy, you could choose from a quite broad spectrum of options— from self-flagellation to indulgence of the pleasure senses, from service to others to pursuit of wealth and power. Obviously the latter of each alternative held the broader appeal for the human species. It occurred to him that he wished he had had a woman sometime in his life. He laughed. It seemed likely that had he arrived at this viewpoint while a free man, he would have been a sensual existentialist. Something of a hedonist. He laughed again. Like all Irish intellectuals he loved a perceived irony, for it is one of the richest veins of the Irish national heritage.

A few days later, an officer of the Justice Department came to talk to him in his cell. He was a bespectacled little man in a vested tweed suit, which Donovan supposed the man thought a reasonable imitation of English ministerial dress. The man seemed to have great difficulty coming to the point, using circumlocutions, euphemisms, and pompous rhetoric to surround his subject without broaching it. Donovan suppressed his ordinary irritation with such silliness. He stared directly into the other man's eyes, when he would meet them. He said nothing. His expression never changed. Indeed, it was difficult to ascertain that his face *had* an expression. This bland lack of response made the man nervous and he ended by telling Donovan more than was intended. Which was as Donovan had known he would.

It was rather simple, really. The Jesuit Father General was very disturbed over his case. There had already been three years of the most repugnant publicity about the outlaw priest and the very mention of his name was painful to the Church hierarchy in general and to the legions of St. Ignatius in particular. It was feared that the long multiple trials, with their attendant sensationalism in the international press, would do great harm to the order and the Church. Father General *and* the Archbishop of Dublin *and,* rumor had it, the Holy Father in Rome himself had made their views known to the Taoseach and his ministers. Accordingly, an arrangement had been decided upon if he would cooperate. If he would plead guilty before a magistrate to the charges stemming from the Sligo raid and waive his right to a jury trial, all other charges against him would be dropped. Since there was no murder at Sligo the maximum sentence he might expect would be eight years in prison.

"What about Patjo?"

The little man sniffed. "You'll be meaning Hogan."

"Yes."

"His case is different. He'll have to stand trial for the lot."

Donovan shook his head. "No."

"No?"

"The arrangement's all right if Patjo gets the same as I do. Otherwise I plead nothing, I demand a jury trial on each incident and I'll make a three-ring circus of it all with my testimony." The little man sniffed again and straightened his spectacles.

"I see." He argued with Donovan or attempted to, but Donovan merely shook his head. He would only utter the one word.

"No." Presently the little man went away. Upon reflection Donovan was surprised to realize that he had made his first choice as a man of free will. He had apparently decided that loyalty to one's friends was the initial rule of the new personal code he would have to manufacture for himself in whatever remained of his life. He also noted that, apparently, whatever options he exercised, he was going to commit himself to them to the extent of risking his life. That was hardly surprising in a man of his character and experience, but it made an interesting point he never forgot. If you are willing to lose your life, to die—nothing else can really be done to you.

A week later the little man came back and said the terms would be met. Patjo would be included in the arrangement. Donovan seemed not to feel much upon learning that he would go on living a while. It still did not seem to matter much.

The formalities of pleading and sentencing were accomplished within ten days, with only a few small items in the press. They both received sentences of eight years.

Prison life was disagreeable in the extreme. Donovan decided he wished to survive it relatively intact so he adapted the spiritual exercises of St. Ignatius to his new existential

85

frame of reference. He began a careful contemplation of the options that were available to him and assembled a personal code from whole cloth. Loyalty (to those he chose), courage, and calm were his trinity. The desire to experience the pleasures of life that he had previously forsaken became his goal. He evolved a weekly cycle of meditations upon the means of meeting his goal and upon the closeness of his conduct to his code. After two years of these exercises, they bored him. He didn't need them any longer. He had become his code and his code had become him. He was a seamless, spiritual entity incapable of acting other than in the manner he had consciously chosen. It made him a man apart again, a man whom other men automatically looked to for leadership—even his jailors treated him with respect and deference. It also made him, in particular situations, as ruthless and remorseless a man as ever lived.

In the spring of 1959, Donovan and Patjo were among several classes of prisoners granted pardons and freed. They had been in prison three and a half years. They went to London. Patjo secured a job as a bus driver and Donovan found work as a librarian. They shared a small flat in Brixton. They lived an irresponsible, relatively carefree life for nearly two years. Patjo indulged in his life's love—beer and whisky; Donovan indulged in food, wine, and women such as his pocketbook would afford—he was mildly surprised to find that many women found him attractive; he concluded that it had been utter foolishness to reject sexual love for over thirty-one years.

In time, he met a man at a party who was a friend of Mike Hoare's. He pursued the contact. He and Patjo enlisted as Congo mercenaries. His quality and ability—he was a naturally gifted soldier—allowed him to rise quickly to captain and command of a company. He pulled his company out after the last breakout in Stanleyville and he and Hogan returned to England. There were a few sporadic jobs of arms-running and the like, though they were not much to his taste. He also began to study military history and tactics.

When the Angola opportunity came along he was contacted by the CIA. In the first Angola independence war, he was a major and commanded a larger company than he had in the Congo. He got his men out in time and none of them stood trial or were executed. In the second Angola war, the CIA brought him back again, but this time as a colonel with command of two companies. He saw the end coming early, and, much to the CIA's displeasure, pulled his men out once more. Again, none were tried or executed.

In the intervening years, he and Hogan lived modestly but comfortably on the profit they had taken out of the first three wars. But he chafed. He had been on the losing side three times. He wanted a chance to win. When Assam Azyad approached him on behalf of Colonel Kadafii, he jumped at the prospect. And it had been one more irony. He had assembled the cream from his previous companies. For two years they had fought tough, brilliant, hit-and-run war against superior numbers. At the decisive battle of Simba Pass, the government troops had been crushed, though the IWACs took heavy losses. And when they returned triumphant to Port Imbann, Ossungi had tried to throw them in prison. They had to fight their way out of the city and up the coast highway. And Kadafii had double-crossed them as well, hadn't paid them.

Donovan crushed the bitter memory with the stub of his cigar. He supposed, in one sense, this whole undertaking—Captain Jackson had dubbed it the Money War—could also be viewed as Donovan's revenge. Well, he had to do something for the boyos. After the muck-up. And they were all a bit like children. Lost without him. He looked at his watch. Close enough. He got down from the cab and started walking toward the garage.

As Donovan walked, confusion grew inside the bank. The central security office in the Federal Reserve Bank of St. Louis is a medium-sized room with large windows on two sides. It is jammed with alarm and security systems, electronic equipment, direct connections to neighboring Fed banks in Louisville and Kansas City, and a large radio transmitter—but all these devices require power.

Cronin could not bear to sit in the dead room any longer. He walked out and leaned against one of the window walls. The men he'd sent down to the generators came running along the hall, breathless, gasping.

One managed to wheeze, "Al, the generators've blown."

"Blown? Something blew out in them? How could they go at the same—"

"No, Al, they've *been* blown up!"

"Blown up? Those weren't very big explosions. More like something overheating and blowing out."

"I know, they must not have used very much explosive in them, but they're cracked open and gutted."

"They . . ." They. Of course. They. If the generators had been blown up, someone had done it, some *they*. One of the men he had sent to keep the check department calm came along the corridor from the other direction.

"Al, there are men and trucks outside. Men on the roof and in the parking garage."

"Show me."

The four guards went sprinting back toward the check department. Their flashlights bobbed and moved with their arms as they ran. The beams made crazy arcs, crisscrossed like airport searchlights, bounced along the floors and walls. In the check department, they had to shoulder people aside to get to the windows. People who knew him called his name, asked useless questions.

"Al, what's going on?"

"Is it a robbery?"

"What are you going to do, Al?"

"Should we leave, Al? Should we go home?"

"We aren't in any danger are we, Al?"

It was hard to see, even though the snow was not falling nearly so thickly now, was more like a flurry than a storm. He could see the two large semis on Fourth Street alongside the parking garage and some men moving around. He stared at the men on the roof of the parking garage a long time. They looked strange. He couldn't quite make out why. They seemed to be carrying what looked like a ladder down off the roof. They took it to the back of the front truck. There were two tubelike things coming out of the back of that truck. They seemed to go up the side of the original building, but it was hard to see clearly. It was quite dark and the snow covering made everything look like various shades of white. Cronin shook his head in disbelief. Jesus Christ. It must be a robbery. Absurd, but what other answer was there? Strange way to go about a robbery, fiddling around on the roof of the parking garage. He turned away from the window.

"All right now, everybody calm down. Everybody just relax. You check department people just sit down and don't worry. We'll handle it, whatever it is. Guards, come with me."

He led the way to the weapons supply, handed out shotguns, two M–16s, extra ammunition. They made their way toward the night door.

Cronin outlined the tactics. "Jerry, you take half the men and circle around the bank. We'll give you time so we can come up on them from both sides at once. We'll fan out on both sides of the street so they can't get away. Any resistance at all and we start shooting. Anybody who would try to rob the Fed must be pretty dangerous. Jack, as soon as we get outside, you hightail it over to headquarters, police headquarters, and get them to send us a ton of men."

When they opened the door they found themselves staring at the metal plate. They shined flashlights all around it, saw that it completely covered the doorway. They pushed it. Eight or nine rammed it with their shoulders simultaneously. Nothing. It did not even quiver. Cronin motioned them back with his flashlight.

"All right, everybody get well back."

He stepped back about five paces, took his pistol and

aimed at the center of his flashlight beam on the plate. The shot reverberated in the high stone hall and they could hear the ricochet pinging wildly around in the dark. Cronin walked over to the plate. He found the mark of his shot. A large concave bubble with blister marks around the edges.

"Shit."

He got one of the M–16s, had all the men lie flat on the floor. He lay prone, had another officer beside him shine a flashlight at the plate. He squeezed off the entire clip in three long bursts. The sound was deafening inside and the madly pinging ricochets eerie. They approached the plate. It was pockmarked like a gray moonscape with the blistered concave bubbles, but nothing more.

"All right, we'll check the other doors." Cronin led them on a tour of the bank doors. Each time they came face to face with another gray metal plate. They tried the same experiments on all of them, with uniform results. Nothing. By the time they decided to try shooting out one of the large extra-thick safety-glass windows, it was too late. They were walking along a corridor toward the windows they considered best for an exit.

"After we shoot away the glass, we'll play hell getting those bars loose."

"They're old, Jerry. Enough leverage and the masonry will give way if the bars don't. Unless you'd like to try some of the upper stories. I don't fancy myself as a second-story man."

"No. Me either. Not in this weather."

"Not in any weather."

There was a gasp and one of the men staggered into two others, then fell. The other two men were knocked down and flashlights and equipment clattered around the floor. Cronin turned, irritated.

"What the hell's going on? You guys doing your three stooges routine or what?"

"Jack fell down and knocked the other two over."

"Well, what's the matter with Jack?"

One of the men knelt over him and shook him. "Hey, Jack, what is it? What's the matter?" He shined the light in his face and then felt for a pulse in his wrist, then throat. "Christ, Al, he's dead."

"Dead?"

"Yeah. As a stone."

"What'd he do? Hit his head?"

They half lifted his upper body and examined him for marks, found none.

"Well, what the fuck. He must have had a heart attack."

"You wouldn't think it, a young guy like him."

"Ah, well, you never can tell. He was overweight. I was always after him about . . . hey, Jerry, what's the matter?"

Two more men had sat down and leaned against the wall. Cronin prodded them with his foot but they did not respond. One groaned.

"Jerry, Jerry! What's the matter." His friend mumbled and he knelt to hear better. "What was that? What'd you say, Jerry? What's the matter?"

"Sick . . . feel sick."

"You feel sick?" His friend did not answer. He closed his eyes and slumped sideways. His head hit the floor with a loud, sickening crack. Cronin felt for a pulse. Wrist. Throat. Nothing. He was dead. Three more men staggered and went down. Most of the rest were swaying, muttering. Cronin stood and felt dizzy. He had a headache he hadn't noticed before and he felt pressure in his ears. He noticed some of the men were bleeding from their nose or ears or mouth or all three. He tried to think. His head seemed fuzzy. The strange-looking men. Asbestos suits. The tubes. Hoses. The roof of the original building. Ventilation shafts. Gas.

He staggered and tried to shout, "Gas." His voice came out soft, almost a whisper. He tugged at several of the men. Tried to lead them. There were some masks with the weapons, he thought. It was hard to think. The men were going down quickly now. He staggered away. His face was sticky.

He wiped at it. He turned his flashlight on his hand. Red smears. Something wet dropped on the lens of his flashlight, spread slowly, turned the light pink. The flashlight was very heavy and he needed all of his strength to move his thick legs. To stand, even. He dropped the flashlight. He was walking in its beam, a curious, thinly pink light. He was fascinated by his shadow. He hit a wall, couldn't remember staggering. His head hurt. He didn't know when he fell. Everyone in the bank was dead.

McGregor came up, saluted. Donovan returned it.

"Perimeter secure, sir. No penetration. Scouts report that there is practically no activity in the area. One man saw one car headed away to the north, but that is all."

"Very good, Sergeant-Major. Keep me informed. I'm going down to the garage now."

"Yes, sir." They exchanged salutes again and McGregor walked off. Donovan went into the parking garage. When he got to the lower level, he did not need his flashlight any longer. The men had set up the two portable spotlights, bathing the area in a harsh intense light. The containers were neatly stacked against the wall near the lights and the Dragon. The forklift truck was parked near them. The containers, a startling shade of Day-Glo orange, seemed to vibrate in the hard light. The forklift truck was necessary because, although the empty containers were relatively light, loaded with currency each would weigh slightly over three thousand pounds.

Sergeant Oxhall saluted. "Everything's ready, Colonel. Whenever you give the word."

Donovan glanced at his watch. "About ten minutes more, Sergeant. We have to be sure about the gas. I'll be back then to see it done."

Oxhall grinned. "Yes, sir. You always like to see it done proper, Colonel. We all know that."

Donovan smiled. "That's right, Sergeant. We want it done proper. Manchester, isn't it, your home, Sergeant?"

"That's right, sir."

"But you'll come up to London with the rest of us after this is done, won't you, Sergeant?"

"Yes, sir. I'm looking forward to living like a proper London gentleman. No more o' that north England for me."

"That's grand then, Sergeant. I'll be back in ten minutes."

"Yes, sir." They exchanged salutes.


### ST. LOUIS, MISSOURI/9:14 p.m., CST/LT. ARTHUR ADAMS


Art Adams had made a bad mistake and he knew it. He had done what he feared Donovan's ambiguous orders had meant he should do. He had stayed too long. He had thought 8:50 or until serious reinforcements showed up. At 8:55 he had noticed a quantum leap in the firepower coming their way. There were a lot more men shooting at them. Twenty at least. They had been driven off the island and up into the mouth of the cul-de-sac where their cars were parked. Two of his men were dead and two were wounded so badly they might as well be. The 510–4s were holding the police off, but that was all. They were going to have a hell of a time getting out of there. It was like Port Imbann all over again. He saw a shadow move by the wire fence across Kingshighway. He loosed three or four rounds at it. Why was the image so familiar? He shuddered.

As they approached the bridge to cross into Port Imbann it was dusk. The shack villages were alight with cooking fires. Crazy patterns danced against the galvanized iron shanties. Adams glanced down the line of the wire fencing. Things moved on the wires. Adams sucked in his breath. Rows of bodies hung from the fences. Donovan followed his gaze and nodded.

"Ah—an example of the new justice under General Ossungi. Seems to be much like the old justice under General Attigo."

93

The people in the city mobbed them, cheered them, crowded the streets as their personnel carriers rolled through. It was probably why Ossungi tried to arrest them at the hospital. Everyone knew that Donovan and the IWACs had won the war for Ossungi. He hated Donovan for that. They had heavy losses from Simba Pass, but Donovan took one look at Colonel Somutu and formed the men up. Shooting started. The trucks got going in great disarray and under heavy fire, followed Donovan's command car across the city to the coastal highway. They were pursued for a day and a half, all of it under fire, until they were within three miles of the border. Of the original company of over four hundred, only a hundred and nineteen made it out.

A pistol shot closer than before brought Adams back to St. Louis. He tried to see the new position the shot had come from. He was frightened. The fire, still untouched by the firemen, had nearly consumed both plants, but by some freak of luck had not spread across the street to the houses. The towering blaze lit the scene fully; fire engines lined up at a distance, their men hiding behind them; what looked like a dozen police cars blocking the street in both directions; policemen moving from cover to cover, trying to make their way into the houses overlooking the cul-de-sac and so flank the IWACs with crossfire; water was leaking from one of the fire engines, gasoline from one of the police cars, another was in flames, having exploded after taking, apparently, a shot in the gas tank; four bodies lay some distance apart—two IWACs, two policemen. Adams squeezed off a long burst of fire, then cursed. A policeman had gained a porch three doors down from the houses overlooking the opening of the cul-de-sac.

He heard the sound of shattering glass behind him and spun. Another IWAC was standing up and firing into a window of the house on the right.

"Get down, stupid—"

The rapid roaring of a pair of pump-action shotguns cut

his voice off. The standing man was blown away, screaming. Adams and the other two men still capable of fighting
emptied their clips into the house in a long, steady stream
of concentrated fire. They heard one loud yell from the
house.

Adams began working his way back to the cars. The men
behind him didn't notice and kept firing at the house. As he
slipped into the driver's seat, he glanced back and saw pistol
flashes coming from the house on the left. He started the
engine, left the lights off. He drove to the end of the cul-
de-sac, up into a driveway, and turned around. He waited,
poised at the top of the slight rise, and watched. More police
were crawling up to flanking positions. Adams waited. He
wanted as many police at the mouth of the cul-de-sac as
possible. If he got a running start, he might be able to bust
through the line and away. One of the last two men fighting
went down. No more time.

He put the engine in neutral, revved slightly, slipped it
into drive. The tires spun for a second, then he shot down
the street. He saw a fragment of the one IWAC left standing
as he shot past; surprise, then quickly anger. The windows
of the car were shattering all around him, but he was not
hit. The sound of tearing metal was constant as shots ripped
the sides of the car. He was going forty-one miles per hour
when he hit the island, bounced up, spun his tires and slid
sideways across to the curbing alongside the Rexall plant.
He could feel the heat from the fire. He gunned forward.
His only chance was to slip down the side street between
the two plants. Kingshighway Boulevard was blocked both
ways. He fought the wheel as he began to yaw on the slick
street. He made the turn awkwardly, began to gain control
and shoot forward again when he felt both rear tires go at
once. The car slammed into the curb, rocked as if to tip
over on its side, fell back onto its wheels again, rocking
gently.

He sat stunned for a few seconds. He shook his head. He
had been thrown across the seat against the passenger door.

He forced it open and jumped out. The heat from the fires on either side of him was terrible. As he ran, he knew he was a perfect target outlined brilliantly by the blaze. He began to weave erratically, as if running some long-remembered high school football pass pattern. He heard the shots behind him, pistol and shotgun. Then the sound of the 510-4 on full automatic in an unrelieved burst. He knew his man was shooting at him. He felt only a series of terrible blows to his back, as if he were being clipped in football, when the burst of automatic fire shredded his spine. He rolled in the street, flopping like a terribly torn rag doll.

Pvt. Mickey Rivers smiled when he saw Adams fall. "Good on you, you double-crossing son of a bitch." He decided to surrender and began to stand up. He did not remember to throw away his rifle and raise his hands fast enough. Two shotgun blasts at close range hit him in the chest at the same time that a revolver shot tore through his throat.

Only one of the IWACs on this detail was left alive, and he died on the way to the hospital, unconscious the whole way. At 9:43, the firemen were finally able to move in and begin putting out the fires. The two plants were total losses and extinguishing the blazes was a long, tiring, and mostly preventative task—the only thing left to save was the surrounding buildings.


### 9:45 p.m.: PATROL SGT. HARRY GROOVER

Groover was tired. He'd been at the arena since dispatch had sent him over at 8:40. He was shaken, too. He had nine years in on the force, but he'd never seen a real riot before. His body ached from the blows he'd taken—kicks, punches, body blocks, his arms were leaden from swinging, poking, and prodding with his nightstick, but the worst thing was the fear of what he'd seen. In the back of his mind, he was already wondering if he might not look for some other line

96

of work. A policeman might be called upon to perform crowd control duty any time. He did not know if he could make himself face another riot. If dispatch told him "There's a riot at Busch Stadium" this summer, would he be able to respond? He wondered.

When the riot fever finally broke, those people who were not dead or injured, or had not fled on foot or managed to escape in their cars early on, were herded back into the arena. Groover estimated there were still ten or eleven thousand in the crowd. He had some of his men interviewing people, trying to discover who or how the riot first began. That was a hopeless task, but he would have to write a report tomorrow, and he wanted to be able to say that he had tried.

There were more than one hundred fifty wrecked cars in the lots, and he'd sent a couple men to round up tow trucks. He didn't yet have an accurate count on the dead and injured, but the total would be over two thousand. He had sent men to St. Lukes, Jewish Hospital, St. Johns, Fermin Des Loge, Bethesda, Glennon, Deaconess, and the city hospitals for ambulances for the injured. The first ambulances from Deaconess, St. Johns, and Jewish Hospital had arrived and he was putting injured policemen in them. The animals could wait, he was going to take care of his own. That wasn't the way department regulations read, but the hell with that. They could can him if they wanted. He just didn't care. One of his men came up to where he was sitting in the front seat of his patrol car.

"I've got the numbers, Sergeant."

Groover sighed. "Okay, let's hear them."

"Fourteen officers killed."

"Fuck."

"And thirty-four seriously injured."

"Animals! Fucking animals! I'd like to shoot them all!"

The young patrolman who had collected the statistics was nervous. He had noticed that Sergeant Groover was acting peculiar since the riot had ended, muttering or swearing to himself. He waited until he was sure Groover's outburst was over before continuing. He glanced down at the sheet of notebook paper.

"We think nearly a thousand civilians dead so far."

"GOOD! I hope more of them die!"

The patrolman's hands were shaking now. "And probably more than a thousand injured, so far as I can tell. There may be twelve hundred to fifteen hundred." Groover muttered something. The patrolman leaned forward. "I didn't get that, sir. I didn't hear you."

Groover looked at him. "I said, maybe some of them will freeze to death or something."

"Yes, sir." The patrolman waited. After a minute of silence, Groover began muttering to himself again. The patrolman waited a few more minutes, but when it became apparent the Sergeant was not going to pay any more attention to him, he began to edge away. He was twenty-two years old and a rookie with less than eight months on the force. He had been scared silly by his first riot also, but he was doing a better job than the older officer of keeping what was left of his nerve. He walked across the lot toward the ambulance that had just arrived from St. Lukes to see if he could help.

Groover leaned his forehead against the steering wheel. He stared through the rim almost without seeing, his eyes followed details of the activity going on around him, but he did not think much about them. He was shot and knew it. He wanted desperately to go home to bed. To sleep. To forget. He shivered, not from the cold.

Groover did not notice the police car pull up next to him. He heard a car door open and close, but took no note of it, did not raise his head. A gloved hand tapped him lightly on the shoulder and he looked up into the unsmiling face of Major Noah Peterson.

"Pull yourself together, Sergeant."

Fuck you, thought Groover, but he straightened and got out of the squad car. All he said was, "Yes, sir."

"Where's the chief of detail?"

"Dead, sir. He got stomped to death by the . . . crowd."

"Who's in charge, Sergeant?"

"I'm senior man present, sir. Was until you came."

"Your name."

Coldblooded prick, thought Groover, staring at Noah's hardeyed face. "Groover, sir. Sergeant Harry Groover."

"All right, Groover. You come with me. My son is in this crowd and we're going to find him."

Groover felt the nausea rise again; Jesus God, his son! He fought to keep the shakes from starting again as he walked toward what was left of the arena with Peterson and his driver. As they walked through the debris, the stained snow, the abused and dying cars, past lines of ambulances, stretchers, bodies, Groover described the terror, panic, insane chaos of the riot. As they passed people being loaded onto stretchers or bodies lying on the ground, Peterson would stop and look at each one. Peterson's face was a cold, neutral mask, but Groover noticed as they approached bodies or stretcher victims, the Major's body stiffened and he moved with the solemn rigidity of dread. He did not interrupt the work of police or ambulance personnel often, only issuing an occasional order that helped expedite a foul-up. Groover remembered talk among street cops that Peterson was a good, tough man. A cop's cop. And once as he described the stomping death of the chief of detail he saw the fury in Peterson's eyes that he himself felt.

When they reached the remains of the crowd clustered near or in the arena, Peterson moved through them carefully, scanning the faces. Now that the fear and panic had been burned out of them through the orgy of violence, they stood quietly, blank-faced, will-less as tired sheep waiting to be nudged in some direction. Any direction. Groover's hatred dissipated. What in them was worthy of righteous anger? But contempt, ah, contempt—that was all these were worth. He noticed that people seemed to recognize Peterson as someone of importance. Some reached out and

99

touched him. Some asked questions. He marveled that Peterson could be calm, did not flinch from the laying on of hands, was able to answer questions in a mild, reassuring manner. He did not notice when his own back began to straighten again, was not conscious of the moment when he began to respond to questions with the measured confidence of the professional, but when a man gripped his arm firmly to stop him for a question he realized he was not going to recoil with distaste, but would listen to the man, help him, soothe him. He was on his feet, moving, acting, doing the job he was paid to do and in which he had often taken pride. He did not think about it at the moment, but later he remembered how shattered his spirit had been and how quickly he had recovered not only his professional competence, but his dignity. Once, late at night, on an uneventful shift, he would recall the incident for his patrol car partner.

"In fifteen minutes, just by being there, Peterson made me a cop again."

Noah left Groover and his driver behind as he moved into the arena. It was dark, eerie. Voices, flashlights, people moving about aimlessly, police and rescue workers trying to dig through the rubble in the center of the stadium, searching for trapped victims. Or bodies. Noah borrowed a flashlight from a patrolman and searched the crowd, clumsily sweeping the clustered faces, startling some, angering others. A woman who had been raped was weeping in the arms of another woman. An ambulance attendant was trying to help a man who was obviously dying of shock. Some people from the crowd were helping search the debris. And Noah held on to himself desperately, as if his sanity were an acrobat on a high wire in a fierce wind and the desire to fall a delicious temptation.

He began to search the debris with the others. The third body he found was his son's. Pulling at a large board and part of a steel girder tumbled aside a heavy mass revealing a pocket beneath. Noah Peterson III, in blue jeans and Webster Groves High School letter jacket, lay as if sleeping, looking much the same as always, blond hair with a high hairline, the blue eyes and compact build that made him so much a reflection of his father. Only a piece of falling concrete had crushed the back of his skull. And the flashlight brought closer revealed the bloodless skin, the rigor mortis, the shrinkage of the form, the change from living human to a sack of cold meat. And Major Noah Peterson sat down in the ruins and held that which had once been his son and cried just like any other father.

### 9:45 p.m.: PIERRE LACLEDE JONES

The slim red candle stood in a rippled puddle of melted wax in a jelly dish. Situated on the table in the breakfast nook to one side of the kitchen, it did not really illuminate the room, but rather produced a small pond of light to one side with points of light on metal and glass surfaces and shadows that moved with the rhythm of the flame. Pete Jones stared at the flame with a half-drunk concentration. Occasionally, he took swallows from his glass of Jack Daniels or got up to get more ice or refill the glass. He had been drinking steadily since he got home at eight and he had had quite a bit to drink before he arrived. The bottle of Jack Daniels on the table was more than a third consumed. It had been unopened when he started. The table top was a lustrous pearl-white with an irregular pattern of thin gold lines running through it. Sometimes he traced one or another of these lines with his index finger or simply stared at the contrast of his brown hand against the white table. For the most part, though, he stared at the flame.

Jenny was upstairs quieting the children, trying to get them to sleep. They had used the power failure as a wonderful excuse to scare themselves Jenny was angry with him, he knew, even though she controlled and suppressed any outward display of temper. She did not like him to come home half drunk. She did not like his uncommunicative mood. She did not like him to drink heavily in front of the children. She did not like—oh, piss on that. She would like the money just fine when she found out about it. She would like the money and would never know where it had come from. She would like the money and she would not have to carry the load of responsibility, guilt, fear, and disillusionment that he was bearing.

His conscience was bothering him. He thought he'd come to terms with all this, but he hadn't. He had merely suppressed his fear and anxiety, which is a very different thing from making peace with yourself.

He did not know any details of the plan, but he knew it was happening as he sat at the kitchen table. The power failure was a confirmation. He was sure Al's group was responsible for it. People must be dying. He was sure of that. No matter what the plan was, it couldn't ever hope to work without some violence. And Al's warning implied something he was truly afraid to consider for very long. Was it possible that everyone in the bank would die? He shuddered. He took another swallow of whisky. Why else was it imperative for him not to work tonight?

And he was afraid the plan would fail, would end in a shambles of incompetence. Al would be caught. He would talk, implicating Pete. Life imprisonment or execution.

And Al. Had he really been ready to kill him if he didn't go along, didn't supply the information? Did he remain ready to kill Pete if he didn't keep quiet after tonight? Pete was sure of it. He believed it. In many ways that was the hardest thing to accept. Killing in the abstract, killing strangers, killing in large numbers were all ugly and painful ideas. But they were not as painful to him as the idea that Al could have killed in the particular, the singular and a friend—his best friend—that very first night they had gone to the ballpark and the proposition had been made.

And Pete had mentally reversed the roles and discovered that he could envision himself doing what Al had been pre-

102

pared to do. He had had to be honest and admit to himself that he could have killed his best friend, Al Jackson, given a particular set of circumstances.

It was this last that was fully depressing. It exposed the sham of the comfortable, respectable, middle-class existence he had worked so hard for. He, as most men, liked to think of himself as a relatively decent human being. Apparently, that was not true. He merely was able to live a life where he was not faced with difficult moral dilemmas regularly, or where the moral quality of his acts was shielded from him by his relative obscurity in a large society. Faced, for the first time in many years, with an obviously immoral and obscene temptation, coupled with a mortal threat, he had shown himself both cowardly and venal with little or no resistance. He supposed this was what was meant by the rather abstract phrase, losing one's soul. Another candle in a jelly dish came into the room bringing a second, wider pond of light. Jenny followed it, set it on the opposite side of the table. She sat. She was frowning at him and the bottle.

"Why don't you give it a rest, Pete?"

He stared at her without speaking, but eloquently raised and drained his glass. She sighed. He uncapped the bottle and refilled his tumbler. It was a deliberately contemptuous act. Self-hatred is a powerful emotion that few can long sustain. Invariably it begins to seek targets outside the self.

"You want to talk about it, Pete?"

"No."

"Then I'm going to bed. One of us ought to go to work tomorrow and it's for sure you're not going to make it."

"Absolutely. Good, sound thinking. I'm not going to work tomorrow. Maybe I won't ever go to work again. You go to work. I'll sleep in. That sounds like an ideal arrangement."

She stood, looked down at him, shook her head. "Good night, Pete. I'll talk to you tomorrow after work. When you're sober." She took her candle and walked out of the

103

room. He heard her footsteps on the stairs. He took another
swallow of whisky and resumed his attentive observation of
the candle's flame. He laughed.

"I won't go to work tomorrow because there won't be
any work to go to."


## ATLANTIC OCEAN/11:49 SAN JUAN TIME/CPL. ASSAM AZYAD

Assam Azyad was not, strictly speaking, an IWAC,
though he had been Donovan's orderly for two years in
Imbannailand. He was the youngest of six sons of the
Azyad, head of the "Arab Rothschilds," as El Ahram had
once referred to the shipping and banking family that held
multi-million-dollar interests all across the Middle East and
Western Europe. Assam, at twenty-seven, educated at
UCLA and the Harvard School of Business, had approached Donovan on behalf of Colonel Kadafii, and when
Donovan accepted the job had gone along as orderly and
Kadafii's agent on the spot. There was no direct remunera-
tion to either Assam or the family for this mission, but it
was this type of favor, performed by younger members of
the family for Arab heads of state, which kept the Azyads
in political grace in all the nations where their business interests touched. Assam had been performing these chores
for over six years. It had been a long, distasteful, dangerous
task, but it had presented Assam with an opportunity to
present the family with a major financial windfall—one way
to hasten the climb up the family pecking order, which was
ordinarily governed by the aging and attrition processes.

The *Casablanca* swung gently to meet a small swell. She
was an aged, twenty-two-thousand-ton freighter from the
family shipping fleet. She had been chosen by Assam because he was familiar with her and because of the two
heavy-duty winches on her main decks. She had unloaded a
cargo of weapons and drums of Agent VX the previous
week in New Orleans. The transfer had been made at night

and illegally, with the help of a bribe to a customs official Assam had worked with before. A large delivery van had taken the shipment to St. Louis. Now the ship was holding station 22.5 degrees north latitude and approximately 69.5 degrees west longitude, some two hundred fifty-plus miles northwest of San Juan, not far from the Tropic of Cancer. There was a freshening breeze coming down from the northwest. It was a quiet, warm night with a clear sky and a beautiful mural of the heavens.

Assam could not sleep. In a few hours he would know if his major coup was successful. He calculated time two hours backward for the tenth time. It would be 9:50 in St. Louis. They would be well along at the bank. If all had gone well. Irritated with himself, with his restlessness, he walked along the deck and peered over the side. A deck hand was sitting in a rope cradle that dangled twenty feet down the side of the ship. Halfway up the rope a lantern hung to illuminate him and the side of the ship. He used hand signals to indicate to the two men on deck when he wanted to be raised or lowered and at what speed. He was unrolling three-foot-wide strips of tape as he stuck them to the ship's plating. The tape had been cut into twenty-foot lengths and he was crisscrossing them to make a series of long fat Xs all around the side of the ship. The tape was a thick, salt-water resistant, cloth-backed material in a bright Day-Glo orange, the same shade as the containers at the bank. The Xs on the deck and the funnels of the *Casablanca* had already been completed. They would make the ship extra visible and easily identifiable for Captain Imman in the morning.

Assam was nervous. There were dangers, risks, possible repercussions if the operation went badly. But he was not frightened. Tense, yes, but he did not frighten easily. He *had* been frightened when, after fighting their way out of Imbannailand, Donovan had learned, in London, that Kadafii had not paid the promised money into their bank. Assam had never seen a rage like that. Donovan did not speak. He did not storm or smash things or, in fact, move at

105

all. But standing stock-still in the hotel room he vibrated terrifying energy, angry energy like a high-pitched frequency that makes your fillings ache. Assam had been sure he was a dead man. Captain Jackson's idea and Assam's proposal—seed money, laundering the take, a draft copy of the Damascus Agreement for insurance after the act—these had saved him. He had made the offer to Donovan without qualifications, though he hadn't known if he could sell the idea to his father and the family council. But he hadn't had a choice. If he hadn't done it he would have been dead. And Donovan had been blunt as Assam left for home, for Rabat. If the family didn't agree to the proposal, somewhere, sometime soon, an IWAC would find him. Would kill him. He had still been frightened on his return to Rabat, but he had assumed a calm, unruffled exterior. It was essential for his dealings with his father and the family council.

The August Atlantic was an uncanny, unforgettable blue banked in the eye forever and the sun was a distant fire surrounded and all but overlaid with blank, terrible, white shadows. Even with his silver sunglasses on, Assam could not let his eyes rest in one direction more than a few seconds at a time. His glance bounced restlessly like a hand-held camera image in a low-budget motion picture: the flawed facets of the sea, high scorched sky, marshmallow white marble of the city at a distance, hot pink of the family's rococo villa—finally, he closed his eyes for an impatient rest. He hated waiting for his father on the terrace, hated having an important discussion in the discomfort of the unrelieved midday sun. That was his father. He had said one o'clock. They both knew he would be late. They both knew Assam would be punctual, would suffer the discomfort, would grow impatient. They knew it was one of his father's ways of seeking advantage even before discussion began. One did not forsake the habit, even dealing with one's family, one's children.

It was nearly one thirty and Assam had sweated through

106

his shirt and the thighs of his trousers. On his face and neck, in his scalp, the sweat no longer dripped, but rather flowed continuously. He lifted his glasses again and wiped moisture away with a handkerchief. His father waddled out of an arched glass door and Assam rose to greet him. Before they sat, his father unfurled and raised the umbrella table awning, which Assam had not dared do.

"There, that's better. You must be hot, my son." The Azyad clapped his hands and a hovering servant came. "Lemonade." The servant disappeared. They talked inconsequently of his report to Kadafii, the progress of various family business matters, Assam's willful dilatoriness in producing more grandsons for the Azyad—who already had eleven, but was compulsively avaricious in this as in all his appetites. The servant brought a tray with a bucket of ice, glasses, a pitcher of iced lemonade and several small plates of tiny date and fig cakes. The Azyad poured.

When his father had finished his first glass of lemonade and eaten several cakes, he leaned back and sighed, his hands folded over the mound of his grotesque belly—he was perhaps a hundred and fifty pounds overweight. He closed his eyes and Assam began to rapidly sketch the plan and proposal. When Assam touched upon the use to be made of the Damascus Agreement, the Azyad's eyes opened wide, initially in surprise, then quickly in hostility.

"By the beard of the prophet, education at the hands of the running dog Americans has robbed the child of respect for his elders. No one gave you leave to meddle in those affairs."

"If I have offended, such was not the intent, my father. I merely thought to use this valuable information to further the family estates." By the beard of the prophet was a favorite oath of the Azyad, which amused Assam since the family was at least nominally Christian and, in any case, the prophet was never specified. But it was a certain sign of his father's displeasure so he assumed an attitude of penitence and contrition. His father, satisfied that the son's disrespect was properly chastened, drained a second glass of lemonade, popped a cake whole into his mouth, closed his eyes and fluttered the fingers of his left hand for Assam to continue with his recital. When he finished, his father gave no sign of even having been listening for some time. He sat immobile as if dozing. The silence must be born patiently, Assam knew. It was another of his father's devices. Finally, he sat up and opened his eyes. He poured another glass of lemonade and indicated that Assam might help himself to a second glass. He popped another fig cake into his mouth and spoke while chewing.

"What makes you think the Americans will suffer such an outrage to protect the Damascus Agreement?"

Assam smiled confidently. "It is the coup necessary for their President to be re-elected next year. With it, he has a strong chance. Without it, he might as well not bother to run. He will do *anything* to protect it. And his Secretary of State hopes to win a Nobel Peace Prize, which he will no doubt receive if the agreement is fulfilled. He will do *anything* to protect it. That seems obvious."

His father nodded. "Perhaps you are right." He fell silent again for a moment. Assam knew he was sorting the rest of his objections for the more important ones. "Between one and two million dollars to finance the operation—that is a great deal of money to risk."

Assam nodded. "That is true, but a one-hundred-million-dollar profit in a space of a few months is a fantastic return. The family has risked more money for a lesser return in the past. And twenty percent is a generous fee for laundering money when the sum is so large."

"Yes, but the risk was not so great as this is and it was done upon the recommendation of older and wiser heads than yours, my son. We have no knowledge of the quality of this Colonel Donovan and his men other than yours."

"True, but I have spent two years with them and you have said yourself that I am not an utter fool when it comes to judging men."

108

"Of course not. You are my son." He hesitated. "The proposition would be more attractive to the family if there were a way to appropriate all of the money for the Azyads."

Assam shook his head. "With all due respect, my father, something might be tried, but I doubt the success of such an attempt. The containers will be wired and armed with plastique. Any attempt to open them without the proper tools in the proper sequence will result in a total loss of the money *and* the life of those who try it. I would not be willing to attempt it."

"Some arrangement with the Swiss?"

"I have thought of that. Alas, unfortunately, so has Colonel Donovan. The bankers in question are the family of his executive officer, Major Turrman. And even so, they are warned that they will be killed if they should come to some arrangement with us."

The Azyad's eyes widened and he nodded thoughtfully. "A prudent man, this Donovan."

"Yes. For we are to be warned as well. The entire Azyad family, men, women, children will be killed, should we attempt any arrangement with the Turrmans."

"Could he carry out such a threat?"

"He could and would. He has the ability, the temperament and the loyalty of sufficient men to complete the task."

"It would seem that he has foreseen the possibilities." It was the opening Assam had been waiting for. He sank the barb he knew would sting his father like salt on flayed skin.

"He is the coldest, most ruthless, cleverest, most far-sighted, and dangerously brilliant man I have ever known." The Azyad leaned back swiftly as if Assam had flung a steaming scoop of pig dung on the table. It was an intolerable insult to rate another man higher than one's father and his anger and hurt left him speechless. Assam had counted on this, but he knew the remark would carry all the more weight as an endorsement of Donovan once his father began to think about it. He watched his father's eyes closely as they mirrored the emotional changes he was undergoing. When they began to slide back to their habitual cautious neutrality, he knew his father was beginning to consider the proposition seriously. It was another ten minutes before he spoke again. Assam's head was beginning to ache from the terrible heat.

"What would be your reward, should the family actually undertake this headlong folly and it actually succeed?"

"A two percent finder's fee."

"Nonsense. A hundred thousand pounds might just barely be possible—I promise nothing. The council will have to decide, but I will attempt to get you such reward as I can." Assam knew it was all right. They were merely haggling now. His father had made up his mind to recommend the scheme.

He shook his head. "Two percent. And—"

"*AND!*" his father roared. "BY THE BEARD OF THE PROPHET, the child *has* lost all respect. Two percent *and*, he says." Shouting was, of course, one of his father's common techniques, but not a very effective one. Assam suspected it was merely an honored face-saving device.

He spoke calmly. "And the Paris assignment. Director of family affairs for Western Europe."

"Absurd. You could perhaps assist your brother in Athens or even, just possibly . . . I'll try my very best to get you the London suboffice. You can't hope for better at your age, my son." Assam shook his head. He knew he was in a strong position. He was already dreaming of French food and women, the Continental lifestyle. He could not wait to get out of Morocco. Often, he hardly thought of himself as an Arab at all.

Assam forced himself to stand still, lean against a deck railing, try to relax. The salt breeze was a pleasure on the face, in the nostrils. He was glad of the good weather. The drop this morning would be a near enough thing as it was. He had been reliving his fear of Donovan, but now he began to feel it slip away. Donovan was dangerous. What was it the war correspondent had said about the Colonel? Oh yes, Donovan was like a bad stretch of mountain road traveled too frequently by cars going too fast. Donovan was like an accident waiting to happen. That was very clever. And quite accurate.

Well, Donovan was an accident that wasn't going to happen to him. The Azyad had summoned the family from all across the Middle East and Western Europe. He had broiled all eighteen of them in the sun for an hour. Then Assam and the Azyad had made a smooth presentation; they ran it right through, although the debate about Assam's rewards had been quite spirited. Near the end, his eldest brother, from Athens, coveting the Paris directorship for himself, had stalked from the meeting. But the council submitted to the Azyad's will. Assam laughed. He remembered his father's summation.

''Now we must vote, but before we do, I remind you of the words of Omar Ibn Al-Halif:

> 'Four things come not back:
> The spoken word;
> The sped arrow;
> Time past;
> The neglected opportunity.' ''

The Azyad had opened a large, hairy, clenched fist to disclose an empty palm.

Assam chuckled again. There seemed no doubt now, that when his father died, Assam would succeed him as the Azyad. This would probably not be for some years, of course. His father, fifty-nine, obese, indolent, still afflicted with satyriasis and gluttony, seemed, nonetheless, perfectly capable of retaining leadership for another twenty or thirty years. The legendary, original Azyad had continued to run family affairs until his hundred and fourth year. Still, Paris was the ideal place to await, in sybaritic pleasure, his eventual ascendancy. The gently rolling rhythm of the ship moved him. He began to think about his mistress.

111

The M–47 Dragon is a tube launcher for small guided missiles. The tube is forty-four inches long with a bipod at the rear. The operator sits with the front section of the tube resting on his shoulder, and sights through a monocular eyepiece; he fires by depressing a thumb switch safety and squeezing the trigger grip; he must maintain the target in his cross wires until it is hit. It was designed as an anti-tank weapon and has a great deal of sophisticated electronics, infrared tracking detector and course correction side rockets for accurate shooting at up to a thousand meters. These features were not important to the IWACs since they were to fire at a stationary target from a distance of less than thirty feet. They had chosen this weapon for its lethal qualities—it would easily penetrate three feet of steel-reinforced concrete.

Donovan knelt beside Sergeant Oxhall. They had both donned heavy flak jackets and helmets. The other men had been sent to the upper level to wait. The risk of being injured by flying rubble was little enough in this situation, but Donovan didn't believe in unnecessary risks for his men, however slight. He glanced at Oxhall.

"Ready, Sergeant?"

"Ready when you are, sir."

"Right, then. At your pleasure."

Oxhall ducked his head to the eyepiece and began breathing slowly in a controlled rhythm. He held his breath and fired. The concussion was so overwhelming they felt intense pressure on all surfaces of their bodies at once. They were pushed slightly backward, but not enough to knock them down. The noise was so complete that it was less like a distinct sound than a totality similar to an absence of noise. Small pieces of concrete block sprayed outward, but the bulk of the rubble was driven inward and a jagged irregular

112

hole more than five feet in diameter appeared in the wall. Donovan moved quickly across to it and shone his flashlight through. The missile had sufficient force after penetrating the garage wall to make a dent in the vault wall beyond, but had not penetrated it.

Donovan went quickly toward the ramp and motioned Oxhall to follow. They were met at the top of the ramp by one of the men in an asbestos suit. Donovan motioned him on down and he descended, carrying a glass beaker of clear fluid with a rubber seal top.

The original bank building which contains the vault is not used by the night shift. It is sealed off from the newer sections at night by massive hydraulic doors. Since the gas had been pumped into only two ventilation shafts which run to the new additions, presumably there was no gas in the old building, but the vault area had to be checked for leakage.

The man climbed down into the room and found a guard desk with his flashlight. He set the beaker on the desk and carefully cut away the rubber seal. The fluid was a special chemical compound which would react differently to normal air than to air contaminated by Agent VX. If the air were pure, the fluid would turn color over a period of five minutes to a violent Day-Glo chartreuse. If even an infinitesimal amount of Agent VX were present, it would become a milky yellow in five minutes. The man climbed back out and went up the ramp to wait.

Sergeant-Major McGregor came into the garage, saw Donovan, and crossed to him. Salutes were exchanged.

"One of the scouts has spotted a police automobile in the area, sir. He can't tell yet if its patrol will penetrate the perimeter."

"All right, Sergeant-Major. Keep it under observation. If it comes too close, bring them in however you have to. The operation's gone beautifully. No errors now."

"Yes, sir."

The man glanced at his watch. Six and a half minutes. Long enough. He descended the ramp. In the vault area, his

113

flashlight beam picked out the beaker even before he got to the desk. The Day-Glo chartreuse of the liquid radiated like some live, volatile thing in the pale beam. He crossed to the desk for a closer look, then returned to the ramp and the upper level of the garage. He pulled off the head covering of his suit as Donovan met him.

"No gas, Colonel."

"Ah, that's grand, then."

Donovan and Oxhall returned to the lower level. Oxhall reloaded the Dragon while Donovan moved one of the floodlights so that it shone directly through the hole in the garage wall, gave good illumination to the vault wall beyond. He knelt beside Oxhall and nodded at him. Oxhall sighted on the dent in the vault wall. He fired. Very little rubble came out into the garage and the concussion and noise were slightly diminished. The missile had ripped a hole in the vault wall slightly more than two feet in diameter. Donovan reloaded and Oxhall fired again at the lower right edge of the hole. The hole was enlarged to almost four feet. Donovan reloaded and Oxhall fired at the lower left edge of the hole. The hole was enlarged to more than five and a half feet in diameter. Donovan crossed to peer in. He straightened and nodded.

"That's a lovely hole, Sergeant. Pack that thing on up to the truck and we'll put the lads to work."

"Yes, sir."

Donovan went up to the first level and motioned the working parties down. He descended in the lead. He removed his flak jacket and helmet and gave them to Oxhall. He crossed to a pillar and sat leaning against it to watch. He lit a cigar and sighed. He was tired and his legs hurt a bit.

The first working party brought picks and sledges and quickly set about the business of clearing the rubble. They heaved most of it into the vault area away from the holes in the walls. They used the picks and sledges to level off the bottom edges of both holes. It was hard work and slow because of the confined area. After twelve minutes, Donovan crossed to them and observed the progress.

"Just level off that last corner a bit more, Corporal, and that'll do." The men nodded.

A second detail had brought down a long section of planking nailed together with two-by-fours for cross braces, battery lanterns with heavy-duty suction cups affixed to the back plates, a number of cloth-sided refuse containers on wheels that were filled with trays of light, thin plastic. The plastic trays were to hold the money and would fit into the Day-Glo orange containers for shipment. The cloth-sided refuse bins would hold all the five- and one-dollar bills the IWACs could stuff in them. (Since ones and fives raised the weight total of the money substantially without raising the dollar figure significantly, the refuse bins of money would be left with other equipment in the warehouse as incriminating evidence against the Afrikaners). Three men went down into the vault and began sticking the lanterns to the walls with the suction cups and switching them on. Six lanterns completely illuminated the interior of the vault. They edged the section of planking down through the holes until it was firmly in place with cross braces down. It made a solid ramp from vault to garage floor. A third detail had taken the Day-Glo orange containers and spread them at convenient intervals across the garage floor, leaving adequate space to move about between them. They removed the covers and set them aside.

The vault was separated into sections, each section containing wheeled carts upon which the money was stacked. As the first cart was wheeled up to the garage floor, Donovan rose and walked across to it. He lifted a stack off the top and looked at it. One-hundred-dollar bills. Several million dollars on that cart alone. He held it up and turned toward the men in the garage. He removed the cigar from his mouth with his left hand.

"Gentlemen, the object pursuant to this exercise in the

martial art. Money." The men cheered and laughed. He tossed the packet back on the cart, waved it on, and walked back to the pillar to observe. A *money war*, he mused, that's all this really is. He liked the phrase. Turned it over in his head. *The money war*.

The Federal Reserve banks of the United States band currency in packets of one hundred bills regardless of denomination. All bills, regardless of denomination, are approximately two and one half inches by slightly more than six inches. The plastic trays, stacked in the refuse carts, were twenty-six inches wide by sixty-two inches long by six and a half inches deep so that one hundred stacks of six packets of bills would fit uniformly and snuggly into each tray. The trays had snap-on plastic covers, thin and snug. Each Day-Glo orange container would hold ten trays firmly in grooved slots. Thus six thousand packs of bills would go into each container. All fully loaded orange containers would weigh three thousand and twenty-seven pounds, and one packed with fifty-dollar bills would hold thirty million dollars.

The men began loading trays quickly and placing them in containers. They took only bills of ten dollars or larger denomination, threw the ones and fives into the refuse carts. Donovan descended into the vault to guide the men in the selection of the bonds which were usable for them. The men were joking and laughing as they handled the money. They seemed slightly giddy. Donovan glanced at his watch. 10:39 p.m. Right on schedule. The tip of his cigar glowed.

The floor of the vault was littered with coins. The missiles had hit the left front section of the vault where the coins were stored, as had been the intent. Bags of coins had split open and scattered and ricocheted around the interior. Two bags of half dollars had been subjected to such intense flash heat that they had partially fused into a lumpish collage of several hundred liquid images of John Fitzgerald Kennedy.

Donovan quickly sorted through the collections of bonds, indicating those to be taken and those to be left. When he exited the vault, the forklift truck had a loaded container on its forks and was starting up the ramp to the upper level of the garage. Donovan followed it. As he passed the cloth-sided refuse containers, two men were dumping packets of one- and five-dollar bills into them.

Outside, the forklift truck crawled down the street to the second trailer. A heavy-duty steel ramp had been angled from the street up into its belly. The forklift drove slowly up the ramp and to the front of the interior of the trailer. The container was eased into position and strapped down while the forklift backed slowly out and returned to the parking garage.

Donovan walked on to the lead trailer. The doors were open and five men were storing equipment. The compressors and the empty gas canisters and the extension ladder were snugged. They were moving the Dragon and its extra shells into place for stacking. Donovan nodded to one of the men.

"Stack it carefully. The refuse containers will take a lot of space, lad, and you won't be being able to stack them."

"Yes, sir."

The hoses were flapping slightly in the wind as they dangled down the side of the building. They would be left, as would the metal door plates. They merely needed enough evidence to be clearly incriminating, not every piece of equipment.

Donovan threw his cigar away. It made a wet hiss in the bank of snow. He was glad the snow had stopped. The roads would be difficult, but not impossible. And they had plenty of time. He walked back toward the second truck. The forklift had deposited another container and was returning to the garage. He stopped and listened. Popping sounds on the wind seemed to come from the northwest corner of the bank. He quickly turned the corner and began walking along the north side of the parking garage. He stopped at the door. The sounds were louder. He glanced in the door, saw four men standing about.

117

"Private! You four come with me. Have you an extra rifle there?"

"Yes, sir."

The four men came trotting across to him. One tossed him a rifle. Another handed him six spare clips. They followed him up St. Charles toward Broadway. The popping sounds grew louder. Donovan cocked his head as he walked. He identified some of the sounds as 510–4s on automatic. He picked up the pace.

### 10:44 p.m.: CPL. PATRICK JOSEPH HOGAN

He was driving too fast, he knew. He couldn't make himself slow down. He didn't know how long he could remain conscious. He was afraid he would pass out before he got to Chicago. To the airport.

He looked at the speedometer needle. It was between ninety and ninety-five. He tried to calculate what that was in kilometers per hour, but his head wasn't clear enough for the math involved.

These American roads were good. Two lanes each direction separated by a wide island which was sometimes flat and sometimes a ditch. He'd come far enough north that the roads were clear. The storm hadn't hit here. Traffic was moderate. He was afraid of being stopped by the police, but he was more fearful of passing out, so he held his pace. His side was sticky when he touched it—still bleeding and the pain was intense. The pain had been good at first. It had helped him stay awake. Now it was so strong and had been going on for so long that it was beginning to have a numbing effect. With his window halfway down, the cold air was some help, but he was beginning to get the first feeling that it was losing its effect as well.

The overhead road signs were confusing. They told him of exits to places he had never heard of, route numbers he

118

did not want, lane change decisions he was not quite sure what to do about. Route I-55 and 66 had separated. He was not sure which one he was on now, but the map seemed to show that whenever they separated they rejoined a few miles further on. He had to slow now. He was approaching more signs. Apparently if he wanted to stay on 66, he had to take this exit and follow the beltline road, whatever that was.

After a couple of miles, he came to a stop light. The road was going along the edge of a town. Some place called Bloomington, Illinois. A police car stopped behind him. He glanced back in the rear-view mirror. Two policemen. Joking. The passenger passed the driver a lighted cigarette.

When the light turned green, he started off cautiously. The police car seemed in no hurry, followed him at his moderate pace. There was a series of stop lights and he hit them all red. The police car stayed with him. The road was lined with restaurants, motels, offices. He passed a hospital. St. Josephs. He thought of going to their emergency room. But there would be questions he couldn't answer satisfactorily. At a madly confusing intersection with what seemed a dozen signs and more roads than he could count, there were shopping centers on three sides. America. Insane opulence.

Now he was passing through the edge of another town, though he couldn't tell any difference, couldn't see anything but the sign to distinguish where one ended and the other began. This one was called Normal, Illinois. A wildly improbable name. Endless puns suggested themselves. Normal man bites dog, etc. To his left, across a roll of ground, he could see a huge complex of row houses. Apartments, the Americans would call them. The outer row was illuminated by street lights. Tan brick first stories topped by chocolate and cream-yellow imitation-Tudor second stories. Hogan wondered what it cost to live in one of those homes.

Route 66 was rejoining I-55 as the map had promised. He held a steady fifty, five miles below the posted limit. The police car finally became impatient, passed him swiftly, drifting outward on a sweeping curve. He decided he had better keep his speed down for ten miles or so. He wanted to give the police car plenty of time to get far away. The pain was diminishing now. His side seemed numbed. He felt a sudden gust of nausea break across him. He quickly rolled his window all the way down for more air. He wondered if he was going into shock.

### CHICAGO, ILLINOIS/10:45 p.m., CST/CAPT. ABDUL IMMAN

Captain Imman was normally a cocky, somewhat arrogant young man. He had reason to be. He was chief pilot for Azyad Shipping at the age of twenty-eight; an excellent job, fine pay, responsibility. Of course, since Azyad Shipping often performed extra-legal or illegal tasks, either for profit or political gain, he was, from time to time, involved in unusual, shady, or tricky operations. Ordinarily, this did not bother him. But this job was a bitch and he was not at all sure he wanted to do it. He had to file a falsified flight plan with the FAA, which would cost him his license if he was caught out. And he was going to have to do some fancy flying with a 727, in concert with another 727 doing the same kind of flying. Usually if you were going to fool around it was in some little job more appropriate to the task.

The desk officer was leafing through the papers Imman had filed. He was taking a long time with what was an ordinary matter. It was one reason Imman was nervous.

"You're taking a load of what down to Alton?"

"Machine parts. The invoice is there."

The desk officer looked up at him. "I know it's there. Is there some reason you don't think you should answer questions civilly, Captain? Are you above all this mundane paperwork?"

"No offense intended. I merely thought by your question that you might have overlooked the invoice."

120

"Thank you for your concern, Captain." The man turned his eyes back to the stack of papers and Imman curled his lip. "Funny time of night for this kind of run."

Imman nodded. "I thought so too, but the boss says fly down there at one in the morning, deliver the parts. It's a special rush order he says. The man pays my salary. So if he wants me to fly at funny times, I don't argue."

The man nodded his head. "A most obliging fellow, eh, Captain? That's good to know. After you drop the load at Alton, you're going to ferry down to San Juan?"

"That's correct. I have to pick up a load of electrical equipment bound for Cartagena."

"Yes, that's what it says here, Captain. Thank you, but I *can* read. You know what I mean?" Imman bit his tongue. Literally. The man stared at him. He was openly hostile. Imman knew the type—bored, middle-aged, bureaucrat in a dead-end job, looking for a target for his listless antipathy. "You know what I mean?" Imman remained silent. The man leaned toward him. "I said, 'You know what I mean?' buddy."

Imman leaned even closer and whispered. "May Allah smile on you with the smile of a thousand curses and on your children and your children's children even so unto the tenth generation. Endorse the fucking papers, *buddy*, or I'll have your ass up before a review board. I don't have to take this chickenshit from you or anybody else." They stared at each other with mutual hatred. The man broke his eyes away first. He began stamping papers vehemently.

"Weather's clearing at Civic Memorial. You shouldn't have any trouble. Lambert's closed by snow so there won't be much traffic."

"Thank you."

He handed Imman his copies, kept the rest. "Pleasant flight, Captain." Imman walked away without answering. As he went out the door, he flashed the universal finger of scorn backward without looking to see if the man was watching.

One of the men in the courtyard of the bank had opened up on the police patrol car too soon as it came down St. Charles Street. It had stopped across the street in a vacant lot, had not completely penetrated the perimeter. The men in the used-car lot had coolly held their fire since they were not behind the police and did not have them trapped. Donovan lay on his stomach in the courtyard. He had reduced the firing to one rifleman while he watched and decided tactics. He had all the men save the one rifleman well concealed in the shrubs and snow. They waited quietly, patiently. The important thing was not to spook the police into running. If they got away . . . They were crouched behind their car for the moment, firing occasional shots at the rifleman. They could not have very clear sight of the situation at that distance and at night. Else they would have run already.

Donovan motioned for one of the men to come to him. "You and one other lad are going to have to hop the wall here. Go around toward their right, make it look as if you're trying to flank them. That should move them around toward this end of the car, put the lads in the lot behind them."

"Yes, sir."

"Get your man."

"Yes, sir."

In a minute, two men dropped over the wall of the courtyard and began running diagonally across Broadway as if to flank the police car. They fired their rifles on automatic as they ran. One policeman raised up to fire his pistol.

Donovan shouted, "Make them keep their heads down." He and the other five men in the courtyard opened up on the car. The windows and sides were quickly riddled, and the policemen could be seen moving to their left, away from the apparent danger. When they reached the end of the car, the three men in the parking lot, who had worked their way through the parked cars to nearly point-blank range, shot them both quickly. Neither patrolman had a chance to do much more than spin around in surprise at the attack from the rear. The bodies were dumped into the back of the patrol car and it was driven, limping, down to the parking garage and on in. The IWACs suffered no casualties in the skirmish.

When Donovan returned to the garage, McGregor was waiting for him. Donovan handed his rifle to one of the men and returned McGregor's salute.

"No further activity on the perimeter, sir. Except Private Jensen in the mall over there said two drunk civilians came out of the Holiday Inn at one point. He convinced them it was a bad night for a stroll and they went back inside. Nothing further."

"Very good, Sergeant-Major. Wait here. I'll see how the loading is going and be back with your final orders."

"Yes, sir."

Donovan walked to the back of the second truck. The forklift was inside the trailer, stacking a container. The driver came up.

"Last one going in, Colonel. The equipment truck is loaded and closed."

"All right. We'll move out in a minute."

"Yes, sir."

The forklift backed away from the containers. The operator shut it off and put double chocks around all the wheels. Donovan climbed into the trailer and counted the containers—twenty-four, right enough, and checked to see that they were well secured. When he came down from the trailer, he nodded at one of the men. The ramp was slid up into the truck and the doors closed and locked. The men were assembled in the garage. Donovan approached and grinned.

"That's well done, lads." They laughed, clapped. A sort of ragged cheer went up. "The truck details are moving

# RETREAT

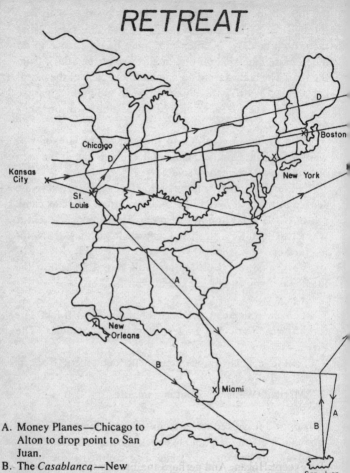

A. Money Planes—Chicago to Alton to drop point to San Juan.
B. The *Casablanca*—New Orleans to San Juan to drop point to Marseilles. (This area not to scale.)
C. IWACs—Auto to Kansas City, air to Boston to Shannon.
D. IWACs—Auto to Chicago, air to Shannon.
E. Donovan—Auto to Peoria, air to Washington, layover, air to Shannon.

out now and the rest of you best get off." He turned to McGregor. "Wait until the trucks are under way and then you may disperse the perimeter guard, Sergeant-Major."

"Yes, sir."

They exchanged salutes and separated. Donovan went with the driver to the money truck. Two men were in the cab of the equipment truck. They shifted into gear and began rolling. The men in the garage began walking the few blocks in separate directions to where their cars were parked. In five minutes, Sergeant-Major McGregor dispersed the perimeter guard. They lay down their weapons on the spot and began walking to their cars. At 11:19 p.m., the money war was over.

### ZURICH, SWITZERLAND/6:30 a.m., ZURICH TIME/ MAJOR JEAN TURRMAN

Turrman checked his watch. It would be 11:30 in St. Louis. They would be about finished up at the bank. He did not have any doubt that it had gone well despite the intricacies and difficulties. Turrman was a cold, efficient, hard man who believed in only three things in this world—money, war, and Colonel Donovan. Even the final African fiasco hadn't shaken him. Donovan did things right. He had been Donovan's executive officer since the first Angola war, more than ten years, and he knew him better than anyone else except Hogan. And perhaps the French war correspondent. Turrman grimaced. He didn't like the correspondent. But he had faith in Donovan.

He was dressed in a bankerly charcoal suit and was having his second cup of coffee. He had arisen half an hour early today. He wouldn't go into the office until seven-thirty, as usual, but he had been unable to sleep any later. The telegram had come yesterday afternoon: IRISH WAGER AT CLONMEL GOES TONIGHT.

125

It had been signed, DONOVAN. A very direct man, the Colonel. And that was much the best way. Turrman put down his coffee and yawned. The routine at the bank was dull. After a month of it, he had remembered why he hadn't gone into the business with his family twenty years before. It bored him. There was no difficulty with it. He was an intelligent man and had quickly mastered all the basic work of his department and many of the nuances. He supposed it would be of greater interest once it was partially his money he was managing. Certainly he had formed some ideas about what to do with the account. He was anxious to propose them to Donovan. He was secretly quite proud of the formula he had worked out for their money. He knew he was anxious for Donovan's approval. It was a thing that had become very important to him. It did for many of the men. You had such absolute faith in Donovan's . . . well, judgment was the closest word, that you wanted him to approve any idea you had. Think well of it. Think well of you.

It was strange. Wanting Donovan's approval. Like a father, though Turrman was less than ten years younger. Turrman shrugged. Whatever it was—it was. Funny, though. He didn't give a damn about his own father's opinion. Or his older brother's. He never had.

Major Turrman broke open the double barreled shotgun and slipped two shells into the cylinders. He turned to his older brother.

"But Andre, I thought the family would be pleased to have the prodigal son return to the bosom of the family and join the firm permanently." Andre Turrman completed a similar task with his shotgun. He was shorter than his tall brother, heavily built and, now in middle age, his hair was rapidly turning white. He smiled at his brother.

"Of course we are, Jean. We have always hoped that you would one day forsake these adventures of yours and return to the fold. I am merely saying that we have to consider the proper position for you in the bank. You're not a young man

126

any more, Jean. Next year you'll be forty. Normally, we'd start you off as a clerk, but that would have been twenty years ago. That wouldn't do now."

"No, that wouldn't do at all." They began walking through the small patch of trees at the edge of the field. The barely post-dawn air was cool, here near the lake, even in August.

"But we can't very well put you in charge of even a department with no experience to speak of. Father and I haven't thought of a solution yet. That is all I am saying." The dog, sniffing the damp earth ten meters ahead of them, stopped. In a few seconds, she came to a rigid point. They closed and raised their shotguns and began to edge forward quietly, cautiously. They were nearly upon the dog when the birds burst from cover eight meters away. Four of them rising instantly to flight made no sound save the sudden whirr of flapping winds. The deafening explosions of the four shots came one on top of another with no perceptible pause between. Two birds fell immediately. One flew away untouched. A fourth yawed downward, tried to regain altitude, then fell heavily. The dog trotted off to fetch the kill.

"You always were a better shot, Jean." Major Turrman smiled.

I've always told you, Andre, you're a microsecond too impatient. That's the difference."

They broke open the guns, extracted the spent cartridges. They were warm to the touch. They dropped them into side pockets and reloaded.

"I've always thought it humorous, Andre. You the solid elder, with the painstaking method in business."

Andre shrugged. "Different kinds of patience." The dog returned with a bird in her jaws. He took it and dropped it into the game sack as the dog ran to fetch again. They lit cigarettes while they waited.

"I don't want you and father to worry any more. I already know what sort of position I want." Andre turned a cautious, neutral expression toward Jean. "I shall supervise the investment of a substantial trust account which I shall be bringing to the bank as new business. That will be my only interest to begin with. Later we can see."

"I don't know, Jean." He shrugged. "A trust account, that's merely clerking for the most part. Even several million francs is in the province of a very junior trust officer. You know that. We can't make you a director immediately, but we're not proposing that you begin as a functionary. We didn't mean that at all. We just need time to design the right sort of opening. You should know we're not going to treat you shabbily, Jean. That was not what we meant. We just didn't want you to assume that you could become a full partner overnight." The dog waited, breathing lightly, for Andre to remove the second bird, then ran off to find the third. They began to follow slowly.

"I understand all that, Andre. *You* misunderstood *me*. I'm not talking about several million francs, I'm talking about a substantial account. Even by our standards." The older brother shot the younger a quizzical glance as they walked.

"Can you be more specific, Jean?"

He nodded. "The precise figure will not be certain until the amount is deposited, but the minimum figure will be over eight hundred million francs and it might go as high as a billion and a half." Andre stopped and stared at Jean. Jean smiled. The look of surprise pleased him. It was not often he was able to shock Andre sufficiently for it to show.

"Where does this money—where will it come from?"

"It will be deposited, originally, say in fifty or sixty days, in an account in the name of the Azyad family, one of their companies. You know who they are?"

"Of course. Any European banker does."

"All right. Then, it will remain dormant in that account for another thirty to sixty days. Within that time frame, it will be transferred to an account in the name of the Irish West Africa Company."

"That is the name of your mercenary company."

"That's right. That's the account I will manage. Ten percent of that money will be mine." He smiled when he saw an even more incredulous expression on Andre's face than before. "That's right, Andre, your little brother will soon be the richest member of the family." The dog came to them and Andre took the bird. They followed her as she resumed her sniffing on a diagonal across the field away from the trees and the lake.

"Of course this makes a great deal of difference, Jean. Father will be enormously pleased. Can you tell me what the money is for, mmm, why it is to be paid to the, your company?"

"Obviously, Andre, the Azyads are to pay us in exchange for a somewhat larger sum of money that we will be delivering to them elsewhere. A twenty percent larger sum of money." Major Turrman smiled at his brother, "Laundering is the term, I believe. The Azyads can return the dirty money we give them to circulation without difficulty through their banking channels worldwide."

Andre frowned, "Dirty money?"

Jean laughed, "Come now, Andre. Don't play squeamish with me. Money is money—right?" He clapped his brother on the shoulder, "On the day of the transfer I will receive a ship to shore cable confirming delivery and a cable from America with the exact figures of the money."

Andre nodded, "I see. Can you tell me where the dirty money comes from or is that to remain secret?"

"When the time comes, it will be quite clear from public accounts of a sensational nature where the money comes from, but there will be no slightest chance of its origin causing us any difficulty at all. The Americans will be angry, but there will be nothing they can do."

Andre snorted. "The Americans! Fools and children. They never pose difficulties. They aren't clever enough."

"The one thing we have to talk about, you and I and father, the transfer of funds from one account to the other. There must be no misunderstanding about that."

"What do you mean, Jean?"

"Simply this. The Azyads might well try to cheat my company if they could find a way. That is why I am using the family. There will be a finder's fee in it for you and father, of course. Perhaps a million francs apiece."

Andre nodded. "Of course. Very generous. And it goes without saying that you need not worry about the Azyads attempting to cheat you." The dog came to a point again. They approached cautiously as before. The sun was shining fully now and gleamed off the blue metal of their shotguns.

Jean whispered, "I mean there can be no misunderstanding of the consequences of treachery. Even amongst our family members." They paused and looked at one another closely for a few seconds. "Even if I wanted to prevent it, I couldn't. And I wouldn't prevent if if I could. The penalty for treachery is death, swift and sure." The birds flew up suddenly, two of them together, mates. Jean quickly raised his shotgun and fired. Both birds fell instantly. He looked at Andre, the sun reflecting winking points in the center of his silver-tint sunglasses. "Others would handle the Azyads if it should come to that, but I would handle you and father myself. Personally." He smiled and shrugged. "So, of course, I'm not worried. I'm not worried at all. As you say, it goes without saying that you will insure that the Azyads do not cheat us." He put an arm around his brother's shoulder as they walked toward the fetching dog. "After all, if you can't trust your family—why then, you can't trust anyone at all."

**12:00 MIDNIGHT: COL. TERRENCE DONOVAN**

They were on Route 111, north of Horseshoe Lake, rolling smoothly along at a comfortable forty-five mph. The road was only spotted with patches of snow or slick spots.

Most of the storm had abated over St. Louis—very little traveled this far east. The driver, Private First Class Lars Amundson, was a taciturn Swede who had been with Donovan since Angola. They did not converse much. Their silence had the ease of men who have been long together and have an established relationship with which they are comfortable. Donovan checked his watch. Plenty of time. He lit a cigar and cracked his window for a little air in the stuffy cab. Presumably, since they were traveling at an easy speed on a moderately good road, the half-dozen men in the back of the trailer were having a comfortable enough ride.

"What are you going to do with your money, Lars?"

The Swede shrugged. "How much will it be?"

"Well, let's see . . ." Donovan consulted the slip of paper Captain Jackson had given him: *$233,888,000.00 Cash. $319,108,000.00 Bonds.* A total of $552,996,000.00. Twenty percent for the Azyad family. That would leave roughly $440,000,000.00. Ten percent for himself, ten percent for Turrman, ten percent for Jackson would leave $308,000,000.00 to divide by approximately one hundred. "Something over three million dollars."

"If I leave it in the general account with the others, how much would I have a year?"

"Major Turrman feels that a ten-percent return, even with highly conservative investments, is not unreasonable on a sum of that size."

"Three hundred thousand dollars a year?"

"Yes. If you spend it all. If not, it will increase."

"Yah." The Swede was silent for a few moments. "That is what I will do then. I will pay off the mortgage on my father's farm. And the rest, I will leave in the general fund."

"That's grand, then. That's what most of the lads will be doing."

Donovan yawned. He was tired. And he had a long day ahead. There was still the touch-and-go with Washington. Still, it had gone well. The men had performed well. McGregor had been worried. He thought they might be rest-

131

less after Imbannailand. And he was afraid of the court-martial during training. It wouldn't sit well with the men. He was afraid Donovan might lose control of them. Donovan had smiled and shrugged.

"It's no good backing off, Sergeant-Major. Either they follow me or they don't. We're going to be doing a hard thing over there. We'd better find out if the men still have the discipline now. We can't have it breaking down in the middle of the operation."

The men had been working hard in the long beautiful summer days on the peninsula. Donovan's farm was the base. The barn had been converted into a barracks for the men. Calisthenics for all in the early morning; then breakdown into teams and familiarization with tasks and equipment; in the afternoon, Donovan lectured on the total picture with maps, photographs and the scale models Jackson and Hogan had made. In the evening, the men could visit the local pubs until midnight. Two rules were stressed again and again. No trouble with the locals (Mick Doyle's IRA boys were edgy enough about Donovan's return and the men). No contact with the local women. None. And one of the men, drunk, raped a local girl on a hill behind Durrus. Donovan prosecuted Private Ingram. McGregor acted for the defense. The girl's brother and Mick Doyle observed. The men were the jury. Two thirds were necessary to convict and sentence. The verdict was guilty, the sentence—death.

McGregor and Donovan sat in the kitchen, drinking tea. The late afternoon was still sunny and fairly windless.

"The firing squad will have to be limited to three men since that is all the rifles we have here." McGregor nodded. "Full clips in each rifle set on fully automatic. Instruct the men to empty the clips completely." McGregor said nothing, but he looked at Donovan in surprise. Donovan nodded. "I know, Andrew. It will make a bloody hash of the body, but that's better than firing five or six rounds into the

132

poor bugger—none of them lethal—and leaving him squirming and flopping about to be finished by a pistol bullet in the ear."

"Yes, sir."

"Firing squads are always nervous, Andrew. They don't like shooting one of their own and they are prone to bad marksmanship. Set them at twenty paces, kneeling position, and twenty shots apiece. It will look like hell, but in the end it'll be kinder to poor Ingram."

"Yes, sir."

"You know the men who are particular friends of Ingram?"

"Yes, sir."

"Exclude them from the drawing of lots. It's bad enough business as it is without that."

"Yes, sir. Begging the Colonel's pardon, but that's just what I've been thinking. It's a bad business to be starting off an operation with."

Donovan rubbed a grooved, dark, burn mark on the tired wooden tabletop with his forefinger. He pushed his tea cup aside and leaned back in his chair.

"I couldn't agree with you more, Sergeant-Major, but what's our alternative? We're on an operational basis. The standing orders were clear and agreed to. Ingram has come quite close to jeopardizing the entire operation."

"I realize that, sir—"

"And so do the men. Over ninety percent voted to convict, over eighty percent voted to sustain."

"That's so."

"And he did rape the girl. Nothing will satisfy the IRA boys but what we've elected to do. They could still sabotage us rather badly."

"That is the other point I would like to raise with the Colonel. Legally, this will be murder. Doyle will be a witness."

"Just so, Andrew. And not a trustworthy man at all. But I believe we can remedy that situation after the operation is over. After will be quite a different matter. Mr. Doyle will become both expendable and something of a nuisance. We will attend to him. After.''


It was raining hard and the wind was howling in the dark. The men were assembled at a distance and to one side of the barn. Two autos were placed fifteen paces from the barn—Donovan had shortened the range because of the filthy weather—slightly angled so that the insides of their front fenders were nearly touching forming the bottom half of an X. There was a man in the front seat of each auto, keeping the engines running. The firing squad stood between the autos.

Donovan and McGregor led Ingram out of the house and across to the barn wall. He walked stiff-backed and gingerly, like a man who does not want to put his foot in anything. They tied his hands behind his back around a low post driven into the ground. Donovan pulled a long white scarf from his pocket, but Ingram shook his head. Donovan and McGregor walked around behind the cars. They checked the squad's rifles, then tapped the windows of the cars. The headlights came on. They had been focused to shed a strong crossbeam illuminating Ingram and a narrow section of the barn wall quite brightly. The squad knelt. They rested their rifles across the hoods of the cars. Donovan nodded at McGregor.

McGregor's cry, "FIRE!" seemed lost in the wind.

The long, ragged, stuttering volley seemed to go on and on, but was over in seconds. Ingram's body had been whipped back and forth, now lifted, now hammered down, finally hung sagging from the post, legs splayed, head over and down to the left, nearly touching the ground. It twitched and jerked with the final, post-mortem muscle contractions. McGregor crossed to the body. Rain washed much of the blood away, gave the skin a slick, white sheen in the glare of the auto headlights. McGregor knelt to see that he was qute dead. He stood and nodded his head. The automobile

134

lights died away and the engines shut off. Doyle turned to Donovan.

"Justice has been done, Terrence."

"Has it, Mick?" Donovan looked down at the shorter man. "Perhaps. More like expediency, I'd say. We get little justice in the world, Mick. And when we do, we seldom care for it. It's not justice we want."

Later, Donovan told McGregor they would move the departure date up by a week. He did not want the men to have overlong to brood on the incident, and training had been going well ahead of schedule in any case. In the afternoon, he drove to Bantry to send cables to Switzerland, Paris, and St. Louis, advising of the change in schedule.

It had been a bad business, but it was over and the men had held. Not much more to go now. Donovan shut his eyes. It was all moving right along. The equipment truck had been locked in the warehouse. All the rental leases had been taken in the name of John 3X Brown.

The men were on the main roads to Kansas City and Chicago, except the Jefferson City, Baldwin, Meramec, and switching station teams. They were already at Kansas City International Airport. The IWACs were poising for flight.

### ST. LOUIS, MISSOURI/12:32 a.m., CST/MAJOR NOAH PETERSON

He had taken his son's body to an undertaker in Webster Groves. He had pounded on the door until it was opened and he and his driver had carried the boy inside. There were rules, regulations, ordinances, paperwork and Noah brushed all the man's questions aside curtly.

"You know who I am?"

"Yes, of course."

"Then get on with your work and we'll attend to the red tape tomorrow." The man had stared at Noah's face and nodded acquiescence.

Noah had pounded on the door of their family doctor's

135

home also. The doctor, a neat, late-thirtyish man, had looked sleepy and irritated, but Noah had been curt with him as well.

"Dr. Gerard, my son has been killed. I'm going home to tell my wife. You're coming with me."

As soon as Liz had seen the doctor, and then taken a closer look at Noah's face, she broke. Noah held her, shaking, crying, and told her what he knew. And he and the doctor put her to bed and the doctor sedated her. The twins, Cheryl and Charles, had sat on the couch and cried quietly and held hands. Now they were in the kitchen, talking quietly in a kind of stunned incomprehension.

Noah sat in his study chain-smoking and drinking steadily. He felt cold and sober despite four stiff drinks. Tomorrow neighbors and friends would come. And there would be nights and days of viewing the body. And mass. And the burial. And the wake. Hundreds of people passing through the house—eating, drinking, laughing, crying, comforting, graceful and graceless and good-hearted. He knew the ritual of death from deaths in the family, deaths of friends, deaths in the line of duty, deaths out of uniform, departmental deaths, informal and unpretentious deaths, political deaths—pompous and filled with ceremoney. He was a relatively young man and he had seen it all, but he was burned out by the slaughter of this night and the death of his son. And for the first time in his life he felt *truly* murderous, as visions of guns and blood and terrifying vengeance floated through his mind. But whom, he finally wondered, whom should he kill?

## 1:00 a.m.: CAPT. ABDUL IMMAN

Captain Imman eased the 727 forward on the taxi apron. They had been waiting for twenty-three minutes, were finally next up. The 747 charter that had been just ahead of them in line thundered by and began a steep ascent.

136

"Azyad Shipping 868, you are cleared for takeoff."

"This is Azyad Shipping 868. We copy, are proceeding for takeoff."

He made the turn onto the runway, began revving the engines. He liked the 727. It was a good ship, comfortable to fly. He hoped the pilot behind him, Captain Faizeal of Azyad Shipping 864, would remember to use at least eight thousand feet of runway for his takeoff. That would be about the minimum if the planes were fully loaded as the falsified flight plan indicated. Empty, they could lift off after a much shorter run, but that might be noticed by someone in the tower. Unlikely, but a pilot doesn't really want to take *any* chances with his license. At Alton no one was likely to notice anything, even though they would be loading instead of unloading, as the flight plan called for, and taking off with loads of thirty-thousand-plus pounds apiece rather than empty for ferrying to San Juan, again as the flight plan called for. Of course, they would be empty when they landed at San Juan. The ship was straining hard and he loosed her. It was a smooth takeoff and he guessed he had run about nine thousand feet before liftoff, which should convince the tower that he was loaded if anyone bothered to think about it. When he came to his course heading and leveled off at thirty-three thousand feet, he turned it over to his co-pilot and lit a cigarette. One would be about all he could have; about the time he finished it they would be preparing to get into the descent pattern for Alton. It was such a short run down that their flight path was nearly an arc; ascend, level off, descend in rapid order. He exhaled a narrow screen of smoke, sighed, and yawned.

**1:47 a.m.: COL. TERRENCE DONOVAN**

When you enter the roadway at Civic Memorial Airport in Alton, Illinois, you see a series of modest buildings stretching off to either side and nearly dead-on is an equally modest but modern and relatively new hexagonal control tower. The land is flat and nude. There was very little snow here, the merest ground cover. The roadway was damp, but not particularly slick. The airport was nearly deserted. There seemed to be no activity. Donovan directed the driver to swing left where the roadway forked, around behind the short row of small hangars. There were three cars parked behind the end hangar. When the truck stopped by them, Captain Jackson got out of the middle one and walked across to the cab. Donovan rolled down his window. Jackson saluted. Donovan returned it and they both smiled.

"Evening, Colonel. You're right on schedule."

"That's so, Captain. 'Twas well done."

Jackson walked ahead of the truck to a gate in the chainlink fencing, opened it. The truck pulled through and Jackson shut the gate after it. Donovan helped Jackson slide open the doors to the hangar he'd rented and, after they were closed again, Amundson swung open the doors to the truck. The men climbed down and begun walking around, getting the cramps out of their legs. Jackson stared at the containers. He smiled and shook his head. He laughed aloud.

"Son of a bitch! I can't quite believe it. I've been thinking about robbing that fucking bank for fifteen years."

"Well, it's not thinking any more, Captain. It's done."

"Son of a bitch!"

Donovan took a cigarette that Jackson offered, accepted a light. He looked at his watch. 1:56 a.m.

"The planes should be arriving soon."

Jackson nodded. "If they took off at one or so, they should be here in the next fifteen minutes." Donovan turned to the men standing in a close semicircle.

"All right, lads. We might as well get ready."

The men moved into the back of the trailer. They positioned the ramp. The forklift operator unchocked the wheels, started the engine, and eased the forks under one of

138

the containers. He backed down the ramp and pulled up to the door of the hangar, shut off the engine. They waited. In a few minutes they heard the engines of the first plane. Jackson walked out of the hangar across toward the apron area where the jets would stop.

Jackson had arranged for a night ground crew to top off the jets' fuel tanks while they were being loaded. The operation took thirty-nine minutes. Jackson and one other man boarded Captain Imman's plane, two others boarded Captain Faizeal's. Imman took off at 2:48 a.m., quickly followed by the second plane. The truck was left in the hangar. The remaining men, three to a car, left for Chicago. Donovan took the third sedan. He traveled alone because he was only going as far as Peoria.

### 3:00 a.m.: CPL. ERNST HAUPTMANN

Mundt and Hauptmann had finished refilling the gasoline tanks for the oversize van and its generators for the last time. The transmitter, fully automated, would now run for approximately three more hours. They stood in the lot between the two vans. They checked their watches.

Hauptmann nodded. "Three o'clock. Time we left, Liebchen." Mundt nodded and cut a loud, wet fart.

"Ach, der sauerkraut." Hauptmann cuffed him affectionately on the ear, as they began walking across the lot toward their sedan.

"Yah," said Hauptmann, "Der sauerkraut undt the chili undt the beer. See you finish that gas off now. I don't think I can take any more of it at close quarters." Mundt farted again. "Ach, what a stink. Your insides are rotten, do you know that?"

Mundt giggled. "Undt yours are no perfume either, mein Corporal." They got into the sedan and warmed it up for a minute, pulled out of the lot. The other transmitter crew, near Edwardsville, left five minutes later. They were the last IWACs to leave their posts. All were in retreat now.

### 3:12 a.m.: CPL. PATRICK JOSEPH HOGAN

Hogan had made it to O'Hare. He had found a parking slot in the main lot in the inner arc of the great terminal. He was a hundred meters from the international building. He sat and gazed across the lot at it. His vision blurred from time to time and he was weak and tired. He did not feel as if he could make it to the building. Not now. He needed rest. He could sleep a while. His flight wasn't due to leave for hours. None of the others would have arrived yet. If he went into the building, someone would surely notice his condition, try to help, ask questions. No, better to rest here for a while. Sleep, perhaps. He found the pint bottle on the seat, took the cap off and tilted it to his mouth. Still empty. He could only squeeze a drop from the neck. Damn. He wished he had a drink. A bit of whisky and a nice snooze go so well together. He swore under his breath, though there was no one to hear him. He was a fool not to have brought several pints. When they got back to Eire, he'd buy Paddy's by the gallon. Ah, wouldn't that be lovely. He'd drown in a vat of Paddy's. What was it the American movie comedian had said, "Drowned in a vat of whisky, eh? Death, where is thy sting?" Hogan fell asleep.

### 3:33 a.m.: CAPT. ABDUL IMMAN

"Azyad Shipping Flight 868, this is Memphis Center. A Pan Am 747 will pass your flight angle approximately four miles ahead of you and three thousand feet below you in four minutes."

140

"Memphis Center, this is Azyad 868. We copy. Will monitor." Imman yawned. Routine traffic calls were about all they would have to deal with until they passed Grand Turk. He glanced at the I-NAB inertial guidance system readout. In red numerals, like a digital clock face, it gave him a course reading measured down to minutes and seconds. Sitting on the ground at Alton, he and Captain Faizeal had set the coordinates for the meeting with the *Casablanca*. With it, you could "automatic" your course and arrive within a couple hundred yards of a precise point. They would need it. They would only have time for one run at the *Casablanca*. He wasn't sure what their cargo was, but he knew damn well he couldn't land at San Juan with it still aboard. He felt his co-pilot stiffen and as he glanced, his heart stopped. Directly ahead and less than a third of a mile below them he could see the outline of a 747. He imagined in the fraction of a heartbeat that he could see figures illuminated by interior lights shining through the jumbo jet's windows. They were past so fast his hands didn't have time to start shaking until miles separated the two planes again. He stared at his co-pilot, whose face was flushed, a sure sign that he was nervous.

"Did we see that?"

"Yes."

Imman got on the horn, his voice rising in rage, "Memphis Center, this is Azyad 868. What the fuck is going on down there! You cocksuckers asleep or just pulling your wongs!? That 747 just passed under my nose so close the pilot asked me if I wanted a drink and the stews were flashing beaver at my co-pilot and navigator!"

"Azyad 868, this is Memphis Center. The 747 pilot made a minor course correction that we didn't notice quick enough. He thought you were below him instead of the other way around. Sorry about that."

"Jesus Christ, Memphis, sorry doesn't get it! We're swimming around in puddles of urine up here. It may just look like two blips merging down there, but that fucking jumbo looks like the side of a mountain up here. I'm going to have to file a report at San Juan. Providing you jerkoffs on the ground get us there."

"Okay, 868, we're still sorry . . . how did the beaver look?"

"I can't tell you. You can't get a hard-on after your heart stops." He got off the horn and sighed. He muttered, "May Allah smile upon you with the curse of the slow death, infidel." His co-pilot nodded agreement.


### 3:59 a.m.: PATROLMAN EDDIE DAVIS


Eddie Davis was a twenty-two-year-old rookie. He was nervous. He had never soloed before, but with forces spread so thin most men were taking a car by themselves and covering a large area. He was patrolling the riverfront business district, which was virtually deserted. He hadn't really any reason to be nervous. It wasn't likely that he would have to confront any kind of emergency situation at all. Still . . .

He was driving north on Fourth Street, passing the Fed Bank for the third time in an hour. As he came abreast of the parking garage, something moving in the wind flicked across a corner of his peripheral vision. He slowed to a near halt and looked left and back slightly. Two white lengths of something dangling from the roof. Hoses? That's what they looked like. What kind of hoses would they be using at the Fed Bank? He shrugged.

Something about the bank had been bothering him each time he passed it, but he couldn't think what. It was nerves, no doubt. It was a spooky night. All the trouble at the jail and everywhere. All the buildings dark and shadowy. Dark? He stopped the patrol car at the intersection of Fourth and St. Charles. He looked up at the rows of windows. The Federal Reserve Bank shouldn't be dark. Even in a power

failure. They had auxiliary power, just like central headquarters and other critical buildings. Hospitals and such.
He turned up St. Charles and pulled up at the night shift
door. He got out and walked up to it. The archway was
covered with some kind of metal plate he hadn't been able
to see from his patrol car. At eye height for a man one inch
shorter than his six-one was a block-lettered sticker of some
kind. He shined his flashlight on it.

> **EXTREME DANGER    NERVE GAS**
> **THIS BUILDING IS CONTAMINATED**
> **WITH AGENT VX/DO NOT ENTER**

Davis backed away from the arch and drew his gun. He
looked down at it in his hand. That was silly. What was he
going to do? Shoot the nerve gas? He holstered the gun, got
back in his car and drove around the bank. He stopped and
inspected each door. They were all covered with the same
metal plates and each plate bore an identical sticker. As he
came abreast of the parking garage again, he stopped. He
got out and walked over beside the wall. Those *were* hoses
whipping in the wind. He stared up at the rows of windows.
He shivered. He got in his car again and turned up St.
Charles. His headlights caught the doorway to the parking
garage. It was slightly ajar. He turned into the driveway so
that his headlights bathed the door. He got out and drew his
gun again. He tested the door of the garage and it gave,
opened easily. The lights illuminated a tunnel down the center of the interior. Caught in the left edge of that wedge of
light was the back end of a blue-and-white patrol car. Davis
stiffened. He stepped aside into the darkness. He waited for
his eyes to accustom themselves to the black. After a minute, he found he could still not see much. He heard no
sounds. He snapped on his flashlight and crossed slowly to
the blue-and-white. The back door had red stains from
something that had apparently dripped down the side. He
opened it and saw the two patrolmen.

"Oh, God,"

He checked both bodies. They were dead and already cold. He flashed his light around. There were civilian cars parked, but nothing else. He walked down the ramp to the lower level. The first thing his light picked up was the hole in the wall. He crossed to it, stood on the planking and shined his light down into the interior.

He ran back up the ramp and outside. He holstered his gun and tossed his flashlight into the car. He ran up the street to the night-shift door and took out his pocket notebook and pen. He peered closely at the sticker and copied the wording exactly. He sprinted back to the car and pulled out of the driveway.

Patrolman Davis walked into Captain Harshman's office at 4:41 a.m., breathing heavily and flushed. Harshman looked up at him in surprise and mild annoyance.

"What the hell you barging in here, Davis? You want to see me, clear it with the desk sergeant. Get out of here."

"Sir, the Federal Reserve Bank has been robbed."

Harshman rocked back in his swivel chair and stared at the tall, blond rookie. He looked excited, but not over the edge.

"The Fed Bank has been hit?"

"Yes, sir."

"Have you been drinking, Davis?"

"No, sir." He began to explain what he had found. As he reported, Harshman listened and studied him at the same time. He wasn't drunk or hysterical. When Davis showed him the notebook page with the sticker wording it began to come home to Harshman. If Davis had been clear-headed enough to take down the warning, the rest of his report must be fairly accurate.

"Noah was right."

"Sir?"

"Never mind, Davis. You come with me up to the Command Post."

It was still dark as Donovan entered the roadway to the Peoria Airport. The look and size of the building seemed about the same as the Cork City Airport. The parking lot held only about a dozen cars. Donovan chose a slot some distance from the others. He retrieved his handbag from the trunk and walked under the concrete archway into the lower level. The rental-car and other service booths with their overhead, lighted-plastic signs in primary colors were deserted. Two janitors were running a large buffing machine across the already-gleaming floor. The stainless-steel carousel at the base of the baggage chute was spinning for some reason at this odd hour. One frayed, tan, two-suiter rode continually, like the last girl at the party whose escort left hours before. Donovan rode the escalator to the upper level.

A sleepy ticket clerk checked his handbag through and fiddled with figures on the flimsy pink opaques of his ticket booklet. They exchanged only a few monosyllables during the transaction and the clerk yawned rudely as he gave the customary parting.

"Have a good trip, sir."

Donovan did not bother to answer. He crossed to the coffee shop and ordered a hearty breakfast. Eggs and chips, french fries the Americans called them, and ham and coffee. When he finished, he went back to the lobby and sat on one of several couches. High against one wall was a large-screen color television. Something called the "Today" program was playing. Activity in the lobby was increasing, but it wasn't really busy. Donovan checked his watch against an electric wall clock. Forty minutes until his flight to Washington. It was light outside now and the glass walls on either side of him at a distance filtered the cold gray rays before letting them sift through the broad lobby. An elderly man and woman sat on a couch opposite. The man aimed his putty-colored eyes at Donovan. He seemed as if he would like to start a conversation and was sorting through his repertoire of opening gambits. Donovan took his sunglasses from a breast pocket and slipped them on. He lit a cigar. The man turned away and began talking softly to the woman.

### 6:24 a.m.: CAPT. ABDUL IMMAN

Imman had taken back the controls from his co-pilot. They were coming up on the Caicos Islands and it was the first critical point. Just about the Caicos or Grand Turk they would pass out of the Miami Center's signal range and would not yet be in range of San Juan. Miami Center has a computerized set that calculates not only course, but altitude; San Juan does not. It was 7:24 EST and a cold sun was already shining across the sea below. Imman saw the Caicos off to his right, ahead. They appeared in the early sun as a slightly truncated, spiny, green seahorse. He called over his shoulder to the navigator.

"Tell them in back to get ready. We're going to take a quick ride down." The navigator returned in a minute.

"Okay, Abdul. They're set."

Imman nodded. "Okay, here we go."

They had been fighting slight headwinds for over an hour and the rapid ride down was a little bumpy. The sea rose steadily to meet them, beckoning them to take the final plunge and slip into her silver blue arms. Imman fought the amazingly sweet seduction, shaking his head jerkily several times. At two thousand feet, the calm sea was like a grainy marble floor. Imman leveled out. They had dropped thirty-four thousand feet in three and a half minutes.

He checked the inertial guidance system readout and corrected his course slightly north for 22.5 north latitude and 69.5 west longitude. He sighed and relaxed a little.

146

"Okay, in about twelve minutes I'm going to cut speed back to about three hundred and we'll have to start keeping our eyes open. We should run across them in about eighteen minutes." His co-pilot nodded and bit off the end of a fig bar, began chewing.

Jackson shivered. It was cold in back with the containers. He and Private Conyers, a solid, taciturn Lancashireman, sat on the floor with their feet propped up on containers. The containers sat in a tight row on a specially designed automated treadmill. They were clamped into position by a series of metal bars that would release them when they reached the end of the treadmill at the ventral door. Their parachute rip cords were attached by leather thongs to the positioning bars, so that once a container was clear of the aircraft, its chute would open. The whole process was automated. Jackson and his men were merely insurance to see that all the containers got out. They wouldn't even start the treadmill. The navigator would open the ventral door and start the treadmill on instructions from the co-pilot, more or less like a bombing run. Jackson yawned. He was sleepy. What the hell, he could sleep on the flight from San Juan to London. And enjoy being a millionaire all the way. He hoped they would have a nice steak on the flight. He was hungry. Two steaks.

Imman slowly cut the speed back to three hundred. "Now let's open our eyes. We could pick them up at any time now."

"If they're on station."

"They will be. That Assam is a bright boy. He doesn't screw things up. He'll be the Azyad one of these days."

"He'll have to wait a while. The old bastard isn't ready to lay down and die yet."

Imman checked the wind reading. He would swing south of the ship when they made the run. With the wind head-long, the chutes would drift toward the *Casablanca* that way.

After a few minutes, the co-pilot grunted, "What's that

dead-on?'' Imman stared straight down the nose. He saw an orange and black dot.

"That must be it.'' He called over his shoulder, "Open the ventral door.'' After a few seconds the navigator's voice came.

"Ventral door open.''

Abdul edged the nose slightly south of the dot, which was beginning to separate into the outline of a ship with orange Xs all around her. As the range closed, he could see orange Xs on the deck as well. The plane was bucking a little, probably because the ventral door was open. He calculated the range again.

"Automate the treadmill.'' As they came down almost on top of the ship, the navigator answered again.

"Treadmill automated.''

Abdul could see figures on the deck waving as they passed overhead. He held course for two minutes.

"Close ventral door.'' A pause.

Then, "Ventral door closed.'' He began the swing back to the San Juan course and, on it, began climbing, leveled off at twelve thousand feet for the run in. Well, he was ten thousand dollars richer for this little job. All he had to do now was explain why he had changed altitude. Trouble with the cabin pressure was the best excuse. They might think it a little funny, but what could they really suspect? What could they really do?

Jackson looked across at Conyers. It had all gone so smoothly they needn't have been there. "Looks like we were just along for the ride.'' Conyers stared at him in silence for several minutes until Jackson had begun to wonder if he had been heard.

Conyers cleared his throat. "Ah, well, that's the Colonel, then, isn't it? The ones who take precautions don't have the problems.''

Jackson nodded agreement. "You are absolutely right. The Colonel is one sharp son of a bitch.''

"That's right,'' said Conyers, "and Irish too.'' He shook

his head in amazement. "I would never have believed it. The smartest man I ever met and he's an Irishman." He shook his head again in plain wonder.


**6:51 a.m.: ASSAM AZYAD**

The planes had come one after another and within three minutes of each other. They had been so low they seemed to come out of nowhere and drop down almost on top of the ship. They had shit a neat stream of Day-Glo orange bricks, like pigeons dusting the heads of a regularly formed file of tourists. Assam had counted the parachute pops—a dozen per plane. As expected. The *Casablanca* had moved swiftly, the men were hoisting the first container aboard when the second plane ended its drop run. Now there were two aboard, and the mate was driving the men to move quickly. Assam and two of the crew were using binoculars to keep sight of the drift of the outer, most distant containers. By the time the close ones had been hauled aboard, there would be quite a spread between the outer ones. Fortunately, the bright orange coloring (Donovan's idea) was an excellent choice—the containers could be seen for miles. Assam yawned. He was sleepy. He had not been able to make himself sleep the whole preceding evening.

The power winches on either side of the ship were operating simultaneously now and two containers were swung aboard at once. The first fifteen or so would be gotten in fairly quickly before they had much of a chance to drift. The last eight or nine would take a while longer. Two hours. Perhaps three. Then they could get underway and he could cable Switzerland. He yawned again. Then he could sleep until they got to Marseilles if he wanted to. He put the binoculars back to his eyes and swept the outer edge of the drifting containers.

The Sergeant-Major was worried as he exited the international building of O'Hare Airport and crossed into the parking lot. The wind was whipping ferociously and he had to lean his heavy bulk into it to make way. All the men had arrived on time except the team from Portage Des Sioux. When they had not arrived by seven, McGregor had sent four men to scout the other wings of the airport and six to search the parking lot. One of them had found Hogan in his car and reported that he was in bad shape.

McGregor saw the American black private standing at the rear of a vehicle in the next row motioning nervously to him. When he got to the car, he slid in the passenger side and looked at Hogan. He was pale and shriveled-looking, as if he had started the erosion of death early.

He shook him gently. "Patrick . . . Patrick . . . Patrick. Can you hear me, Patrick?"

Hogan opened his eyes. They seemed soft and unfocused. They glided gently shut again. McGregor shook him again.

"Patrick, can you hear me, man?"

Hogan's eyes opened again, focused. "Like a ruddy great bellowing bull, Andrew. Do you have to shout so? And stop . . . stop shaking me about like a bloody rag doll. I'm . . . not . . . not a shagging pocketful of coppers . . . to be sorted out."

McGregor paid no attention to Hogan's mumbling. He opened his clothes and examined the wound. Fairly clean. Great loss of blood. Shock. He couldn't tell if anything major had been hit.

"What happened at Portage Des Sioux, Patrick?"

"Ah, you should have been . . . there, Andrew. You . . . you should have seen it. Lovely it was. A rare fine bang."

150

"Yes, I'm sure, laddie, but where are the others? Where's the rest of your team?"

"Dead."

"All four of them?"

Hogan nodded. "Three of them got caught by the blast. Guarda . . . no, not Guarda, the . . . oh, you know what I mean, Andrew."

"Police."

"That's right. Police got Perete. I got the two policemen."

"And one of them got you before he died."

Hogan nodded weakly again. His eyes closed again. The black private slid into the back seat. He stared at Hogan.

"What's happening, Sergeant-Major?"

"The rest of the team's done for. Only Hogan got away."

"He looks done for himself, if you ask me. He ain't gonna make it. We'd better let him be."

McGregor gritted his teeth, then spoke. "No one has asked you, Private. No one will ask you. Go inside and find Sergeant Berkley. Send him out to me."

Berkley brought the field first aid kit. They dressed Hogan's wound and then dressed him in clean clothes. They got a wheelchair from Aer Lingus, explaining that he was an invalid, and passed him through customs that way. McGregor had to take the black private into a rest room and slap his face. He was petrified that Hogan would die, the wound be discovered, and the rest of them be given away. McGregor was worried as well. It was a great risk to run. But he was not a man to leave one of his wounded behind. He told the black private:

"I'll execute you for insubordination if you don't get hold of yourself, and leave you in that toilet stall, but we'll not leave Patrick behind." And one would have to reckon with Donovan. Patrick was his great friend of many years. McGregor would not like to be the man to tell him that Hogan had been left, wounded and helpless, in America. That would be too dangerous by half.

It was 10:33 a.m. in St. Louis, but in Zurich the bank was
nearly deserted. Deserted and quiet. Only Turrman and two
clerks and the Azyad remained. Turrman's footsteps made
no sound on the rust-colored carpet. He opened a polished-
mahogany door and entered his office. The Azyad looked
up at him, then saw the thin rectangle of yellow paper in his
hand. Turrman handed it to him and sat behind his desk. He
watched the older man read it.

The Azyad was dressed in an ill-fitting charcoal-gray suit,
white shirt, and black tie. He still looked like a refugee from
a street bazaar. Turrman frowned with a deep distaste he
was having great difficulty concealing.

He was not a racist. He could not have been an effective
officer in the IWACs if he had been. And he was. Of course,
no one but Donovan liked him. That wasn't necessary. But
they respected him. Not like Donovan. But enough. And
they wouldn't have if he had been a racist.

But Turrman preferred a certain . . . style. Even among
hard men he wanted a certain . . . quality. The air of a
gentleman. The Azyad was many things—able, shrewd, avaricious, powerful. He was not in any sense of the word—a
gentleman. Turrman decided he detested him. Ah, well, a
necessary evil.

The Azyad dropped the cable on the desk. Turrman
glanced down at it involuntarily, though he had already read
it three times:

IRISH WAGER AT CLONMEL SUCCESSFUL BY TWENTY-
FOUR LENGTHS

It was signed—Assam. It was a ship to shore cable ra-
dioed from the *Casablanca* somewhere in the Atlantic. To

152

both Turrman and The Azyad it meant that the IWACs had delivered twenty-four money containers as anticipated, and the *Casablanca* had recovered them all.

Now The Azyad was reading Donovan's cable again, though all it contained was a series of figures—the cash and bond totals supplied by Captain Jackson's friend at the Federal Reserve Bank—the amount of money stolen by the IWACs. And delivered to Assam. Turrman stifled a sigh. He would not let this old man know how irritated he was becoming. Finally the Azyad put down the cable and looked at Turrman.

Turrman pulled a sheet of paper from a file on top of his desk. It was a transfer form. It called for the transfer of $442,396,800.00 from an Azyad account to the account of the Irish West Africa Company. It only required the Azyad's signature and the witnessing of the two clerks waiting in the next room.

Turrman passed the form and a slip of paper with figures and percentages jotted on it across to the old man, who took a pair of greasy, black-plastic-rimmed glasses from an inside pocket, put them on, began examining the papers.

He set them aside after a few moments and pulled some soiled papers from a side pocket. He selected one sheet, passed that to Turrman:

## OPERATIONAL EXPENSES

*Rentals*

| | |
|---|---:|
| Airplane Rentals | $ 194,891.66 |
| Automobile Rentals | 14,655.32 |
| Truck Rentals | 5,602.79 |
| Equipment Rentals | 89,324.45 |
| Warehouse/Hangar Rentals | 8,300.00 |
| Rentals Subtotal | $ 312,774.22 |

## OPERATIONAL EXPENSES (*cont'd*)

*Armaments*

| | | |
|---|---|---:|
| Agent VX | $ | 439,951.04 |
| Rifles | | 68,422.00 |
| Ammunition | | 11,512.00 |
| Armaments Subtotal | $ | 519,885.04 |

*Shipment*

| | | |
|---|---|---:|
| Containers | $ | 212,000.00 |
| Casablanca Operating Expense | | 78,777.00 |
| Shipment Subtotal | $ | 290,777.00 |

*Expenses, Men*

| | | | |
|---|---|---:|---|
| Commercial Air Fares/2 Ways | $ | 76,941.88 | |
| Daily Food/Housing/ 17 Days | | 164,000.00 | (Advanced) |
| Daily Pocket Money/17 Days | | 42,500.00 | ($25.00 per man per day/Advanced) |
| Expenses, Men Subtotal | $ | 283,441.88 | |

| | | |
|---|---|---:|
| Miscellaneous (Advanced) | $ | 50,000.00 |
| Subtotals | $ | 312,774.22 |
| | | 519,885.04 |
| | | 290,777.00 |
| | | 283,441.88 |
| | | 50,000.00 |
| Operational Expense Total | | $1,456,878.14 |

Turrman passed the paper back to him. "Very interesting. I often wondered just what this operation would cost. Now I know." The Azyad nodded and sat looking at him expectantly. Turrman returned his stare calmly. Finally, after two full minutes, the old man spoke.

"You will have to alter the papers." He indicated the transfer form. "The figures on this form."

Turrman feigned mild surprise. "I can't imagine why. The figures are all quite correct and in order."

"But the expenses—"

"Come off your end—"

"—must be deducted."

Turrman smiled icily. "Come, come, Mr. Azyad. The agreement was quite clear. You advanced the expenses and will handle the dispersal of the money and bonds. For this, you receive the generous allowance of twenty percent off the top. You must absorb the expenses from your profit margin." He glanced at the paper. "It leaves you a handsome net of over one hundred nine million American dollars. Free of tax."

The old man rubbed the tip of his nose. "We could split them with you, I suppose."

Turrman pushed a button on his desk. "You suppose incorrectly." The two clerks entered the room through a side door, stood waiting. Turrman pushed the transfer form across the desk and offered a pen. "Come along now, Mr. Azyad. This isn't street haggling. This is a proper financial arrangement, previously agreed to by gentlemen. Let's not take too long. I have a dinner engagement with a *very* charming young lady. I shouldn't like to keep her waiting."

The Azyad hesitated, then took the pen. He hesitated again, then slowly signed the form. He pushed it back to Turrman and handed the pen back. Turrman motioned and the two clerks came forward. They signed the document in turn. He handed the form to one of them.

"Please make the proper ledger entries before you leave, Ardemann. The firm appreciates your extra hour's duty. My father will thank you personally in the morning." He waved them away. He rose and walked with the Azyad to the doors

of the bank. He let them out and locked the door behind
him.

## 12:00 NOON: COL. TERRENCE DONOVAN

He lay on the bed of a luxury suite of a downtown Washington hotel. He had come directly from the airport and
checked in an hour before. He was waiting for room service
to send up his luncheon. He would place the call at one-
thirty. He didn't suppose he would get through to the DDP
the first time, but after the DDP got his message, he would
wait anxiously for Donovan to call again.

He closed his eyes. He was fully clothed and did not
intend to sleep. He was not even truly tired. He merely
wanted to relax. The odds would be dicey. He did not know
these men well. He did not know if they could be trusted to
see the direction of their own interest. He supposed they
could, most politicians did if you once pointed it out to them
in cogent terms. Please, God, no moralists. He smiled to
himself. Calling on God again. They couldn't be moralists.
Moralists destroyed the logical sequence. Everything
turned on these men being clear-headed pragmatists. Everything.

Room service came. He signed the bill and waved the
man away. The onion soup was passable, but the Crab
Louis and Beef Wellington were both soggy and the beef
was overdone. He ate only about half of each, pushed the
tray away disgustedly. He opened the bottle of champagne
and filled his glass. Excellent. Wonderfully dry. He looked
at his watch. The men and the money would be well on the
way to Europe now. Only Donovan and the dead remained.
Donovan sipped champagne.

# BOOK II: **WAR CRIMINALS**

4. Also calls upon all the States concerned in the collection and exchange of information which will contribute to the detection, arrest, extradition, trial and punishment of persons guilty of war crimes and crimes against humanity.

*Resolution on War Criminals*
*(General Assembly Resolution 2712), United · Nations, December 15, 1970*

Bucky Walters sat in the DDP's office shaking his head at Philbin Brooke. It was one o'clock EST and the news of "The Great St. Louis Massacre," as one TV reporter had dubbed it, was reverberating across the country.

Brooke sighed. "It's no use shaking your head at me, Colonel Walters. It is as I said before—the President, the Secretary of State, the National Security Council, the Forty Committee do not want to know. But they want the Damascus Agreement saved. At any cost."

"But don't bother them with the details."

Brooke nodded. "Precisely."

Bucky shook his head again. "So we're going to do their dirty work for them. Sit on a moral outrage. Ignore a thousand or more people killed, people shot, people gassed, people stomped to death, arson, murder, assault, and the theft of—what was the estimate?"

"Several hundred millions in cash and bonds."

"Can you stomach all that?"

Brooke nodded. "We cannot allow the personal emotions such as humanitarian empathy, moral revulsion to govern our professional judgment. You've been with the Company a long time, Colonel. You've had to do hard things before."

"Not like this."

The DDP fitted a cigarette in his black jade holder, "Suppose we look at the alternatives. Without the Damascus Agreement peace is not assured in the Middle East. The potential for war is great, confrontation between ourselves and the Russians quite possible. One measures the lives lost in St. Louis against the possibility of nuclear holocaust. As for the stolen money—this treaty will cost us billions in aid to the new Palestinian state, but the oil cost concessions will be worth, perhaps, a trillion dollars in the next decade. Maybe more. Half a billion dollars, if it amounts to that much, is a mere nothing."

159

"So we're going to do it. Help Donovan."

"Yes, Colonel, that we are."


When Donovan called, he was surprised to get the DDP so quickly. The conversation was short, direct.

"Brooke here."

"This is your Irish friend. We did something—presumably you understand what."

"Yes."

"You've had time to consider your answer."

"The answer is yes. We will help tidy up for you."

"Grand. We will need a London contact, just in case of later complications."

"Yes, that can be arranged. You will be given particulars in a week to ten days. Is that satisfactory?"

"Surely. And you'll be needing some scapegoats."

Brooke nodded approvingly to himself. "Yes. That had occurred to me."

"If you will meet me at National Airport in two hours, I'll have some documents and information that should help."

"Right. Where?"

Donovan and the DDP met in a cocktail lounge. Donovan explained exactly what had been done and how. He explained the use made of the Afrikaners, and gave papers showing rental receipts for the equipment in the name of John 3X Brown. He explained how money and equipment could be linked to the Afrikaners. He caught his flight and the DDP returned to his office. He explained the briefing he'd had from Donovan to Bucky.

"We'll have to use a couple of our people in Justice and at the FBI to smooth things along, but we should be able to tidy up rather neatly. And quickly."

"No."

"No?"

Bucky sighed. "I don't mean you can't do it. I don't even mean you won't do it. I just mean I'm not going to be involved. I haven't told you everything I know. I had a call from my brother-in-law."

"Major Peterson."

"Yes. He had to drive out of the city to phone—the lines still aren't working in St. Louis."

"And?"

"Noah's oldest boy was killed at the arena in the explosion. Margeret and I have no children. I don't know if you know . . . but we . . . *can't* have children." Bucky moved uncomfortably in his chair. "My . . . my sperm count is erratic and too low."

The DDP nodded sympathetically. "I didn't know. I had wondered. A faithful Catholic couple. I am sorry."

Bucky swallowed. "I wouldn't tell you these things, but you have to understand. Noah III, was my godson. I was very close to him. I taught him to fish; he and his father and I used to go camping every summer. He was a wonderful boy. A wonderful young man." Bucky coughed to cover the strain in his cracking voice. The DDP nodded sympathetically again.

"I see."

"It's too personal. It's too close to me. You do what you have to do. I just can't be involved. I'm going to take several days off to fly out to St. Louis. Margeret and I. For the funeral."

Brooke's voice was buttery soft. "Of course, Colonel. I quite understand. Take all the time you need. And we need say no more about this affair. You need not be . . . concerned."

After Bucky left, the DDP pondered. Should he be worried about Walters? Probably not. The man had been with the Company for many years. Still . . . one might keep an eye on him. He turned to his phone to begin the necessary calls to the Company's people in the Justice Department and the FBI. At least Donovan had given them a good out. And this was the sort of mess that had to be covered up quickly and completely or it would unravel in too many directions.

The city of St. Louis was in chaos. The hospitals, morgues, funeral homes were overwhelmed. Fifty-nine city policemen killed. One thousand two hundred ninety-four civilians killed. Forty-eight armed raiders killed. Over sixteen hundred injured. No telephone communication. Freezing weather and no power. Onto this scene descended a hostile and sarcastic national press corps which tends to view excursions to the interior of America as penance for sins known or unknown. The National Guard was finally mobilized by late evening at exactly the right time to have missed most of the looting which took place sporadically throughout the day, but in time to add to the confusion of an overburdened city police force trying to restore order. The Senators from Missouri and all the Congressmen from the St. Louis area flew back to the city. The Governor of Missouri toured the city. The Mayor publicly attacked the Police Department. The Police Commissioner attacked the Mayor. The President flew in, took a helicopter overflight of the city, declared the area a national disaster, and flew back to Washington.

Noah stayed home. He did not sleep for five days. He held Liz together. And the twins held him together. And neighbors and friends and family were kind.

He hated the hours of viewing. That thing in the casket was not his son. The smell of the masses of flowers was oversweet, too heavy, sickening. And the high mass comforted him not at all even though it was said by the Archbishop of the St. Louis Diocese—he had heard the Lazarus story too often. Even if his son's immortal soul should rise to heaven—why now? Why fifty years, half a century too soon?

And finally it was a relief to put the casket in the ground. And a relief to go back to work, though his concentration was badly broken by the sinful, wrongheaded, terrifying vengeance his heart craved. Someone must pay, but who? Whom should he kill?

The investigation of the raid was a farce. The afternoon of the day following the raid, the FBI had flown in some "heavy" special agents to beef up the local office. They were arrogant and self-serving as usual. They made it clear, at least to the press, that the investigation would be principally a federal affair. All week long they called press conferences to announce pieces of evidence they had "discovered." By week's end, they announced they had "solved" the case. The Afrikaners had done it. They produced refuse bins filled with several million dollars in one- and five-dollar bills, two semi-trailer trucks, empty gas canisters, air compressors, asbestos suits, weapons, ammunition—all neatly stored in a Fourth Street warehouse rented in the name of John 3X Brown. They produced the vans with the jamming equipment and rental receipts also in the name of the late John 3X Brown. And on and on.

And Noah did nothing. He watched. He waited. He listened. Something would come to him. Something. And he would know. Who.

The sun was shining, but it was cold. The Honor Guard formed up at the entrance of the funeral home twelve-strong. The six pallbearers began to carry the casket out to the waiting hearse. The heavy breath of their labor made small steam clouds around their faces. It was the last funeral home that the procession had to stop at and there was only one casket to pick up here.

They had never buried fifty-nine policemen at once before. Probably no one had. Just assembling all the hearses had been a great headache.

When the casket was in place—this last one was Sergeant Ernest Vincente, who had frozen to death in the courtyard during the "Battle of Thirteenth Street"—the procession started again.

Noah rode in the first department limousine with the

Chief and his assistant. In places, small crowds lined the streets. Men removed their hats and placed them over their hearts. Some saluted.

Dieter chewed on an unlit cigar. "I talked to the U.S. Attorney last night. Ralph Bush. Sharp guy. You know him, Noah?"

"I've seen him around."

"He says the grand jury is going to hand down the indictments tomorrow morning. Everything he's asked for, robbery, arson, murder one—the works."

Noah shook his head. "Pretty fast work. The whole thing smells, George."

"Public pressure. We're getting a thousand phone calls a day, asking when these guys are going to be hung. Half of them ask if they can help. Hang them."

"You really think these Afrikaners are the ones, George? I mean the whole thing? I know they were at the jail, but . . ."

"Yeah, I know."

"I know some of those boys. I've arrested a few of them over the years. Somehow it's a little hard for me to picture them masterminding something like this. The press is skeptical too."

"I tell you what, Noah. The FBI comes whizzing in here and goes around the very first day picking up pieces of evidence like candy on Easter morning—now what does that sound like to you?"

"They were tipped. And their source was authoritative."

"That's what it sounds like to me too, Noah."

A small group of young black men stood on a corner. One held a picket sign: JUSTICE FOR THE AFRIKANERS. The others shouted obscenities at the car as it passed.

"I'll tell you what else, Noah. The FBI and the U.S. Attorney's office aren't passing any little bit of their evidence on to us. We get it from their press conferences. They go for indictments in one tenth the time they would normally even think about, and they get them. And the trial schedule has already been set, even before the indictments are handed down.''

"It has?"

Dieter nodded. "That's right. I'm not supposed to know that, so neither are you. Those boys are going to trial in one week."

"One week!"

"That's right. And they are going to go up before the old man himself—Judge Fearing Carter, the last great nigger-hating, right-wing, hanging federal judge in Missouri. Now what does all that sound like to you?''

"Like these boys have had the rails greased right into the penitentiary no matter what the facts may or may not be."

"That's right, Noah. That's what it sounds like to me."

Dieter stuck the unlit cigar back in the corner of his mouth and chewed. Noah lit a cigarette and stared out the window. Many of the shop windows they passed had black crepe hung in honor of the dead policemen.

"I'll tell you another what else, Noah."

"I don't know if I can take any more."

Dieter ignored him. "I have had the Governor, both of our beloved U.S. Senators, several Congressmen, and the like come around and pat my head and hold my hand daily. They tell me what a terrific job the department is doing under difficult circumstances and how wonderful it is that we're cooperating so fully with the federal authorities and if we'll just keep up the grand work we'll all get some lovely publicity and fat pensions out of it and pretty soon the whole nasty business will be over and the culprits punished.''

Noah snorted. "Cooperate! The feds don't even talk to us."

"That's right. But the Attorney-General talks to Bush and the FBI three or four times a day to shove them along, and I know Bush has talked to the White House twice personally."

"The President?"

"I don't know about that, but he has talked to the White

House. And he seems to think he may be in line for a nice federal bench appointment after this is all over. Now what does that sound like to you?"

"Like a personal interest is being taken by the administration to see that this whole thing is rammed through fast and clean. Almost like a cover-up."

"That's right. That's what it sounds like to me, Noah. Only we don't say cover-up any more. We say 'closely defining the perimeters of investigation and information.' "

Noah sighed. They were nearing the church. He put out his cigarette and shook his head. Dieter dropped the dead and mangled cigar in the ashtray alongside Noah's cigarette stub.

"I still say it smells, George."

Dieter nodded. "Yeah, I'll tell you one last what else. It stinks like Union Market in July when the power has failed, but with that much pressure from that many places and that high up a man would be a goddamn fool to buck it. Those Afrikaners are going to be convicted. Bush is going for maximum sentences to run consecutively rather than concurrently, and he's going to use an accomplice rap to pin every count of every charge on every one of the defendants. They're going to come out of that courtroom with several thousand years of sentences for each man, and none of them will be eligible for parole for a couple of centuries. That is what is going to happen. It's one of those things that's on the books. That's it. And I'm not going to buck it or fight it or hinder it in the slightest. And nobody else on the St. Louis Police Department is going to either. That's my last what else, Noah. What does it sound like to you?"

Noah smiled wanly. "An executive directive from the office of the Chief?"

"That's right, Noah. That's just what it is." Noah said nothing, thought—I'll wait.

The Honor Guard formed up at the entrance to St. Louis Cathedral. The leading clergy of the city had decided upon one large ecumenical service and the families and the force had gone along. It took over an hour to get the caskets into the sanctuary.

Noah was at home the next day when the doorbell rang. He answered. A tall, thin, black man stood on their doorstep. He was dressed in a butter-colored leather jacket and boots with cocoa slacks and an open-necked shirt. He was young, but very tired-looking. Noah stepped aside. "Hi, Steven, come on in." Noah noticed his eyes were red and the rims were caked from little or bad sleep.

"I hate to bust in on your time off, Noah, but I don't know where else to turn."

"No problem, Steve. Come on in and sit down." Elizabeth was in the doorway to the kitchen. "Steve, this is my wife, Elizabeth. This is Steve Brooks, honey." They shook hands and Noah and Steve sat in a couple of easy chairs.

"Would you like some coffee, Mr. Brooks?"

"Thank you, Mrs. Peterson, I would." The young man fumbled out a pack of cigarettes. Noah noticed his hands were a bit shaky as he struck a match. He looked at Noah. Sighed. "I guess you know I've been appointed by the court to defend the Afrikaners."

"I heard that, yes. Tough assignment."

"No, it's not tough, Noah. It's too easy. I can just coast since there isn't a thing in the world I can do for my clients. It's all been decided already. They're going to be put so far back in jail they'll have to pump air into them."

"I have heard rumblings to that effect."

Brooks looked at Noah directly. "Doesn't that bother you?"

Noah maintained eye contact as he nodded. "Yes, it does, but I don't see what can be done about it. I've given the matter some thought."

"Yes, I knew you would. That's why I came to see you. Anybody who knows anything about this town, knows you're the most decent man on the force."

Noah waved the remark away with a flip of his hand.

167

Elizabeth brought in a tray with coffee pot, cups and saucers, fresh donuts, sugar bowl and creamer.

"Thank you, Mrs. Peterson, I really can use this. I haven't slept for four and a half days."

"Did you really expect anything else to happen, Steve?"

"No, Noah, I didn't, but this is too much. They're bound and determined to hang the whole thing on my clients and that's a joke. Worse than a joke. Some of those guys can't find their way to the toilet without guidance. And I knew John 3X Brown. He couldn't mastermind a filling-station stickup let alone a half-billion-dollar heist. You want to know what the real scam is?" Noah nodded and sipped his coffee. "Some black dude showed up here late last summer. Knew his way around, had a lot of money to flash. He made contact with Brown through a little wino name of Freddie Greenleaf who has since disappeared. He starts slipping these guys money and promising them automatic weapons and feeding them delusions of grandeur, which they already have plenty of. He had them steal the Dragon from McDonnel-Douglas—the one that was used to blast into the vault—but he fed them some rap about using it on the cops. On that armored vehicle of yours. Anyhow, he set them up to hit the jail, led them there, and disappeared. Nothing was ever said about the rest of what was going down. Especially not about the money."

"So where is this guy now, Steve?"

Brooks shrugged. "Nobody knows. The guy was very cool about the whole thing. He gave Brown some jive name like Ali Mustapha or some such, and after the initial meet on Brown's turf he never made contact with any of the others, and he always met Brown at the ballpark. Not a hope of tracing him through that."

"No, not really. So where does this leave you?"

"Underneath a million-pound shithammer. These guys were set up beautifully to do the heavy work at the jail and take the rap. Their prints are all over the Dragon, the warehouse, the trucks, the equipment. Only not on any of the money or the money baskets that were found. That's interesting, isn't it?"

Noah nodded. "Yes, but not very helpful."

"Don't I know. What I can't figure is why all the pressure to hang the whole thing on my guys? Sure, they've got them on the jail thing and that's bad enough to put them away forever practically, but why the rush to jam the rest of it down our throats? Bush is not a stupid man. He knows goddamn well my guys didn't run this whole thing. But will he talk to me? Hell, no. Will he plea-bargain for information? Hell, no. He doesn't *want* any more information. And the loose ends he wants to cover up or ignore. Christ! The four stiffs out at Portage Des Sioux were white! Sure as hell the Afrikaners don't truck with whites, man. They're as racist as they come. You know what Bush tells me?"

"No."

"Portage Des Sioux wasn't necessarily a part of the rest of the operation. Maybe it was an independent thing. Bullshit! And maybe all you white guys are really niggers who take baths in Beads o' Bleach."

Noah laughed. "You make the point. What else?"

"The black stiffs at the Rexall plant haven't been identified. And Bush says they can't be identified so they're going to bury them tomorrow. I go to court to get an injunction stopping them and the judge laughs me right out of the room. Why? Why is this thing coming down this way?"

"I don't know, Steve. I know there's a lot of heavy pressure from Washington, but I don't know why either."

"Yeah, I know about that Washington shit. Last night I had a talk with a man from the Justice Department. I won't bother you with his name because he didn't give me the right one. He intimates, nothing you could hang him with, just implies in a careful way, that if I'm a good boy, walk the guys through, don't make waves—well, maybe something nice could be coming my way from Uncle Sam. You know, one of those cushy JD slots where you prosecute the cream cases with six waterboys to do the heavy work and

169

they lay fifty thou a year on you because you're so good. That's real sinister, man, because with the hopelessness of this thing and my financial position, I wake up in the middle of the night and find I've been dreaming about a nice tudor house in Chevy Chase. You know?''

"I can't help you with that one, Steve.''

"Don't I know it. I'm just hoping I've got enough integrity left to help myself with it. What the hell, I can't arrest my subconscious.'' Brooks poured himself another cup of coffee. "And the money. Where the fuck is the rest of the goddamn money? You know what they recovered? A few million bucks. All in ones and fives. Can you dig it? That's what a smart operator would leave behind anyway. I figure they carted off about sixty thousand pounds of paper as it is. The ones and fives wouldn't have run their total up much in dollar figures, but it would have just about doubled the bulk. So where is the rest of the goddamn money?''

"I see all the points, Steve, but what is it you want from me?''

"I don't honestly know, Noah. Maybe what you're giving me—a chance to blow off some steam. But doesn't it make you sick that the guys who really laid this thing down are going to get away? You buried, what was it, fifty-four cops yesterday?''

"Fifty-nine.''

"Fifty-nine. And the Afrikaners are going to hang for it sure as hell and the real guys, the heavies, are going to be off laughing somewhere. Doesn't that make you sick? Doesn't that make the force sick?''

"Those who know. Yes. It does. But you know how heavy the pressure is. I can't buck it alone and I know the department isn't equipped or willing to buck it as a whole.''

"The Chief isn't. Dieter isn't.''

"Don't put it all on him. There are others.''

"Yeah, the whole thing is like Watergate revisited. Only nobody is going to blow this one open because the fall guys are perfect. They *are* guilty and they're a bunch of niggers.

And that's the way its going to go down and *almost* every-body is going to be satisfied."

After Brooks left, Noah sat in his study for an hour think-ing about it all. The key question came down to why? What did Washington have to gain by applying all the pressure? His ideas roamed across a hash of different conspiracy fla-vors and dishes, but none tasted right. You could say CIA, but what did that mean? Why would they steal money—the taxpayers gave them unlimited amounts without question. Without a chance to question.

Bucky and Margeret had stayed over for a second week. Perhaps it was time to talk to Bucky.

Bucky and Margeret had taken the twins on a day trip, just a drive into the countryside to get them out for a while. Away. They didn't get back until early dark had come. Noah asked Bucky to come into his study. He had set out two bottles of good bourbon, glasses, ice.

Bucky grinned. "What's this? Getting ready for a long hard night of drinking and reminiscing about the good old days?"

Noah shook his head. "No, long hard drinking and re-membering the bad new days. Sit down, Bucky." Noah poured them both large glasses of whisky, lots of ice, no water. He sat behind his desk across from Bucky. He re-lated everything he knew about the "investigation" to Bucky. Some of it he had discussed with him before, some not, but this time he talked steadily for half an hour, relating the conversation with Dieter, with Brooks, the young black lawyer, everything he knew. They were on their third drinks when he finished. Bucky frowned.

"What do you want me to say, Noah?"

"What you know. You know something, Bucky. You know something about this, I can see it in your eyes when we talk. I've known you too long."

Bucky shook his head. "I can't help you, Noah."

"Jesus, sweet Jesus, what are you saying, Bucky? Will

171

you listen to you? 'I can't help you, Noah'—what kind of shit is that? Goddamnit, Bucky, they killed my boy. They killed him for money! My son, your godson.''

Bucky shook his head. "I shouldn't have said I couldn't help you. I am helping you, Noah. I can't tell you anything. And if I did, you couldn't do anything. Except maybe get yourself killed. And me. And probably Liz and Margeret and the twins.''

Noah stared at him unbelievingly. Bucky got up and poured them both another drink, sat and stared across at Noah. There were tears in Bucky's eyes.

Noah whispered, "My God, Bucky, what the hell is it? What is this all about?'' Bucky shook his head. "I keep thinking about those men at the airport. Those . . . uh, soldiers, mercenary soldiers, wasn't that what you said? Is it them? Did they do it?'' Bucky dropped his head.

Noah crossed from behind his desk, squatted so that Bucky's downward gaze was at him. "Was it them, Bucky? The soldiers? Why is the government protecting them? What is this goddamned thing about? Why did my boy die?'' Bucky was crying. Noah couldn't remember ever seeing Bucky cry before. He didn't sob, snuffle, shake—he sat motionless, staring at Noah, tears running down his bony face. And when he spoke, his voice was tight, but not broken.

"Noah, please understand me. I know things about the way things are that you don't. I can't tell you anything. It will just get more people killed.''

Noah got up and walked behind his desk again. He sat. Opened the top drawer. His service pistol lay there. A Smith & Wesson .38 caliber magnum with a six-inch barrel. Shiny, oily, blue-black, large and heavy and powerful. He took it out and opened the cylinder. Full load of new shiny brass cartridges. He closed the cylinder and looked up at Bucky, who was staring at him. He set the gun on the desk and closed the drawer. Death was in the room.

"I'm not afraid of dying, Noah.''

"I know you're not, Bucky. I'm not either. What I'm afraid of is what I think I'm going to do. Kill somebody. Maybe you, maybe myself, I don't know who, but I'm probably going to kill somebody."

They sat in silence for many minutes. Once Bucky made himself another drink. Once Noah made himself another drink. They sipped them. Smoked. Occasionally one of them would stare at the revolver. They had a hard time meeting each other's eyes.

Finally Bucky broke. Hesitantly, haltingly, slowly, he began to talk to Noah. Tell him what he knew. His voice firmed as he got into it. He spoke steadily after five minutes. Spoke calmly after ten minutes. Spoke uninterrupted for twenty-five minutes. The entire ugly story. Then they sat in silence again for some time. Noah spoke. "You know what I have to do."

"Yes."

"Will you help me?"

"Yes."

"Thank you."


Elizabeth Peterson was worried about Noah. She had made a strong recovery after the first week of helpless grief. Her sense of loss was still strong, still an ache when the thoughts and remembrance came to her, but she was coping. But Noah. He had seemed so strong at first. Now he was distracted. He did not sleep well or regularly. His already modest frame was becoming leaner to the point of ill-health. And his eyes. She hated to admit it, but his eyes were . . . haunted. Spooky. A little crazy. And ever since the night when he and Bucky had stayed in his study drinking he had been worse. He had called Chief Dieter and told him he was taking an indefinite leave of absence. He prowled the house restlessly, but refused to go out. Even for church. And he talked vaguely of a trip to Europe. Alone. "After Bucky calls," whatever that meant. And this morning when the *Post-Dispatch* carried the news of the conviction of the Afrikaners for the ''Massacre,'' he had ranted and raved about ''cockamamie justice'' and ''facist judges'' and this and that. He had finally ripped the newspaper to shreds and dropped the mess on the kitchen floor.

She looked across the living room at him. He was seated in an easy chair. He was reading a paperback book that belonged to one of the twins. A collection of cartoons from a widely syndicated comic strip. This one was about Andy Capp, the insouciant English pub bum. Nothing wrong with that. But he wasn't laughing. Or smiling. He stared, turned a page, stared, turned a page, like some vegetable who cannot comprehend even the pictures let alone the words. How could she reach him? She tried, but it was a difficult role for her. Noah had always been so strong, so self-sufficient. Perhaps too strong. The habit of carrying one's emotional load inside, alone, privately, is hard to break. But what do you do when the load gets too heavy and you don't know how to lean on someone else? Not that they hadn't always confided in each other. Not that she hadn't comforted him in the past as he had comforted her. She knew she had. But Noah always seemed as if he would have survived without the comforting, easily. Now . . .

''Noah?''

He did not look up from the paperback book. ''Yes.''

''Will you think about what I asked you?''

''I have.''

''Will you do it?''

''No.''

''I haven't asked you to do so many things that you didn't want to do.''

''No, you haven't.''

''Then will you please talk to Father Stephanos?''

At last he looked up from his book at her. ''No.'' He dropped the book on the floor, rose and walked into his study, closed the door. She heard soft, rhythmical, *thuk*-sounds presently. He was practicing his dart game.

She supposed it was this that disturbed her most. His

refusal to go to church. Or speak to the priest about what was troubling him. He had always been a better Catholic than she was. Not in practice, but in faith. Probably that was why he seemed so self-sufficient. His faith was a living, real thing to him, had always sustained him. She did so much by rote, not that she didn't believe, but . . . well, habit and familiarity often dulled her sense of mystery. She knew the poetry and beauty of ritual often escaped her conscious perception. But Noah drank a mass like a taster of fine wine, savored its delicacy, subtlety, on the sensitive membrane of his soul. He always came away refreshed, renewed. Now . . .

She steeled herself to pursue him into the study. She must keep trying. Love must forgive the rebuff. Love must penetrate the defense of the troubled spirit. And she loved this honest, proud, kind, and very troubled man.

Father Jonathan Stephanos was a stylish outgoing young priest. He was very popular in this comfortable upper-middle-class parish. He was able to relate to young and middle-aged alike because, unlike so many of his fellow liberal humanitarians, he was not only compassionate and understanding of the downtrodden, the disadvantaged, the youthfully indiscreet—he was also compassionate and understanding of the well-to-do, the overprivileged, the rigidly pious and hatefully self-righteous, the bigots and the cretins. He was only thirty-four, but somehow he had understood the completeness of God's love. All or nothing. No middle ground. Love had to encompass the whining, self-pitying, rich recluse as well as the drug-befuddled, confused adolescent, or it was not love at all.

He wore a white wool turtleneck sweater, chocolate double-knit slacks, loafers and white socks, and a chocolate London Fog trenchcoat for his meeting with Noah Peterson. He smoked a good English briar pipe as he walked across the park. He had soft hazel eyes and thinning brown hair and a comfortably, but not overly, fleshed face.

175

The day was wet, drizzly, but Peterson had not wanted to come to the church or the rectory. Had wanted to meet outside. Leafless tree branches moved arthritically in the wind, snapped and popped with sounds like loose cartilage in the joints. The ground was hard underfoot.

He saw Peterson sitting under a tree on the cold, wet ground. He was a little stunned when he came closer. Peterson had always been a healthy, handsome, meticulously groomed man. Today he was unshaven with a fine light-blond stubble showing on his cheeks. His face was gaunt and his eyes hollow. There seemed to be more gray in his blond hair than Father Stephanos remembered, and he wore casual clothing carelessly. His voice was calm, but, perhaps . . . what? Vague?

"Hello, Father. Thank you for coming."

"My pleasure, Noah, but why don't we sit on one of the benches over there. You'll catch cold sitting on that ground."

"No thanks, Father. I'm comfortable here."

Father Stephanos sighed and sat beside Noah. It would ruin his coat and slacks, but clothing was expendable—souls were not.

Father Stephanos stared at the bowl of his pipe and waited for Noah to begin. After a while he realized he would have to prod him.

"Elizabeth tells me you're . . . troubled, she said."

"My son was killed. For money. Casually, the way you'd swat a fly without thinking about it. Maybe without even knowing the fly was there."

"Yes, but she seems to think there is more to it than that. That your grief has a hysterical quality . . . something disproportionate."

"Disproportionate? Pain, Father Stephanos, pain."

"Pain?"

"Pain is real. It is real. I feel it. It's not subject to mathematical analysis, charts of averages, median statistics, cos-

176

ily conceived normalcy ranges. Pain is real, it exists, it is not abstract.''

Noah was hostile. It was clear he had not wanted to come. He lashed out bitterly, argued, circled. But Father Stephanos was patient. He listened. Argued gently. Prodded. Consoled. Searched. Until Noah began to expand. He grieved for his son and for his wounded city, and he writhed with guilt. Dynamic man. If only he had done this. Or that. Something. This should all have been avoided. This kind of tragedy couldn't, mustn't be allowed to happen. And vengeance. Vengeance must be exacted. He would take the responsibility. He would take the sin upon his head, but it must be done. He was vague about details, but made it clear he knew who was responsible, would soon know where to find them. He lit a cigarette and his hands were shaking. Father Stephanos's pipe had gone out, but he was shaken too—did not think he could bring his hands to fill the pipe steadily.

"It's wrong, Noah, and you know it.''

"Oh, yes, I know it, Father, but what would you do? Can you answer that honestly? What would you do?''

Father Stephanos swallowed. His mouth was dry. "I wish I could answer that. Firmly, easily. Probably some of the priests you knew when you were young could have. I can't.''

Noah chuckled for the first time in weeks. "Father Reilly would box my ears, even now." He sighed. "Sometimes I miss the way it was. I guess it seemed easier.''

Father Stephanos nodded. "I know. But was it better?'' Noah shrugged.

The sky was clearing, but remained a cold gray color. Their faces were moist from the intermittent drizzle. Noah's face had a shine, almost a glow, like a saint or a martyr. The young priest shook his head to clear his eyes of the illusion.

"Murder is a mortal sin.''

"Do you believe that, Father?''

177

"Yes."

"So do I. But God will understand."

He stared at Noah. Then he nodded his head slowly. It hadn't occurred to him before, but he supposed God loved murderers as well as all the other cripples and misfits of humanity.


Noah was glad he had talked to Father Stephanos. It had cleared his head to put so many things into formal language. He realized until that afternoon he had been debating things in his mind. Now the inner turmoil was over. Now he was merely waiting.

Elizabeth was relieved. Noah was kind and cheerful about the house again. He still didn't go back to work, but he ran errands, attended church, seemed much himself again. He still talked about a trip to Europe alone, but she had persuaded herself that it was a good idea for him to get away by himself. And he was very loving. Intense. Almost as if he were memorizing the interplay of their bodies.

When Bucky called, Noah flew to New York the next afternoon. Bucky introduced him to a college friend from some place in Michigan. Albion or some such. The friend was a literary agent and gave Noah as quick a briefing on the business as he could. It was necessary because Bucky thought the best approach was to a French war correspondent who had covered Donovan in Africa and was now writing a book about him.

At the airport, he gave Noah a thin file. "There's not much there—mostly photographs, but it's all I dared bring. I'd go with you, Noah, but that would tip the game right away and we'd never get close to Donovan."

"I know, Bucky. I appreciate all this. How dangerous is it for you?"

Bucky shrugged. "I'm not sure. But I hope you have your affairs in order. Mine are."

# BOOK III: **LAST CASUALTIES**

> They wrote in the old days that it is sweet and fitting to die for one's country. But in modern war there is nothing sweet nor fitting in your dying. You will die like a dog for no good reason.
>
> *Ernest Hemingway*

and papers. He could not really afford this apartment. It was only a few blocks from the life St. Louis in a very expensive area. He could not afford to quit his post to finish the book on Donovan either, but he had lived a life without leisure or pleasure for many years and he could not bring

The correspondent farted. He was fat and happy after several months back in his beloved Paris. He had managed to add fifteen pounds to an already stout figure that years of hard living in Africa had only trimmed minimally. He was sitting at the small table just inside the double doors off the tiny balcony of his apartment. The weather was cold, but the November sun was quite bright and danced swiftly across the surface of the sluggish Seine. He wore a silk lounging robe over his pajamas. He sipped coffee and took another bite of his fresh croissant. Such a pleasure to be a civilized man again. He farted again and sighed. The cassoulet last night had been marvelous. He finished his coffee and croissant and lit a Gauloise. He glanced around happily.

He loved his apartment. It was really one large, high-ceilinged room. He had a pullout sofa-bed, as yet this morning unmade, a very small kitchenette in one corner of the room, and a small bath down a short, narrow, private hall that served him as a clothing closet. His breakfast table by the balcony doors would be cleared and would serve as his desk. The walls were high, white, speckled plaster decorated by two small paintings—colorful abstracts done by a Sorbonne art student. The floors were parquet, dark, interrupted only by a very fine six-by-nine Persian rug. He had a few excellent pieces of spare Scandinavian modern furniture—he especially prized the chrome and glass liquor cart. That was all, save a few shelves of books, his typewriter and papers. He could not really afford this apartment. It was only a few blocks from the Île St. Louis in a very expensive area. He could not afford to quit his post to finish the book on Donovan either, but he had lived a life without leisure or pleasure for many years and he could not bring himself to accept the Athens bureau job after all. Ah, well, one publisher was definitely interested and he had enough money to last more than a year. If he could finish in seven or eight months . . . and there was the American literary agent who had phoned last evening. He began bustling about the apartment. He made his bed and folded it away, replaced the cushions to complete the conversion to a sofa. He washed his few breakfast dishes, cleared the table and set it up for work. After he shaved, showered, and dressed, he allowed himself one more cup of coffee with just a small dash of brandy and another Gauloise.

He was to take luncheon with the American—what was his name? Peterson? Yes. Of course, when the American had asked him to suggest a restaurant, he had chosen the Parfait Plaisir. It was one of his favorites, and it was within walking distance for him. And it was expensive, so he was rarely able to go there now. He had heard that American literary people were quite used to spending exorbitant sums for ''literary'' luncheons. He decided he would have the filet of sole amandine. Ambrosia. He couldn't quite make up his mind which of the wonderful whites to choose to go with it.

He decided he would like *this* American. He had seemed very pleasant, not at all abrasive. He had even apologized several times for his execrable French. Which, of course, he should have, but with Americans—who knew? They often thought you should applaud their terrible French as if they were doing *you* a favor to even attempt a cursory familiarity with your language. And if you spoke English, *that* was considered only the sensible thing to do by them.

He stubbed out his cigarette and prepared to go to work. He was still outlining the narrative attack, shaping his notes, trying to bring a manageable one-hundred-fifty-thousand-word form to the project. And in this preliminary process, he was also discovering the important gaps in his information, the pieces he had yet to put together. Who had paid Donovan in Imbannailand? Perhaps when he had reached that point in the manuscript, he would be able to visit Donovan and, perhaps, Donovan would be ready to reveal some of these facts. He opened his notebook to the page where

182

he had left off the day before. He rearranged a few index cards, licked the tip of a pencil and began to scrawl the beginning of a new chapter heading in his large, oval, childish handwriting. He shifted slightly in his chair to pass gas. One did not fart when one was working.

The correspondent was pleased with the American. He was neatly groomed, intelligent-looking, smartly but not garishly dressed in a black leather leisure suit, gold shirt and tie. He seemed very deferential, polite, low-keyed. He had shown the good sense not even to bother to glance at his menu, but rather asked the correspondent to order for both of them. He was properly appreciative of the sole and the wine and, again, properly apologetic about his poor French. His answer to how he had learned of the work in progress had been a little vague, but the journalist was not sure that was very important.

"How long do you think the book will run? In manuscript—that is, first draft?"

"One hundred fifty thousand words. Perhaps a little more. Certainly not less. Colonel Donovan has had a long and varied career. I could not do it justice in a shorter length."

"Of course not. Actually, extra length is sometimes valuable. It makes the price of the book higher, and that is more attractive to the book clubs. And the paperback publishers."

"I see. What might they be willing to pay? Me."

"Well, I work for a consortium of American publishing houses. Depending upon who I place it with, I think I might be able to get you an advance of forty or fifty thousand francs."

The correspondent almost choked on his bite of sole. When his coughing seizure had subsided, he took a swallow of wine to ease his throat. "What would your fee amount to?"

"Ten percent, but you needn't worry about it. I get that from the publisher as a surcharge on the contract."

The correspondent frowned. He had never heard of a literary agent who operated in this manner before. Of course, he *had* only sold one small book previously. And without an agent. Most of his experience had been in straight journalism, so he was not altogether familiar with book publishing. And should he worry about it if it saved him money? Four or five thousand francs? He decided not.

"Will you need the entire first draft in order to secure a contract and advance from your American publishing house, Mr. Peterson?"

"No. I doubt it. I might well be able to secure the contract on the basis of an outline. Of course, with that arrangement only a portion of the advance would be paid at the signing. The rest would be paid when the completed manuscript was received and accepted by the publisher."

"How much would be paid on signing?"

"At least forty percent of the agreed figure, perhaps half."

There was something faintly off in the way Peterson answered questions. It was almost as if he were reciting something someone had coached him on or he had read somewhere, rather than something he was truly familiar with. Perhaps it was the language difficulty. He did not seem nervous or evasive. Except for how he knew of the book. The journalist could think of no reason for an elaborate hoax to be played upon him. It *must* be the language difficulty. Surely the man was genuine.

"How long do you think it will take to complete the outline? How much do you have done now?"

"Another two weeks. I am almost finished with that stage."

"I wonder if I might read the outline? To see how likely it is that we would be able to secure a contract with it?"

The journalist shrugged. "I don't see why not. It can't hurt anything. I would have to request you to read it at my apartment." He made a small apologetic gesture. "You must understand, I have only the one copy."

184

"Of course. I could come around any time that was convenient for you."

"Come this evening, then. I will not be going out."

"Wonderful. Say eight o'clock?"

"Certainly. I will tell the concierge to let you in." He wrote his address on a scrap of paper and gave it to Peterson. They finished the luncheon in high spirits. The correspondent ordered profiterole for dessert and afterward, at the American's suggestion, an excellent champagne.

The walk back to his apartment in the cold was bracing and helped clear his head. He stopped at his grocer's small shop for some eggs and mushrooms and sausages. He would have an omelet and work straight through until Peterson arrived. He bought a couple of packets of Gauloises and as he passed the wine shop debated the purchase of some American whisky to serve Peterson. The price was far too high and he decided cognac would serve.

Sitting at his desk table, he felt light-headed and sleepy again. He made *café filtre* and forced himself to concentrate. If the American was right—forty or fifty thousand francs would be a considerable sum for him. And from the way the American talked, the advance would not necessarily be all he might receive if the book was successful. In his way, he was a modest man. He hardly let himself dare to dream of wealth or fame such as accrued to a genuinely successful author. Simenon, for instance, was said to have made great sums from his writing. He shook his head against the wine and idle thoughts and resumed writing.

Peterson was prompt. The correspondent took his raincoat and poured coffee and cognac for them. Peterson complimented him on his lovely apartment, which charmed the journalist. He *was* a pleasant American. They chatted for a few moments, as best they could. When the correspondent brought the notebooks, Peterson asked if he might make notes for himself to refresh his memory when making initial talks with publishers. The journalist shrugged. No one could

185

steal his book. Its strength would be his long personal relationship with Donovan. No other author could hope to match that.

"Your French is good enough for reading? It will not give you great difficulty?"

"My reading French is better than my spoken. I took French at my university some years ago. I always read it better than I spoke it."

The journalist nodded. "It is often so. I read English with much greater facility than I can speak it." He went back to his table and continued working while the American read. Occasionally, he glanced at him. Sometimes he would be making notes, sometimes nodding to himself. He seemed to like what he was reading. Finally, when he was finished he set the notebooks aside, put his small pocket notebook away, and smiled at the correspondent.

"Excellent. Really, excellent. I think it will be a fascinating book."

"Really?"

"Without question." The correspondent poured more coffee and a rather more generous measure of cognac for each of them. "If you can bring this project off, it is the type of book which might well become a best seller in America."

"Is this possible?"

"Certainly. I have no doubt that I can secure a contract on the basis of this outline. It would have to be translated and typed, of course, but that is no problem. If it is agreeable to you, I will arrange for it to be done as soon as you finish. And pay for it, of course."

"But that is marvelous. This is the most wonderful good fortune for me. As you must have assumed, my funds are limited. To be paid a partial advance while I am working on the book will be most agreeable."

"I understand. Tell me, where is Colonel Donovan now?"

"He is, perhaps, in Ireland. His home in Cork County. Why do you ask?"

"It occurs to me that, for an American publisher, this project might be made more attractive if we could induce Colonel Donovan to write a brief foreword. Nothing too long or difficult, just some reminiscences about your relationship, perhaps an anecdote or two about some of your shared experiences. It's the kind of personal touch that American publishers like. Adds authority to the book, if you see what I mean."

"Yes, I see. It would be most fitting, but unfortunately I do not know if he would agree. I do not know that he wouldn't, I just do not know. He is a most unusual man. Unpredictable."

"Well, it can do no harm to try."

"No, no harm."

"And if we can secure his cooperation and strengthen the project it could mean more money for you."

"What does, what would . . . how much money might one make from an American best seller?"

"That varies a great deal, but certainly a million francs would not be out of the question."

"Mon dieu!"

The correspondent gulped at his cognac. He stared at one of his paintings for a few moments without seeing it. He waited for his heartbeat to slow to normal.

"That is a great sum of money, Mr. Peterson."

"Yes, it is. That's why it's vital for us to do everything possible to strengthen the book. I wonder if you might agree to take a trip with me to Ireland to see Donovan? To try to secure his cooperation. At my expense. Or if not, you could give me a letter of introduction and I might try to persuade him myself."

"I don't know if I could leave at this moment. In the middle of my work. I am most anxious to finish the outline."

"Then, perhaps, a letter of introduction?"

187

"I'm not sure. He can be a difficult man. I might call him on the telephone and explain. Then you might go across to see him and I could join you later. When I finish the outline. Would that be agreeable?"

"Very much so. I am most anxious to meet Colonel Donovan and I could begin exploratory conversations immediately. When could you telephone him?"

"I suppose I might do it in the morning."

"Wonderful." Peterson took a large wallet from an inside pocket. When he opened it, the correspondent saw a fat stack of notes of various currencies and a thick packet of traveler's checks. He slipped a hundred-franc note out and laid it on the table. "That should cover the expense of the call. Please call me at my hotel as soon as you speak with Donovan. If he is agreeable, I would be ready to leave tomorrow."

The correspondent laughed. "You Americans. You never waste time do you? Hurry, hurry, hurry."

Peterson smiled. "Unfortunately, business often leaves all too little time for the amenities and pleasantries. Time is money, they say. But when I retire, I will squander it profligately."

The correspondent laughed. He did like this Peterson fellow. They finished their drinks and coffee and arranged a time for the journalist to call him in the morning after he had talked with Donovan. Peterson left then and the correspondent went to bed. He lay awake for half an hour thinking of what Peterson had said. A million francs! Was that possible?

Noah lay on his hotel bed. He did not undress because he was not sure he could sleep. He might want to get up and take a walk in a few minutes. His mind was fuzzy and he was tired. The jet lag had not worn off yet, but he had been so impatient he had called the French journalist from the airport minutes after he had gotten off the airplane and gone through customs. Now he was not so sure that he hadn't

188

moved too quickly. He was not at all sure he was ready to meet Donovan.

His cover story seemed to be working well. Of course, it could be expected to with the correspondent. Noah was telling him things he wanted to hear. But Donovan. He would be something different. Donovan would be suspicious. He would be a fool not to be and he did not believe a man could do what Donovan had done and be a fool. He wished he had had more time with the New York literary agent than the layover between flights. He thought he had most of the basics right. It would have to do. The agent probably couldn't have spent more time with him anyway. He had only agreed to see Noah for drinks at Kennedy because he was a college friend of Bucky's. Some place in Michigan. Albion? Whatever.

And what was he going to do when he met Donovan? You couldn't just walk up and shoot the man. He wouldn't be alone. He would have some of his soldiers around. That was why he was frightened by his tiredness. Donovan was surely a ruthless man. A missed reaction or a slip on his part could be . . .

It took the correspondent better than forty-five minutes to get his call through. The Irish operators appeared to be uniformly feebleminded and the Continental operators were not much better. He had had to spell Donovan three times and Ahkista four for the first French operator he talked to.

Finally, "Ahkista nine, Donovan speaking."

"Mon Colonel."

Donovan's laugh sounded tinny, resonated by the poor connection. "Is that you, Charles?"

"Yes, mon Colonel."

"How is your book coming, Charles?"

"Most excellently. That is why I have called. It is only in outline form and that not yet complete, and already a French publisher and an American literary agent are interested."

189

"Ah, well, that's grand. I'm glad for you, Charles. I'll look forward to an autographed copy or two when it's done."

"But certainly. But there is a chance you might be more closely involved than that. If you choose to, naturally."

"In what manner do you mean, Charles?"

"The American says for their edition he believes it would strengthen the book if you would consent to write a brief foreword. A personal remembrance of our experiences. A few pages, nothing too strenuous. He says it would lend great authenticity to the work for the American edition. I personally feel it would be useful to the French edition as well."

"I see."

"The American would like to visit you for what he calls the exploratory discussions if that is agreeable to you. I will finish my outline and then, perhaps, the three of us might discuss it more fully." Donovan was silent for long seconds. "Mon Colonel, are you still there?"

"Yes . . . I've never been much of one for writing myself . . . an American you say?"

"Yes, but most pleasant for a change. A charming man, Colonel. It could do no great harm to listen to him. If you do not wish to entertain the project, then you need not."

"What is this man's name?"

"Eh, Peterson."

"Peterson."

"Yes."

"P-E-T-E-R-S-O-N?"

"That is most correct."

"What's his first name."

"Eh, it slips . . . the Bible, eh, the man with the ship of many animals and the great rain."

"Noah?"

"That is correct. Noah Peterson."

"When would this fellow likely be coming?"

"I am to telephone him at his hotel after our discussion. If you are agreeable, he would leave today."

"He's not after wasting much time, is he?"

"No, he is that much American, but I promise you, he is a most pleasant man. Not, eh, what is the word . . . pushy."

"Can he find his way down here? I'll not be able to meet him at the airport."

"I am sure he can find his way."

"Well, send him along then and we'll see. I'm not promising anything, Charles."

"Naturally. I understand."

"It's grand for your book, though. I'm well pleased."

"Thank you, mon Colonel. I am most happy myself."

After he hung up, the correspondent was surprised to find that he was sweating heavily. The receiver of the phone was moist where he had gripped it. So much depended upon Donovan's whim. If he could draw on friendship . . . but no—he could not honestly say he was Donovan's friend. More than an acquaintance, but . . . there was no word for what you were to Donovan if you knew him for some time.

He sat at his table and composed himself. He finished his coffee, cold by now. He made himself quite cheerful while he talked to the American. He did not want him to feel there would be difficulties. The American might lose interest in the project. He did say that Donovan was a man you needed to talk carefully to, a man you must be patient with. The American said he understood. The correspondent hoped he did. Like an accident always ready to happen.

Donovan stared out the kitchen window at the bay. It was raining, naturally, and gray, and the bay was wild. He sipped his tea. He pondered the phone conversation. An American. He did not like it. He did not like coincidences that could mask deceit or danger.

He left his tea and went up to see to Patjo. His convalescence was becoming difficult. He was a tough old sod, but he had been hurt badly, bled too much, suffered extreme shock. He was mending, but slowly, and he hated being deprived of booze. Only he and McGregor and a couple of the others were still here with Patjo. The rest were already in London. Patjo was awake.

"Ah, there you are, Terrence. I've just come awake."

"How are you feeling, Patjo?" His friend's face was pale and lined. He was an old man, Donovan realized, but then so was Donovan. Perhaps the aging should bother him, Donovan thought. It did so with many people. He did not care. Death did not matter, so how could aging? Do what you want, what you will, what you can. Let the rest go.

"Not too poorly, Terrence. Not too poorly."

"Grand. Will you be having some tea now, then, Patjo? And maybe some sausage or a nice rasher of bacon and an egg?"

"That'd be lovely. And Terrence?"

"Yes."

"Could you see your way clear to spicing the tea with just a little touch of the tincture? Not too much, mind, but enough for the taste of it? I haven't had any in so long I'm beginning to forget the flavor."

Donovan laughed. "I might wave the bottle at your tea cup in passing, but no more."

"Stingy, mean man." Patjo smiled. "That'd be lovely, Terrence. Just a taste."

Donovan nodded. He made breakfast for Patjo and spiked his tea with a decent short shot of Paddy. After Patjo ate, Donovan changed the dressings on his wound. It *was* healing. The oozing had stopped two days before, which probably meant the drainage was complete. Patjo was a tough old sod. So was he, for that matter.

Patjo tired again quickly and went off to sleep. Donovan went back to the kitchen and considered the phone call again. He looked at the name he had written down. Peterson, Noah. It wasn't much to go on. Still.

He found the notebook and looked up the number in London. The man had called a week before. He had said he was their "contact." If they had a problem, they could call him anytime, night or day. He would refer it to higher authority and appropriate action would be taken. He did not know if Peterson was a problem or not. He might be one of theirs, for that matter. Or he might just be a literary agent. He shrugged mentally. Why not? It would be a chance to use the "contact," to see if it was going to be reliable. And if they were trying some shifty trickery, he might be able to tell something from their reaction. He went to the telephone in the lounge.

He smoked three cigarettes before he got through. A slow, low-pitched voice came on the line. "Knightsbridge, four eight hundred."

"This is Wellesley. I want to speak to Vassar."

"This is Vassar. Go ahead, Wellesley. What is your problem?"

Donovan shook his head. Some shagging coding clerk with a sense of humor. Who'd have thought it.

"There is an American, now in Paris, but leaving for Cork today. He is asking questions about me. He purports to be an American literary agent interested in a book that is being written about me. I want to know if he is what he says he is or if he is using cover."

"All right, Wellesley. I think we can handle that without too much difficulty. What name is he using?"

"Noah Peterson. Do you want me to spell it?"

"Just the surname."

"P-E-T-E-R-S-O-N."

"All right, Wellesley, anything else?"

"How soon do you think you can get the information for me?"

"If he's bogus—sometime tomorrow. If he's genuine, it may take a bit longer."

"No news is good news."

A dry, mirthless chuckle rattled along the line. "More or

less. How much longer will we be able to contact you at the, er, Ahkista number?"

"About a week. Ten days at most. Then the backup number in London will take precedence. In any case, Radcliffe can be reached at that number and he can find me." Radcliffe was Major Turrman.

"Very good, Wellesley. I will try to give you a preliminary indication by—oh, say, tomorrow sometime in the p.m."

"Grand."

Donovan stared at the phone after he hung it up. He smiled. Captain Jackson was Smith. McGregor was Bennington. He laughed. As the years passed and the senior command died, they would have to reassign some of the names or they would run out of chic American women's colleges. Presumably, no matter what their personnel changes were, the telephone "contact" would always be Vassar. Could one compose a ringing quatrain to the effect that there would always be a Vassar? Probably not.

He debated sending one of the men up to Cork City to shadow the American, but decided the difficulties outweighed the best possible results. They would know soon enough the likelihood of difficulty with this—he glanced at the scrap of paper, Peterson, Noah. Americans like biblical names. Noah. He searched his memory. Something besides the ark . . . ah, yes—didn't the Bible say that Noah was the first vintner? "And Noah was very drunk." He seemed to remember that. Maybe that was the thing to do. A few smooth-tasting, innocuous-seeming Irish—what was the American word for it—boilermakers. Yes. Paddy and Guinness. A few of those would loosen the tongue. And biblical solutions had such a neat, scholarly, traditional ring to them. He liked that. "And Noah was very drunk." Grand.

On the last Thursday in November, it was one of those strange balmy days that the south of Ireland gets in early winter. The sun was shining and the temperature was in the mid-fifties. Noah could almost think of himself as a tourist. The first sight of Cork City was disappointing. The airport was unremarkably modern, if a bit cramped, and the city was a small, ugly, industrial town. It was outside the city that his breath was taken away. On T65, not far from the city, you enter a long stretch of highway that is straight as a string and lined for miles with a near-uniform row of lush green trees that form a cool, shaded canopy for the road. When you leave it, you are in the gently rolling, lush green countryside of East Cork.

The tiny Fiat he had rented hugged the road cleverly and the surface was good, the drive easy despite the often meandering nature of Irish roads. The towns seemed picturesque at first glance. Narrow streets with long rows of semidetached houses and buildings, most of them painted fairly recently in pink or blue pastels with occasional institutional gray; small cheerful-looking shops, strawberry-faced men in dark suit jackets and caps, plain women in plain clothes; moderate traffic with mostly polite motorists. The towns seemed of a piece with the only difference being that some were larger and some were smaller. They had lovely musical names; Ballinhassig, Inishannon, Bandon, Enniskean, Dunmanway, Drimoleague. It was late afternoon and beginning to rain as he neared Bantry. He had reservations at the West Lodge. He came to it on the southern side of Bantry, before you made your descent into the town proper.

It was a large, modern motor-hotel with the chrome and glass and carpeting associated with such places. Except for the soft lilting accents of the staff, it might have been in Duluth or Memphis.

His fatigue had been reinforced by the moderate flight from Paris to Cork. He had planned to call on Donovan that evening, but now he knew he was too tired. Wisdom told him to get a good night's sleep and go out in the morning. He washed up in his room and went to the lounge bar. The bar was small, a sort of pantry-type arrangement, but the room was spacious and the furniture comfortable, if some-

195

what prosaic. There was even a color television. He watched it for half an hour while he had two gin and limes. He decided Irish television was even worse than American. The dining room was large and conventional. He had some beautiful prawns in a pink sauce faintly reminiscent of thousand island dressing, a rather stringy steak with a strong, gamy flavor which he decided must have come from a grass-fed cow, lovely, small new potatoes and wonderful sherry trifle. He took a gin and lime to his room.

It was only seven-thirty, but he was done in. He studied the road map to see the route out to Ahkista. It seemed simple enough. He took the dossier on Donovan out of his handbag. The man *had* lived an incredible life. The material in the correspondent's outline had not added a great deal to his knowledge of Donovan. He stared at the photographs again. A large man. Burly. He had the look of a modest layer of pleasurable fat over a very strong, very hard, very muscular body. He would be a hard man to kill. The seams of the face were heavily outlined. It was a heavy, sensual face. Where was the asceticism of the man's youth? In all three photographs, two at a distance and one closeup, Donovan wore heavy mirror-tinted sunglasses. The kind American highway patrolmen favor, thought Noah. You can't see his eyes, Noah thought. Frustrating. You can read a lot in a man's eyes if you look carefully. The most recent photo was dated almost two years earlier. Donovan was sitting on the hood of an armored personnel carrier talking to a semicircle of men standing around the front of the vehicle. Noah glanced at the notation on the back:

*Donovan talking to staff officers at base camp near the Zandijari River/Other officers from left to right, Colonel Somutu, Major Turrman, Captain Jackson, Lieutenant Adams, unidentified ILA Major, Sergeant-Major McGregor.*

This was near the beginning of the IWAC entry into the Imbannailand civil war. He looked at the photograph again.

196

He wished he could see Donovan's eyes. The other men were wearing glasses much like Donovan's. Were they imitating him? Was it flattery or sincere respect? You couldn't tell from a photo. You had to be around a man. He stared at one of the black officers. Something very familiar. He turned the photo over to the notation again and then back to the front. Lieutenant Adams. Adams? . . . Art Adams? Yes. The promising young tennis player of a few years back who was always being confused with Arthur Ashe. He stared hard at the photograph. It was an excellent quality print, almost glossy and apparently taken with a first-rate camera. Still, he couldn't be sure. He thought so, but his eyes were tired and he was tired. He put the photos back in the dossier folder and replaced it on the bottom of his bag. He laid out fresh clothes for the morning. And his pistol. He had been surprised at how easy it was to smuggle through customs. In pajamas, in bed, he debated leaving a call for the morning. No. He needed to sleep until he woke naturally. That would clear his mind. He turned off the light. He felt sorry, briefly, for the Frenchman. He was so eager. It was not a decent deception to play on the man. When he realized it was a hoax, the crushing disappointment would be quite cruel. What else could he do? He had to get close to Donovan. He was too tired to wrestle overlong with his conscience. He was doing what he was doing and he would have to pay the price in penance. Later. After. Whatever. He fell asleep to the soothing sound of a gentle Irish rain.

It was one of those gray mornings when rain is inevitable, but the early drizzle is so apathetic one assumes the clouds are having difficulty mustering the energy or enthusiasm for a downpour. The peninsula road was damp, but not particularly slick. It was past eleven when Noah pulled up at the crossroads in Durrus. He sorted out the slightly confusing road signs and took the right-hand road on toward Ahkista. The gray-green surface of the bay was as listless as the drizzle. He passed a postman riding a bicycle, heavily covered with a rubber slicker. He nosed the Fiat in between two battered Morris-Minis in front of Arundel's pub. Inside, two men were shooting darts, two more stood at the bar watching. Four pints of Guinness, in various stages of depletion, were lined up along the short bar surface. A plain girl of indeterminate age was behind the bar. Everyone looked at him with uninhibited, slightly curious stares. He approached the bar and cleared his throat.

"I'm looking for the Donovan place. I was wondering if you could help me out."

The silence and the continued stares went on so long, he began to wonder if he had actually spoken or had merely intended to and imagined the act. Finally, one of the men muttered some short phrase in a soft singsong that Noah couldn't catch.

"I beg your pardon."

The man looked at Noah as if he were daft. He shifted uncomfortably on his feet, reached for his pint, then pulled his fingers back slowly. He repeated the mutter. Noah strained in the dead silence to make it out.

It sounded as if he said, "Which Donovan would that be?"

"Colonel Terrence Donovan. I'm looking for Terrence Donovan. I was wondering if you could direct me to his house."

The silence was even longer this time and the stares were now more guarded than openly curious. Noah began to feel as if he were hallucinating. It was as if he had not spoken at all, or had spoken to them in some strange tongue they did not understand, or something was so awry with his appearance (had he forgotten his pants?) that he appeared as some freak, some aberrant apparition. He restrained himself with some difficulty from touching his clothes to see that they were all in place or turning to use the window as a mirror. The tension stretched until he thought he would shriek.

The girl finally moved down the bar toward him and gave him simple directions. He was not sure he understood, but he was too thoroughly confused and embarrassed to ask her to repeat them. He thanked her, rather too profusely, bought a pack of cigarettes he didn't need and fumbled his way out and into the Fiat. None of the men had moved or taken their eyes off him.

He backed out onto the road and drove into a series of sharp turns amongst trees that sometimes hid the bay from him. Out of sight of the pub, he pulled off the road again and sat to light a cigarette and calm himself. He looked at himself in the small car mirror. There was no bleeding hole in his head or strange unsightly growth spouting from his face. He patted his clothes and looked at them. All in place, clean, pressed. He shook his head and pulled back into the road.

Surprisingly, he found Donovan's house without too much difficulty. Beautiful view of the bay and the mountains. The kind of view that commanded hundreds of thousands of dollars in America.

He walked up the slick white stone steps and knocked on the massive wood door. A man answered, not Donovan, that he recognized from one of the photographs. He was dressed in casual, nondescript trousers and shirt. His accent was not Irish or English. Scottish? McGregor.

"I'm looking for Terrence Donovan. Is this his home?"

"Aye. Come in out of the draft."

He followed the man into a modest, but comfortable living room—lounges, they were called. A large man in clothes similar to McGregor's sat in an easy chair smoking what smelled like a fine cigar. He did not rise to greet Noah. His feet were propped on a padded footstool and he wore silver mirror-tint sunglasses in the gloom of a nearly unlighted room on a dark, overcast day. Donovan.

"You'll be Mr. Peterson, the American literary agent." His voice was softly pitched, but deep, resonant, authoritative. He quietly dominated the room, even sitting down with two men standing nearly over him, like an openly, but strategically placed cannon. Noah suppressed a nervous giggle

199

and resisted the temptation to say wildly, "All right, I'll be Peterson, the American literary agent, you be James Joyce,"

He said, "Yes, you must be Colonel Donovan."

Donovan smiled. "If I must be, then I will. Sit down, Mr. Peterson. Andrew bring us some tea. You'll take a touch of the tincture in it for flavoring, Mr. Peterson?"

Noah nodded as he sat in an easy chair next to Donovan's, though he was not sure what he was agreeing to. Their chairs flanked a smallish fireplace. A cheerful coal fire popped and hissed.

"You've come about the book Charles is writing, as I understand it. An American publisher is interested?"

"No. Not yet. I'm interested in the project. I represent a consortium of American publishers. I scout foreign markets for material that might be suitable for the U.S. and Canada. I try to place any property I represent with the best house at the best price."

"Then *you're* interested in the book about me?"

"Yes, that's correct. I think it may be a very saleable project. As has probably been explained to you, the reason I came is that I feel a short preface by you personally would strengthen the market appeal immeasureably."

"So I understand. Ah, thank you, Andrew." The large Scotsman set a tray on a table next to Donovan. It had a plain porcelain pot, two cups and saucers and a nearly full bottle of Paddy's Whisky. Donovan handed him a cup and saucer. "Tea with whisky and a touch of lemon. The very best remedy for a chill Irish day."

"Thank you." Noah tasted the tea. It was very strong and nearly half whisky. The aroma was rich. It tasted clean, but burned going down. "Very hearty."

"It's a grand brew. You'll stay for a bit to eat? Andrew does a rare fine egg and chips."

"You're very kind, Colonel Donovan."

"Not a bit of it. Two at table, Andrew." McGregor nodded and slipped out of the room. "I'm not sure I'm understanding what you're proposing, Mr. Peterson. I'm not a literary man myself."

"It's really fairly simple."

"Ah, I'm sure of it, it's just my slow West Cork peasant head that takes a bit of time to penetrate." Donovan seemed to be laughing at him. He couldn't be sure. He wished Donovan would take off those glasses. He liked to look at a man's eyes when he talked to him. He took another sip of the hot tea.

"I'm sure that's a little joke, Colonel. For the American market—the mass market—the reader prefers some touch of the personal nature in this type of book. It gives an authority to the work it wouldn't otherwise have."

"I see."

"A few pages, maybe twenty or thirty, in which you might say something about your relationship with the author, recall a shared experience or two, perhaps include an anecdote or two."

"A little bit about myself and Charles."

"That's it exactly. You might include whatever future plans you have that aren't confidential. I understand you're in semi-retirement for the present?"

"I am."

"No, uh, new wars or, uh, adventures to undertake that seem to appeal to you?" Donovan looked at him sharply.

His answer came slowly. "No. No new wars. There aren't many about worth the bother these days. There's this new dustup in Angola, but I'd not be wanting to go back there." He laughed. "I don't believe I'm remembered there with any great fondness." He waved it away with the back of his hand. "There's no one involved anymore who'd be willing to pay me."

"You've made enough to live comfortably through—put enough aside over the years then?" Donovan glanced sharply at him again.

"That's a bit personal."

"I'm sorry, Colonel. No offense meant."

"Well, it's right enough. I've put some aside. A man always likes a bit more unless he's filthy rich. I suppose if I undertook to write this piece you're proposing, I might expect to share in the proceeds?"

"Of course. We would certainly make an adequate arrangement."

"Grand."

As they talked, Donovan refilled their tea cups again and then again. He was rather more generous with the Paddy than Noah might have wished, but he began to like the sharp, slightly brassy taste. The rain finally had some energy behind it and drummed on the windows, which chattered and shook with the wind from the bay. Noah slowly relaxed back into the soft chair. The fire was very bright and cozy now, as Donovan had added fresh coal on top and prodded it with an old bayonet. The escaping gases made bright, fluffy rainbows of fire. He was still tired and hadn't eaten much breakfast and wasn't really a heavy drinker or a morning drinker. The Paddy was beginning to fuzz his mind.

"Ah, sure I read the piece about Imbannailand. It seems General Attigo is gathering money and strength to return from exile and retake power. And it looks as if Colonel Somutu is going to boot Ossungi out anyway. A good man, Somutu."

"You have no interest in the outcome?"

"Ah, well, it'd be grand if Somutu came out on top. I could go back and take my choice of sides and name my price, but I seem to have lost my taste for war." Donovan smiled. It was a broad, charming smile that lit his entire face. If only you could see the eyes. Noah thought Donovan must be very attractive to women. "I'll be fifty soon. I've been at it long enough."

"You were a priest once, were you not, Colonel?"

"Oh, aye. I was, so. A Jesuit in my hot-blooded youth. Are you a religious man, Mr. Peterson?"

Noah nodded. "An ecumencial Catholic."

"A disciple of John XXIII."

"More or less."

When they stood to go in to eat, Noah was appalled at how drunk he felt. His kidneys were burning and he asked to use the toilet facilities. They were upstairs. After he relieved himself he washed his hands and then splashed water on his face. It only made him feel marginally more alert. A door to a bedroom was ajar. Through the narrow opening he could see a man sleeping. He was pale and his breath seemed labored. The bedclothes were in some disarray, and Noah could see the man was heavily bandaged and taped around his right side toward the bottom of his rib cage.

They sat at the kitchen table. The food, fried eggs and sausages and chips, smelled quite good. Noah was unnerved by the sight of pints of stout by their plates. Donovan raised his glass and Noah had no choice but to follow his lead.

"Irish wine. As the boyos say—it's not bad for Protestant stuff. *Slointha Issail.* ' They touched glasses and Donovan drank deeply. Noah took one medium swallow and set the glass down. It was dark, heavy, bitter. Noah ate as rapidly as he thought some modicum of table manners allowed. The food was as good as it smelled. The chips especially were fresh potatoes sliced medium-sized and deep fried a gorgeous golden brown. The food seemed to help his head, but the Guinness *was* tasty with it and he could not reduce his glass by more than half before McGregor came in and topped it off again. As a result, Noah was still woozy after lunch when they went back into the lounge. He was near tears when he heard Donovan instruct McGregor.

"Ah, Andrew, bring us a bottle of the *potheen* and a couple of the Harp lagers."

"Oh, no, Colonel, really I couldn't."

"Ah, you can't come to Ireland without being treated to some of the true home brew. Cigar?" Noah nodded weakly and accepted a light from Donovan. "Cuban blunts. Nothing better than a really fine Havana cigar." McGregor brought a tray with two pint glasses, two cut-glass tumblers, four bottles of Harp lager, and a Paddy's bottle with a clear, oily-looking liquid in it. Donovan poured it into the tumblers, then filled the pint glasses with beer. "A bit raw, the *potheen,* but the lager chases it nicely. Made on the peninsula from the finest peninsula potatoes." It was foul-smelling, raw, burned angrily going down, made him gulp more beer than he really wanted. He sank back in the chair and gave up. He was going to be very drunk and there was no use fighting it. He just hoped he wouldn't be sick. Donovan did not seem to be affected in the slightest. He talked amiably, rebuilt the fire, affected the thoroughly cordial and generous host. The wind had moderated and the rain stopped. Sunlight dropped into the room at an odd angle, making bright shafts and rectangles, leaving dark, shadowed corners. Donovan's deep, soft-pitched voice was soothing. Noah dozed off in the chair. He seemed to hear bells in his sleep.

Donovan went into the large lounge when the phone rang. He had overdone it with the American. He had not only gotten drunk, he had fallen asleep. That was not the idea at all.

"Ahkista nine."

"Knightsbridge four eight hundred calling. This is Vassar."

"Wellesley here."

"Reference your inquiry yesterday in the a.m.: There is a Major Noah Peterson on the St. Louis Police Department. He is presently on leave of absence and his exact whereabouts are not known, but he is believed to have come to Europe. We find no record as yet of a literary agent by that name. We have a description of the policeman—do you want it?"

"Please. That would be most useful."

"Forty-three years of age. Married, three children, RC—"

"What is RC?"

"Roman Catholic."

"Quite."

"He is a career officer, highly intelligent, law degree as well as Bachelor of Science, two years' active service U.S. Army Intelligence during the Korean conflict. Five feet, ten and a half inches tall, weighs approximately one hundred sixty pounds, blond hair with some gray, blue eyes, clean-featured, no visible distinguishing marks or scars. That's all we have at the moment. Does that sound like your man?"

"Yes."

"In that case, I have a query to you from higher channels. Do you wish our department to take any action or render further assistance?"

"Not at the moment. If I find I require your assistance I shall get back to you."

"Very good, I'll ring off now, then."

"Right you are."

Donovan replaced the receiver and went back through the small lounge. The American was still dozing. He went into the kitchen to confer with McGregor. They returned to the lounge.

Noah dreamed someone touched him. He started, awoke. Donovan was stepping back from him. He had Noah's passport in his hand. And Noah's pistol, which Donovan stuck in his belt.

"What the hell—" Something sharp prodded his shoulder and he instinctively leaned back away from it. McGregor was beside him with a large, ugly, automatic pistol in his hand.

"That is a Webley-Scott point four-five-five self-loading pistol. Quite powerful and accurate. Sergeant-Major McGregor is something of a handgun expert. Please do not make any sudden or foolish movements, Major Peterson." Donovan continued to rifle through the pages of the passport as he talked. Noah's head ached and his pride hurt. He felt an incompetent bungler. Donovan tossed the passport into Noah's lap. He sat down in the easy chair and put his feet up on the footstool. He motioned to McGregor and he backed away, sat on a couch a few feet away, rested the pistol on his thigh. "What is the purpose of this deception, Major Peterson? You're no more a literary agent than I am Brendan Behan. You're a policeman from St. Louis, Missouri, in the United States."

"I suspect you know as well as I why I am here, Colonel."

Donovan smiled appreciatively. "That's not a bad gambit, Major, but you'll have to do better for me. Why are you here? Why the deception?"

Noah shook his head. "I don't have to answer that."

Donovan removed his glasses. His eyes were amber, a little like cat's eyes in the poor light. They were a shock. Noah wondered if it were the whisky and beer. Those eyes gripped him, penetrated him. They knew . . . what? . . . He didn't know, but . . . there was an absolute quality to them . . . a finality he had never encountered before. They were quite chilling.

"I don't believe you understand, Major. I can kill you or have you killed and disposed of. Not a flower will be cut, no mass will be said, not a sparrow will cease to sing. It will be as nothing. You will die and there will be nothing more to it than that."

"Why would you want to do that? Why am I threatening to you? Why should you fear me enough to kill me?"

Donovan frowned. "Is this how it is done in America? When you interrogate a prisoner, do you allow him to answer questions with questions?" He shrugged. "Mercenary soldiers make enemies. Some of them have been known to have long memories for revenge."

Noah tried to swallow. His throat was dry. "Could I have a glass of water?" Donovan nodded and McGregor tossed him the automatic, left the room. He brought back a tumbler of water and handed it to Noah. He sat on the couch again.

McGregor had another of the odd-gripped automatic pistols. The water was cool, had a hard mineral taste. Noah drank it all.

"You've had time enough to compose yourself now, Major. I ask you for the last time—why are you here?"

Those eyes were hard to meet. "I suspect you and your men of robbery, murder, arson, bombing, and incitement to riot in my city a few weeks ago."

"Much better, Major. That's very candid. You are referring to the event the press have labeled the 'Great St. Louis Massacre.' "

"Yes."

"What did you expect to do about it?"

Noah shrugged. "I don't know."

"You can do nothing. But your conscience wouldn't allow you to just let it go."

"That's right."

Donovan stared hard at him for a few seconds, then nodded. "Of course, you were at the airport the day I arrived. And at the investigation of the bombing of the bar."

"Yes."

Donovan nodded again as if to himself. "Troublesome things, consciences. They make great difficulties for so many."

"You're implying that you do not have one."

Donovan smiled. The smile reached into his eyes, but it was not a comfortable humor. It was cold, detached, ironic laughter flickering in amber absolute. Noah wished he would put the glasses back on.

"I had one once. It caused great difficulties. I died from it in Sligo in the raid that killed my brother."

Noah was not sure he had heard right. He said nothing. Donovan seemed to go into himself. They all sat silently. Noah was wrung out. He was too tired now even to be afraid. Donovan was not there. The silence stretched for minutes. Finally, Donovan's eyes came back into focus. He looked calmly at Noah for a long minute, judging him, sizing him up. Noah felt his life hanging delicately. Donovan put his glasses back on.

"You have been candid enough, Major. I shall attempt to equal your candor. It is as you suspect." McGregor glanced at Donovan, but said nothing. "Certain arrangements have been made with your government. The thing is ended. You can never prove your suspicions publicly. Should you even try, I would not have to do anything, you would be stopped by your own government. I have no desire to kill you. Or cause you to be killed. That will not be necessary if you accept the reality of the situation. You can do nothing. You are powerless and impotent. You must let it alone. Go home and resume your life. Some things cannot be changed." He paused to light a cigar. "You will be watched now for a time. You have brought that on yourself by coming here, but if you will do as I say, no harm need come to you."

McGregor stirred slightly, but said nothing. Donovan did not even glance at him. Noah stared into the fire. It was dwindling away. Was this evil? The evil beyond the law of man and society, beyond mere criminality? So calm. So bland. So self-assured. The evil of his youth, of the catechism, of the devil was intense, charged with emotion. In his belief it had possessed a malevolence of spirit, a fiery, pure hatred. Was this evil then? Just one more business deal, another contract—sleazy and violent, but unemotional, ordinary, a routine matter.

"Do you feel nothing about what you have done?"

Donovan shook his head negatively. "Not a thing."

"You're another Hitler."

Again Donovan shook his head negatively. "Not at all. I espouse no politics, no nationalism, no religion, no racism—nothing. I have done what I have done for simple, direct, personal gain, and I cloak it in no rhetoric of any sort. I neither applaud nor apologize for my actions. I do not care in the slightest about any man's approval or disapproval.

That is not at all like Hitler. It is better or worse or neutrally different, but it is not the same."

"And God's approval?"

"He does not exist."

"You say that as if you know."

"I do."

"I cannot believe that."

"That is your privilege, Major Peterson."

"You don't proselytize either."

"I don't care what any other man thinks. You have to care to proselytize. You have to be a zealot. And, in any case, it isn't possible. You either know it or you don't."

"Then you must think the rest of us fools."

"Of course."

Noah was too tired to be angry. He felt small and, as Donovan had said, impotent. The fire was almost out. The late afternoon sky had become gray again. Rain was starting to fall once more.

"Will you do what I say, Major Peterson? Will you go home and let it alone? I have no desire for your death, but you must not be mistaken about its inevitability if you persist. In this sort of game, one chance is more than you usually get."

"Am I expected to thank you?"

"Not at all. It wouldn't move me. Will you do what I say?"

"I don't seem to have much choice, do I?"

"None at all. Death or life, whichever you prefer, but that is the extent of it."

Noah sighed. "I shouldn't have been so naive. All right, Colonel Donovan. I'm going home."

"Good. That's grand then. Your family will be happy to have you back, I'm sure."

"How do you know I have a family?"

"I have been at pains to make it clear, Major, arrangements have been made with your government. I only needed to lift the telephone receiver after talking with Charles to learn who you really were. I need only lift the receiver again to dispose of any difficulty I encounter.''

"The CIA?"

"Does it matter?"

"No. I suppose not." He put his passport back in his pocket and rose slowly. Donovan and McGregor walked behind him to the door, their pistols hanging at their sides.

Afterward, McGregor argued that they should have him killed. Donovan disagreed.

"I don't think so, Andrew. That can always be done if it is necessary, but overreacting can cause problems of its own. His death would not undo us. It would be handled competently, I'm sure, but each further act increases the risk, however slightly. I don't believe in unnecessary risks."

Noah drove quickly back to the West Lodge. He packed and paid his bill. He was on the road to Cork in fifty minutes. He felt defeated and foolish. He thought he wanted nothing further than to get out of Ireland that night, depart for home the next day. He caught the night flight to London. He had not even booked a room. He read his travel guide on the flight. He decided on the Cumberland across from the Marble Arch in Hyde Park. The book said it was a large, American-style, commercial hotel and that was all he wanted. A clean, anonymous room.

He went out for a late dinner at a nearby restaurant—a Chinese room near the Cordon Bleu cooking school. He hardly tasted the food and the wine disagreed with his already disrupted physiology. What could he do? He had butchered it. Now he had no gun. Donovan was alerted. He was probably being watched. Perhaps he was not cut out for murder. Wasn't ruthless enough, no matter what rage he felt.

As he stopped at the circular desk for his key, he noticed across from him a black man who looked familiar. He heard the man speak. He was an American, from his accent probably from one of the border states. In his room he took out the dossier again. The man was in the photograph with Donovan and the other staff officers. Captain Jackson. The arrogance. There they all were going about their lives as if they were perfectly respectable citizens instead of what they really were. Damn them! The anger was beginning to come again. But what could he do? There were so many of them.

When he came out of the dining room after a late breakfast the next morning, he saw the black mercenary, Jackson, crossing the lobby. He followed him out. The sidewalks were crowded with pedestrian traffic and Noah had no great difficulty in following closely without being too obvious.

Jackson crossed to the south side of Oxford Street and within a few blocks turned south on one of the less busy side streets. Here Noah had to fall back a little because pedestrian traffic was much lighter, but he could see Jackson at a greater distance. This was the chic Mayfair district. These side streets contained rows of elegant brownstone houses. Some had been divided into apartments or very elegant offices or housed wealthy clubs—a few remained residences. Not far south of Oxford Street, Jackson crossed the street, turned in at the entrance of one such building. Noah crossed and began to approach at a slow pace so that he could get a good look on one pass.

The houses he was approaching were four stories high with short flights of stone steps to massive double wood doors. Most had discreet brass plates by these entrance doors with the name of the family or club or business within. Noah began studying them as if he were looking for a particular address. It would give him longer to look when he came to Jackson's building. He was one door away when he stood completely still, stunned. The brass plate he was staring at read:

### IRISH WEST AFRICA COMPANY

But he was *sure* Jackson had gone in the next door. He moved along to it. It had an identical brass plate with an identical inscription. As did the next two doors as well. Four brownstones! Like some posh club for retired officers from the Indian service. Noah walked on down the street and turned the corner. He stopped and leaned against a railing. He had no words for the anger he felt. Damn them!

He went back to the Cumberland and told them he wished to extend his stay. He had only booked the room for one night. They were quite agreeable, especially when he paid two weeks' rent in advance.

For several days, Noah observed the brownstones of the Irish West Africa Company. He generally walked by on the opposite side of the street, though not always. He never made more than one pass in an hour and he varied his dress and pace quite radically. There seemed to be workmen about much of the time; carpenters, plumbers, plasterers, furniture and appliance delivery men. From overheard conversation and a few casual remarks he passed with some of them, he learned the brownstones were being renovated into something like ninety suites or apartments.

"The extra delux, I can tell you, governor. These 'ere gents must be the real quality. You wouldn't think it by the look of them. Right ordinary blokes they appears. But I don't know no ordinary blokes what lives in digs like these 'ere."

One of the photographs in the dossier had Donovan with most of his men. It was not a particularly good photograph, but Noah began studying it at night. He became familiar with all the faces in it. More and more, during his daytime observance he saw faces from the photograph entering and leaving the brownstones. Apparently the company was moving into its new quarters. It seemed the first three brownstones were completed and the fourth nearly so. He saw Captain Jackson several more times, and once the executive officer, Major Turrman.

During this time, Noah was careful to observe if *he* was being tailed. He was sure he was not. He *had* changed taxis several times on his way from Heathrow to the Cumberland and he *had* registered under an assumed name. They weren't on to him yet.

Toward the end of the first week of December, he went out for a night observation. He had become so obsessed with the IWACs that he ate, slept, and observed. He did almost nothing else. The night was very cold, but clear and windless. He was dressed warmly and carried a flask of single-malt Scotch, which he found very soothing these days. He had found a basement entrance across from the fourth brownstone from which he could observe at night. He took a roundabout route and came up from the south. Sounds carried clearly on the windless air and he began to place his footsteps as noiselessly as possible as he approached.

There was a line of three taxis waiting in front of the IWAC brownstones. They were facing north so he was able to slip into his basement entrance unobserved. He sipped some of the Scotch. It was his first drink that day. He found he was having to watch himself, force himself to wait until evening to have his first drink else he would likely be bagged earlier and earlier each day. He pulled the collar of his overcoat up. He was cold.

There were many lights on across the street. He could see figures moving back and forth across the windows. In one of the first floor rooms, a party of some sort seemed to be in progress. Some of the figures were attractive women. Everyone was dressed to the hilt. He saw champagne glasses and people laughing.

He took several long swallows of Scotch. He knelt below ground level and lit a cigarette. When he stood up, he held the cupped cigarette at his side, ducked down when he wanted to take a drag on it. He was worried about Elizabeth. He hadn't called her for three days because the last conversation had been too painful. He hadn't much he dared tell her and she was worried and miserable. St. Louis seemed a time warp away, as if it were not only a different place but from some other lifetime of his. He ground out the cigarette, then picked it up and flicked it through the railings. His fingers grazed the cold metal and he wished he had remembered to buy gloves.

He took two more long swallows of whisky. It gave him the illusion of warmth for a short while and it didn't seem to be getting to his head as quickly tonight. Probably because he had eaten a decent supper. For a change.

He was horny too. Noah and Elizabeth had remained constant and frequent lovers throughout twenty years of marriage. They were rarely separated and rarely continent for more than a day or two. And Noah was not the kind of man who could seek out a convenient, paid or unpaid, surrogate. The doors of the brownstone he had followed Jackson to the first time came open. Bright light from within flooded out and down the steps. Three couples came out. They were all in lavish evening clothes. Captain Jackson and a tall blond dream. Major Turrman and a heavy-breasted redhead. A young blonde, even more spectacular than Captain Jackson's. The last man was Colonel Donovan. He said something Noah couldn't hear. They all laughed. Donovan seemed to glance around and Noah stepped back instinctively though there was no way Donovan could see him. They were all still laughing as they entered the taxis. The laughter haunted his ears long after the taxis had pulled away. It had had the unmistakable ring of people in the midst of pure pleasure. He sank down and sat with his back against a cold stone wall. He paid little attention to how long he sat there or to the cold. He finished the flask of Scotch and several cigarettes. That was it, then. He'd played out the string. He had to try again. Coldly. Quickly. No mercy. He would have to get a gun. He had a sudden urge to get back to the hotel. He had another bottle and a half of single-malt Scotch in his room and he was desperately thirsty. He took no care to muffle his footsteps now. They were clear on the night air. As he walked north toward Oxford Street, he glanced up at the brownstones. The party was still going on.

Chief Inspector Sir David Ramsey of Scotland Yard was a handsome silver-haired, fit-looking man in his late fifties. His office in the new Yard building was modern and spacious and luxuriously furnished. He was a busy man, but he was also a gracious man. He was very patient and cordial to Noah.

"So you're on a bit of busman's holiday, er," he glanced down at the credentials Noah had presented him, "Major Peterson."

"Yes, that's it, Sir David. And no policeman from anywhere on the globe could pass up the opportunity to visit Scotland Yard while in London."

Ramsey smiled. Nice American chap. Not like some of them. "I should imagine you'd like a bit of a Cook's tour, so to speak."

"I would indeed, if it wouldn't be too much bother for someone to show me around. I'm sure you're far too busy, Sir David. I hadn't intended to bother you, but when I spoke to the Sergeant, he was insistent upon taking me to you."

"Quite right, too. We're all busy here, but not too busy to preen a bit for a brother officer. Hands across the sea and all that."

"You are most gracious, Sir David."

"Yes, well, hmmph, this morning is a trifle crowded. I wonder if you might be able to return after luncheon and I could show you around then?"

"Certainly. That's very kind of you."

"Not at all, my dear fellow. Glad to have you."

After Noah had left, Ramsey sat at his desk in thought for a few minutes. He didn't like to do it, but unannounced as he was, the fellow had to be checked out. He looked in a small notebook in a desk drawer to dial the number properly.

"Knightsbridge four eight hundred. Vassar speaking."

"Ramsey of the yard, here. Wonder if you might run a check for me on an American police officer who dropped in here this morning unannounced. Fellow seems all right—just wants a tour, but we like to check these things out."

"Certainly, Sir David. That's what we're here for. If I could have the officer's name?"

"Peterson. A Major Noah Peterson of St. Louis, Missouri. I took his passport number on the qt, if that would help."

"Very much, Sir David."

Ramsey read the number and the voice asked him to hold the line. Ramsey doodled on a telephone pad as he waited.

"Sir David?"

"Still here."

"That is the correct passport number for Major Noah Peterson of the St. Louis, Missouri, Police Department. Blond, blue-eyed, average build, fortyish?"

"That's the man. Chap's all right then."

"A distinguished law enforcement officer. You wouldn't happen to know where he's staying? The Ambassador might want to invite him to cocktails while he's here."

"MMmm, believe he mentioned something about the Cumberland. I can check with him this afternoon if you like."

"If you would, and ring me back, Sir David. And don't mention the party to Peterson. The Ambassador loves to spring surprises on VIPs, as you know."

"Yes, of course. I haven't forgotten my last birthday. A real shocker, that was. I'll ring you back after he's left."

"Thank you, Sir David."

Damned prompt and efficient information these CIA johnies had. Better than some people gave them credit for. Ramsey turned back to work. If Peterson was all that distinguished, he would have to clear enough time to give him the number one tour. Couldn't really do less.

After lunch, Ramsey gave Noah the top of the line tour. He rather liked Peterson. Nice chap. Properly impressed with the history and the marvels of the Yard. Quite interested in the down to earth details of British law enforcement, especially handgun control.

"We can't get the laws through Congress that we need to control handgun traffic. The politicians won't do it."

"We're very fortunate in that respect, Major. It doesn't keep the guns out of the hands of hard case fellows, but that really isn't the point, is it? It cuts the number of family murders in the heat of argument."

"Yes, that's the idea. Do you have much trouble with illegal traffic in handguns?"

"Not too much. The hard-nosed chaps have them, of course, and just now we've got some problems with the IRA johnies, but we've a great deal less trouble than I should imagine you run into at home."

"Yes, some days it seems everybody in America has a gun or two in the house. We do what we can with undercover squads after the illegal trade, but when guns are so readily available legally—it hardly scratches the surface. Do your men do much undercover work on your illegal trade?"

"Not a great deal. It's a difficult thing to put a cap on. We try to keep informed, of course, and we go after the IRA fairly hard, but that's most of it. If someone really wants a gun they can go into some of the Irish pubs and get one easily enough. Fortunately, our tradition is rather the opposite. It's only the few who want pistols."

"I wish it were true in America."

After Noah left, Ramsey rang up the Knightsbridge number and confirmed that he was staying at the Cumberland. The man thanked him on behalf of the Ambassador.

Noah took a taxi straight back to the Cumberland. He packed up his handbag and checked out. He didn't know how long he had, but he was sure it wasn't much time. Ramsey would *have* to have run a check on him, credentials or no, and that would get back to the CIA or whoever was helping Donovan. They would come after him.

He walked less than a dozen blocks to a very small hotel, the Ryder Street Chambers. He had a suite for less than his room at the Cumberland had cost. It had overstuffed furniture, clean, but ancient wallpaper and a generally Victorian flavor. The elevator seemed as if it might date from the Victorian era. He was not much concerned with his surroundings any longer. He knew he hadn't much time left. Certainly none to get comfortable in.

He went to several large clothing stores looking for what he imagined might pass for working-class clothes. He settled on wash pants and a gray shirt, Clark's desert boots and a brown leather aviator jacket and cloth cap. He took the purchases back to his suite and did what he could to rough them up, take the newness and stiffness out of them, to age them. It wasn't much, but at least they didn't look as fresh off the rack as they had. He put them on and slipped out again. It was early evening now.

He had a list of pubs that he'd managed to cull from a conversation with the desk Sergeant. They were spread out across the city and by the third one, he was not at all sure where he was. The first four didn't seem right, but at the fifth he thought he heard more Irish accents and the atmosphere seemed more that of an enclave, a refuge in foreign, perhaps hostile, territory. He drank quietly for an hour. The only gambit he could think of was darts. He was the fifth best shooter in the very active St. Louis league. He took his pint and walked over by the row of three boards. He watched for a while, then asked politely, shyly, if he might join one of the games. There was a hesitation, then one tall, dark-haired man shrugged.

"Ah, sure. If you like."

He took a set of house darts, chubs—too heavy, really, and took three practice shots. He was keyed and intense. His first two shots were close to the center and the third was a dead bull. The men looked at him a bit differently. The tall man said his name was Dan Conners. They shook hands as Noah introduced himself as Liam Kennedy, an

American of Irish extraction. Fourth generation. Conners suggested they play a game of 301 for a pint.

"You do know the game?"

Noah smiled. "I do."

Connors won the cork shot to see who would shoot first. He didn't get his double to start scoring until his third dart—a double sixteen, leaving him two hundred sixty-nine. The men sucked in their breath or made small whistling sounds with their teeth as Noah broke with a ton—two double twenties and a single twenty, leaving him two hundred one. Connors shot well, but Noah shot better. His eleventh dart was a double sixteen, putting him out and winning the game. Connors ordered a fresh pint for each of them and Noah ordered a Paddy for each of the six men at that end of the bar.

Connors and Noah teamed up in doubles against all comers for pounds bets on each game. They won eleven straight matches in an hour and then gave up their board to fresh blood. They sat in a booth. Connors was a little smashed and very enthusiastic about his new friend. Obviously, eleven pounds was a good windfall for him.

Noah sipped his Guinness. In undercover work it was bad to push too hard too fast, but he didn't have time to set Connors up over a period of weeks or days. He just didn't know how much time he had. When Connors made some offhand remark about the trouble in the north of Ireland, Noah slipped in. He talked about Irish-American sentiment for the IRA. He said since he was from St. Louis, in the middle of America, he didn't have the contacts Boston or New York Irish had, but he had been thinking about donating some money. He gave Connors a hundred-pound note to give to whoever he might know that would see it got to the boyos.

Connors was very drunk by closing time and insisted Noah come back to his flat with him. It was a short walk to a dingy brick row house cut up into apartments. They sat on hard chairs at the table in the tiny kitchen. They drank straight from the Paddy's bottle Noah had bought as they left the pub. Connors's head drooped and his speech was fairly thick, sloppy, inarticulate. Noah steered the conversation to guns. He wanted to buy one as a souvenir to take back to America. A gun he could say had fought for the old sod, even if it hadn't actually done so. For show, like. Connors seemed to try to sober up. He forced himself upright in the chair and tried to focus on Noah's face, meet his eyes. His drunken glare was so absurd, Noah had to suppress his laughter.

"You wouldn't . . . be being," Connors waved his arms broadly in a gesture of contempt, "be being one of those . . CID lads out to trap a poor stupid paddy?"

Noah said, "No," quietly.

"Sure and you wouldn't. American. You're an American lad."

"Yes."

Connors produced a nasty little German automatic and some ammunition from a closet. A Walther .38. They haggled good-naturedly over the price and drank whisky. They settled on forty-five pounds only a few minutes before Connors passed out. Noah pocketed the pistol and ammunition, left the money in Connors's shirt pocket, and eased him into his bed. He left him lying on it fully clothed.

Outside, he walked rapidly in the cold until he was out of the district. He finally found a main thoroughfare, he didn't know the name of, got a taxi to take him back to his hotel. He was very drunk and tired, but he left a call for six a.m.

The young priest was tired. It was cold in the confessional and he hated having to take the early morning hours. The soft voice on the other side of the screen was American. The priest was frankly bored. He had not been paying a great deal of attention this morning. He chastised himself mentally, but apathetically. Suddenly, he stiffened. The tense and content of the man's last statement penetrated his indifference. He thought the man had said, "Forgive me, Father, for I am going to sin. I am going to kill a man."

Donovan lay naked on the bed of his apartment. He was both pleasantly relaxed and pleasantly aroused. The bed was wide and firm with fawn-colored silk sheets. The walls were a creamy tan and the carpet thick gold. He had decorated in an understated, non-stark, modern mode. The furniture was chocolate-brown and buttery leather and dark teak and a touch or two of chrome and glass like the five-foot cocktail table with chrome rim and legs and a top of cut crystal with a pattern of clean, simple squares. He had a large set of cut crystal chessmen that could be set up on it when he and Turrman played. They had close, exciting games of tournament caliber which Donovan almost always won or drew. He did not have a kitchenette, only a hot plate for tea because he did not like to cook, and the IWACs had retained an excellent chef, full-time, anyway. There was a luxurious bath and a small wet bar and a liquor closet with a full stock and a sixty-space wine rack. No television. He despised it. A top-quality stereo which was presently playing Charles Ives's "Three Places in New England." One wall of the bedroom was floor-to-ceiling book shelving that Donovan was only just beginning to fill by reading and rejecting or keeping volumes that pleased or displeased him. His apartment was the largest, both rooms twenty-four by twenty-four, and on the top floor with a lift just outside the door. A love of luxury and the money to satisfy it. What more could a man ask for?

Ginger Heath came out of the bathroom, toweling herself dry. His penis throbbed erect. She had green eyes, a sharp little nose, wide liquid mouth, what seemed at times an enlarged and serpentine tongue, and short blond hair with discreet flecks of red cut in something called a shag. Flawless tanned skin, slender body with high, modest, conical breasts, small nipples, and gold pubic hair. She was nineteen, an aspiring actress who had done two television commercials and a minor film part, liked marijuana and champagne, was not terribly bright, but amusing. She was savagely in love with Donovan, as only an intense young girl could be, and had even once mentioned the possibility of a child, which caused Donovan to laugh and, later, check her packet of pills to be sure she was taking them. Even after some years, Donovan was amazed at his attraction for women. It was one of the very few areas of his life which still held the ability to surprise him. Ginger also was more than fond of fucking and most forms of lovemaking. She smiled and set the towel on a chair.

"Come here, pet."

She crossed to the bed and, without preliminary of any sort, knelt between his legs and took his penis in her mouth. Donovan closed his eyes and felt his scrotal skin tighten as she licked his balls. She crawled forward, her legs outside his. He opened his eyes and watched her inch slightly forward and down until the head of his penis entered her vagina. She slid down very slowly. Their eyes met.

"God, how I love you, Donovan."

He pulled her forward until she lay atop him. Their tongues tangled, hips began rhythmic rock.

"You're a darling girl, Ginger. I love you as I can."

"I know. I know. I know. I know . . . I . . . know . . . I . . . know . . . DONOVAN!"


The correspondent was amazed by the luxury of Donovan's apartment, the IWAC's quarters. Donovan was giving him lunch and a beautiful lunch it was. They must have a wizard of a chef. He wondered where the money came from. He couldn't believe the Imbannailand expedition had been *that* profitable.

"So you're going to America, after all, Charles?"

"It was a piece of great good fortune, after you advised me that the literary agent wasn't genuine. The editor of the magazine rang me the next day to see if I wanted to be their

White House correspondent. How could I refuse? The salary and expenses are very generous and I believe I shall have time to finish the book in a year or so. Perhaps by then I will have made contact with American publishers and can do an American edition anyway."

"That would be lovely for you, Charles." Donovan poured more Chablis.

"I still do not understand, mon Colonel, why the American practiced the deception on me? To get to you?"

Donovan did not answer at once. He opened a gold and leather cigar box. The correspondent declined. Donovan bit off the tip, lit the cigar, blew smoke upward. He took a drink of wine. The correspondent was patient. He had known Donovan long. You could not hurry the man if he was deliberating an answer.

"What kind of man do you think I am, Charles?"

The correspondent frowned. *That* was a difficult question to answer. Not because you had to be diplomatic. Donovan was not easily offended. What kind of man was Donovan? He had been thinking about this very thing as he worked on his outline.

"A strange man, perhaps. You have such a unique history. Also a compelling man, fascinating and dangerous." He smiled. "I have a line I shall use in the book. I thought of it the day you told me the Imbannailand war was going to end." He coughed lightly. "I thought—he is like an accident always ready to happen." The correspondent flushed slightly.

Donovan nodded. "I think that's fair. A good line too." He tapped a quarter inch of ash into a tray. "Do you think I'm a vain man?"

The correspondent laughed. That was not a hard question. It was simple. "No, mon Colonel. You are a proud man, a hard man, self-contained—remarkably so—but I would not say you are a vain man."

"That seems about right, Charles. Yet I do have one small vanity that you have helped to prick with your idea

223

for a biography. I wish to be fully known. Not understood, analyzed, but known. What I have done.''

The journalist made a small self-deprecating gesture with his hands. "In my modest way I shall try to satisfy that modest vanity."

"That is the problem. You can't, Charles, because you do not know it all. You do not know the final campaign. And you cannot know it unless you agree to certain terms. If you do, I will explain why the American practiced the deception."

"What are the terms, mon Colonel?"

"How old are you, Charles?"

"Forty. What has that to do with it?"

"A great deal. More wine?"

"Please." Donovan poured.

"You must agree not to publish what I tell you until after, not only I am dead, but after all of the Irish West Africa Company has shuffled off this mortal coil. Since the youngest members are in their late twenties, it makes it likely that you would have to write this final chapter as an addition for an expanded edition that would be published after your own death. Unless you live to be a hundred or so. You would have to give it to a most reliable man along with a list of the company members and sufficient funds for them to be kept track of. I would be willing to supply the funds for that. If you or anyone else tried to publish this information before such time, you would be killed."

"Mon dieu."

"Yes."

The journalist thought. Posthumous publication was not a terribly attractive proposition. He liked literary benefits that came in one's lifetime. Still . . . if the information was sufficiently spectacular and it seemed likely to be . . . one would gain a certain literary immortality . . . which did have a certain appeal. . . .

"All right, mon Colonel. I agree."

"You must be sure, Charles. No journalistic fervor or moral qualms after I tell you or you're a dead man."

"I understand. You have known me, mon Colonel. You know I am a man who can keep information to himself."

"Yes. Otherwise I wouldn't consider this." Donovan drained his glass. He tapped a half inch of ash off his cigar, puffed on it. "You say I am like an accident that is always ready to happen. I have happened. The American was a police official from St. Louis, Missouri, in the United States of America."

"I do not understand, mon Colonel."

"Of course not, Charles. I'm telling you. Where do you think all the money for this luxurious club has come from?" The correspondent shook his head. "We fought a kind of *money war*. Which would be a fine title for your final chapter. You remember what the international press referred to as the 'Great St. Louis Massacre,' which occurred last month? You read of it?"

"You? Your men? The Irish West Africa Company!" Donovan nodded slowly.

The correspondent could not speak, could not even ask questions as Donovan laid out the entire campaign from the first conversation with Captain Jackson on the flight from Imbannailand, through the planning, procurement, invasion, operation, retreat, and the encounter with Noah Peterson.

It was mid-afternoon. "Now you know, Charles. But beware. No matter how tempting a press coup it seems, they would not get all of us fast enough, and either one of us or the CIA would kill you. And probably cover up the story so that your death would be totally in vain."

"The story does not tempt me, Colonel Donovan. I am not even sure it should be published after the death of the company. I am not sure it should ever be published."

"Ah, well, you can do as you like, Charles. Under the stated conditions. I would prefer to have it all known some

225

day, but when the time comes, I shan't care. Use your own discretion. As long as you observe the conditions."

"Certainly. I shall have to think about it."

Donovan smiled. "Let me know what you decide."

The correspondent nodded. "I quite understand. Quite."

Donovan offered to take the correspondent to a rather fine restaurant that evening for an after-theater dinner. He was about to decline, but at that moment, Ginger Heath came in from a shopping expedition. She was one of the most exquisite women the journalist had ever seen. She had a not as spectacular, but still quite beautiful friend with her. Donovan introduced them. It was arranged that the four of them should go to the theater and dine afterward. They had a short drink together to seal the bargain. The friend *was* beautiful. And friendly. Charity Whitney or some such ridiculous name. The journalist went back to his hotel. He would not have believed any man in the world but Donovan. Donovan was not a fanciful man. If he told you a serious thing, it was so.

Donovan removed the bottles of champagne and Guinness stout from the ice bucket and opened them. He retrieved four completely iced, tulip-shaped champagne glasses from the freezer in his wet bar. He set them on the counter and began pouring.

"Donovan's Black Velvet. Three parts champagne to one part Guinness. Champagne first and gently top with Guinness so that the heavier stout glides down and through without bruising the champagne." He handed the glasses around. "A drink fit for Gods and Goddesses."

The correspondent smiled. "Napolean's favorite drink."

"Yes, but he used more stout. Too heavy that way." Donovan came out from behind the bar. "I say, Charles, you are looking elegant tonight. I didn't know you had it in you."

The journalist flushed slightly. He *was* unaccustomed to evening clothes, but the midnight-blue jacket with vest rather than cummerbund did reduce the portly appearance of his figure. Donovan, as always, seemed at home with whatever he did. His black-on-black brocade double-breasted tuxedo with Continental tie and pale-blue ruffled shirt seemed to fit like skin. The young ladies were stunning in matching silver metallic gowns and fur wraps.

"I should have to be elegant to travel in this company."

"Very good, Charles, your English is improving rapidly. You see, ladies, I told you he was a delightful man."

The Whitney girl, who was clinging to the correspondent's arm, giggled. "I think he's adorable. I just love Frenchmen."

The correspondent smiled broadly. "On behalf of myself and my fellow countrymen, I thank you. I shall endeavor not to disappoint you in the slightest way."

She giggled. "Adorable."

Donovan mixed his concoction three more times in forty or fifty minutes. They nibbled cold shrimp cocktail, oysters on the half shell, lightly breaded, deep fried mushrooms. Everyone was very gay and animated. The correspondent, whose fortunes with women were not always good, was entranced. The Whitney girl was affectionate and had already whispered that they should adjourn to her apartment after dinner. It was obvious, to even a naive eye, that Donovan and Ginger Heath were lovers. Even their casual touches were so charged observers could feel the electricity.

The correspondent shook his head to himself. He did not know what to think of Donovan. So many things Donovan had done should repel him. He was a, more or less, average French-style nominal Catholic. A priest who abandoned his vows was a mad, renegade creature. Terrorism, IRA brand or any other, was personally repugnant to the journalist. Donovan had been a no-quarter combat officer and for pay. And his . . . *money war* in America was almost a synthesis of evil.

But he was often, personally, charming. He was a good

. . . *friend* came closest to the right word but was not exactly correct. He was always competent and at ease with what he did, and occasionally he was brilliant. He was tough, ruthless, self-contained, and unemotional. In some ways he seemed a synthesis of the qualities that were generally considered admirable in a twentieth-century secular man. The urbane and civilized man with no hatred or vengeance in his heart; quite capable of murder when deemed necessary; with a healthy self-interest closely calculating profit, loss, risk. Would not Sartre or Camus have understood Donovan perfectly? They would not have applauded him, certainly, but they could not *honestly* have condemned him.

"Mon Colonel, I have decided you are right. The whole story should be known. At the appropriate time."

"I'm glad you agree, Charles. In some ways it might prove an illuminating glance at our century."

"I was thinking along similar lines."

It was snowing as they came out of the brownstone and began to descend to the waiting taxi. The Whitney girl was huddling close, ostensibly for warmth. It was a most agreeable sensation. He saw a figure walking across the street toward them. He did not pay much attention. Some working-class man in rough leather jacket and cap. He and Donovan stood by the taxi door to hand the ladies in. The man was only five meters or so away when he glanced at him again. It was the American. He looked terrible; unshaven, pale, shaky; he had something in his hand. A gun.

"Mon Colonel—!"

Flame came from the barrel of the gun and the three explosions overpowered the rest of his exclamation. Donovan was smashed back against the door of the cab, nearly ripping it off its hinges and then he slipped to the ground. He lay half upright with his head and upper body propped by the taxi door. The young girls were both screaming incomprehensibly and Ginger Heath was trying to claw her way

228

past the correspondent to get to Donovan. The American stood staring down at Donovan. The correspondent was frozen in place. Shocked. He held the girl back. Red stains were soaking through Donovan's evening clothes at three places on his broad chest. He reached up in an agony of slow motion and removed his sunglasses.

Donovan smiled, "The one just man theory, Major Peterson?"

"Nothing that sophisticated, Colonel. My oldest son was killed by your bomb at the Arena. You can't just let that pass."

Donovan nodded, "Quite right. You'd better run now. My men are coming. You've done me, but you can't kill them all." McGregor and a dozen other IWACs came lunging out the door and down the steps. Peterson turned his gun on them. They stopped for a split second. McGregor looked down at Donovan and then back at Peterson. His face was filled with grief and rage.

"You!" he spat and began walking toward Noah. The other men began to follow him.

Donovan shouted, "Sergeant-Major!" Blood sprayed past his lips. "Not here. Not now." McGregor and the men halted, stared at Donovan in confusion. Donovan looked up at Noah. "Go now, Major. You will be killed, but not here, not now. Go now and I promise you nothing will happen to your family."

Noah sneered, "You promise!"

Donovan smiled, "I have never broken my word to any man."

Noah hesitated, then put the gun in his pocket, turned and walked away without looking back. Donovan motioned McGregor to bend down close to him.

"Andrew, you must follow him. See where he goes, but do nothing to him. Phone Major Turrman and report his location as soon as you can."

"Yes, Colonel."

"Good man. Off you go." McGregor motioned the other men back and began walking after Peterson. Donovan coughed and blood came out of his mouth.

Major Turrman came out. He directed the men to carry Donovan inside to the executive study. He gave the taxi driver a hundred-pound note and told him to get lost, which the frightened man was only too happy to do. The correspondent helped the sobbing girls up the steps and inside.

Donovan was laid on a couch in the study. Turrman allowed the correspondent and Ginger Heath in the room. No one else. The girl sat holding Donovan's hand. She managed to stop crying when Donovan asked her to in his most gentle voice.

"There's a good girl, my pet. Major."

"Yes, Colonel."

"You know what has to be done."

"Yes, Colonel."

"You must tell the . . . police . . . " He paused, laboring for breath. "Tell the police no one recognized the assailant and he got away . . . probably a grudge killing from one of our . . . African campaigns."

"Yes, Colonel."

"You'd better make the call now." Turrman nodded and went to the desk phone, dialed.

"Yes, Vassar, this if Radcliffe. Wellesley has been shot by Major Peterson. A man is following him and will phone me as soon as he comes to rest. I'll pass his location on to you as soon as I have it . . . not yet, but soon. . . . No, no question about the identity." He hung up.

"You'll have to look after the lads now, Major."

"I will, Colonel."

Donovan smiled at the correspondent. "Ah, well, now you've seen it all, Charles." He tugged slightly at the girl's hand. "Give us a kiss, pet." She took his head gently in her hands and kissed him softly on the lips. "Grand. You're a darling girl, Ginger. The love of my life." He coughed and blood sprayed from his mouth. He closed his eyes and sighed. He stiffened and then relaxed. Turrman took his hand from the girl and felt for a pulse. He touched the side of Donovan's neck for a pulse. Held a raveling from his jacket within an inch of Donovan's nose for respiration. The correspondent could see that it didn't move. Turrman took two florins from his pocket and put them on Donovan's eyes.

"The Colonel is dead."

The girl started to weep again, but softly this time. The correspondent looked down at his hands. They held Donovan's sunglasses. One silver lens was cracked and the sidepieces were bent. There was some blood on the glasses. It was caking now. The journalist noticed that some of it had soiled his fingers with dark red smudges and flakes. He took a handkerchief from his pocket and wrapped the glasses carefully. He put them in a side pocket of his jacket. He did not cry. His emotion was not like that. He felt some terrible void where he had not known anything rested. Such a strange man. He supposed it was because you rarely met a man who was so wholly of a piece. Such a strange man.

Much later, he took the Whitney girl back to his hotel room. She spent the night because she did not want to be alone. He had never experienced such intense lovemaking in his life.

Noah lay on the bed in his hotel suite in the dark. Waiting. He knew they would come. He was too tired to run. Too tired and sick at heart. And if he did get home, it would only put Liz and the kids in danger. And Bucky. They would come for him there.

"The one just man theory," Donovan had said. Nothing like that at all. Just bitter, angry, vengeance. Simple. Direct.

He heard the ancient lift clattering upward. That was about right. He had been lying on his bed for over three hours. He found he was terrified. He reached for the gun, then pulled his hand back. No. There was no way out.

Sounds came of someone fiddling with the lock on his

suite door. He lay perfectly still, breathing lightly, but he could not make his muscles stop tensing and his heart seemed like a machine gun in his chest.

A needle beam of light shone in the sitting room. Three men slipped in the door. The last man in was Major Turrman. One of the men came to the door of the bedroom. He shone the light in Noah's eyes.

"He's here."

The other two followed the man into the room. The one with the pencil light also carried a revolver with a silencer on the end. Major Turrman seemed unarmed. The third man carried a small black bag.

"Looks to me like he's figured it all out. Decided to take it sensibly. The easy way, Major Peterson?" Noah did not speak. "Good."

Turrman snapped, "Get on with it!"

"You're here on sufferance, my friend, as an observer. So you just shut up and keep shut up."

"I'm here because I told your *superiors* that I needed to come and they responded to my wishes. Now stop this sadistic cat and mouse and get it done."

The third man had been paying no attention to the squabble. He set his bag down and opened it. He removed an empty hypodermic, a medium-size bottle, and a cloth. He laid them out on the night table and turned to the first man.

"Shut up yourself, Harry. And put that stupid revolver away." He held up Noah's gun. "He has a pistol right here. He could have killed you easily." The man dropped Noah's automatic into his bag. He opened the bottle and began dousing a cloth with liquid. Noah smelled chloroform. He looked at Turrman.

"Is Donovan dead?"

Turrman nodded. "Yes. The Colonel is dead."

"Good!" Noah was surprised at the emotion with which he spat the word. Turrman shook his head negatively.

"No. But it is done and cannot be changed. I am truly sorry you have meddled in this, Major."

The man pressed the cloth over Noah's nose. He forced himself not to struggle. He breathed deeply. In a few seconds a creamy sleep quality came over him and he drifted out of consciousness.

After a minute the man took the cloth away. He dropped it into the bag. He capped the bottle and put it away. He undid Noah's belt, loosened his trousers and pulled them down halfway. He rolled him over on his stomach.

"Give me some light here, Harry."

He picked up the syringe and looked at it. He had the man move the light about until he found a large blood vessel on the back of the leg, just above the knee. He inserted the needle quickly, depressed the plunger, and withdrew it. He carefully sponged away the tiny bit of blood, redid Noah's trousers, and turned him over.

"Air bubble?" asked Turrman.

"Yes." They went into the sitting room. "Open the window, Harry. We want the chloroform smell gone when they find him in the morning. Nothing to worry about. Myocardial infarction. Happens to men in their forties sometimes. They never look for the needle mark if they don't know to look." Noah was dead less than four hours after he had shot Donovan.

When the report came to the DDP, it took him less than thirty seconds to recognize Noah's name and the context in which he knew it. He talked with no one, but decided himself what action had to be taken. Brooke thought about taking it up with the NSC, but no.

He smiled contemptuously to himself. "My dear Brooke, you know it's the sort of thing they want done but do not want to know about. See no evil, hear no evil, speak no evil."

Bucky was getting out of his car in front of a restaurant on a side street. He got out on the street side, slowly. As he walked toward the front of the car, a black sedan came

233

down the street behind him at sixty miles an hour. He didn't even have time to look back. He was thrown into the air and across the row of parked cars, hit the side of a brick building, and bounced on the pavement. He was dead before Margeret could run the short distance to his side. The car had turned a corner and was gone.

# EPILOGUE: **PEACE**

Truly, to tell lies is not honorable;
But when the truth entails tremendous ruin,
To speak dishonorably is pardonable.

*Sophocles*

On Christmas afternoon at precisely 1:11 p.m., scheduled thus so as to slide neatly into a twenty-three minute slot between football games and thus offend no fans, the President of the United States commandeered air time from all three networks for a major television address. Rumors had been circulating for three days that there would be a major foreign policy announcement, and ratings published later indicated that seventy-four percent of all the television sets in America were tuned in to the presidential speech.

The President, for once, was looking alert and exuberant and nicely turned out in a blue suit with maize pinstriping, blue shirt, and maize tie. He sat at his desk in the Oval Office and smiled broadly into the cameras like a horse-player who has just cashed in on the eighth and ninth races after seven long lean ones.

"My fellow Americans, it is with great, and I believe justifiable, pride that I announce to you today the signing of a major peace treaty that will end the years of tension in one of the most troubled areas on our globe—the Middle East. This treaty, which the signatory parties have designated as the Damascus Agreement, contains four major points

"First—the recognition of the State of Israel's right of existence by all the major and neighboring Arab states and the initiation of normal and peaceful diplomatic relations between Israel and those Arab states.

"This will finally guarantee the security of our great and good friends in Israel in the only way it is truly possible—amicable relations with her neighbors. It will also allow her to divert some of her resources from military funds, which has in recent years been a crushing budgetary burden, to ordinary domestic uses.

"Second—an independent Palestinian state is to be created, taking its territory from parts of Israel, Syria, Lebanon, and Jordan. A constitution has been drafted by leading

Palestinian spokesmen, with input from all the signatory countries, and free elections, supervised by the United Nations, will be held within six months. Diplomatic recognition will be immediately granted by the signatory states and the United States. Further, the United States and the signatory states have agreed to provide monetary and technological aid to the new nation in generous proportion. I shall be sending to Congress in the near future a special appropriations request for fifteen billion dollars spread over the next six years.

"This agreement will finally relieve the plight of the Palestinian refugees and meet their just demands for an independent national homeland. We believe that with aid and the good will of nations, the new state of Palestine may rapidly fulfill the long frustrated dreams of her people.

"Third—the city of Jerusalem shall become an independent, free, open city to be governed by the United Nations. This will guarantee free and hospitable travel for followers of three of the world's major faiths to that city, which is sacred and special to each of these religions.

"Fourth—while the United States is not technically a signatory party to the agreement, but only to certain provisions, since much of the delicate and difficult negotiation was done under the guidance of and through the good offices of our esteemed Secretary of State, the oil-producing Arab states, commonly referred to as the OPEC nations, have agreed to make recognition of this contribution by granting "most favored nation" status to the United States and Israel. This status, under the agreement, will allow the United States and Israel to purchase their needed supplies of oil for importation at a price to be fixed at thirty-three and one third percent below the world market price on the date of any given purchase.

"This status will allow the United States, and Israel, to compete far more equitably in the world trade markets, since our lower fuel price will in some measure compensate for our higher labor and production costs. We believe this

238

agreement will once again return the United States to pre-eminence among the industrialized nations, bring back full employment and great prosperity."

The President set aside his text and stared directly into the cameras. He beamed. He knew the canary would digest well.

"I can hardly express the great joy I feel in being able to bring you this magnificent news on this very special day. I wish to offer my heartiest congratulations and the gratitude of the nation to our brilliant and able Secretary of State on a job well done. And it is with this added significance that I can wish you, my fellow Americans, the most joyous of Christmases and we may all look forward to a wonderful new year." His image faded from the screen and network commentators began to fall over one another in slavish praise of the presidential announcement. For about five minutes. Until the next football game came on the air.

The White House Press Secretary was jovial and relaxed in the press room. Questions came quickly and often, as always, but there was a mood of euphoria and, for once, none of the questions was sharp or hostile.

The correspondent was bored. Since he had known in great detail what was coming, he had already written his story and now merely needed to file it. He listened with bemusement to the excited chatter of his fellow journalists. The only sour note he heard was the wry crack of a reporter for a San Francisco paper.

"Trust a typically sensitive and imaginative American politician to schedule an announcement of major impor-tance to Jews and Moslems for Christmas Day."

The correspondent laughed at that. There were ironies in the day, but that was certainly not the major one. It amused him to sit amongst these colleagues who treated him with polite but barely concealed contempt and know that he alone knew the high price of this treaty, this peace. Some of them were already talking about this as a major turning point in twentieth-century history. He laughed and several reporters near him stared at him. When the full story was told years from now, after his death presumably, these arrogant men's words would appear ludicrously naive.

How he wished he could see it. The outline of his book was finished and the writing was coming along nicely. If only one could include that final chapter—what had Donovan's suggestion for the title been?—oh, yes, *The Money War*. What a sensation it would be to tell that now. Of course, one couldn't. The risk was . . . probably . . . no, no—not probably—rather certainly too great to take.

The voices around him babbled on, speculating about how high the stock market would shoot up, how soon full employment would be attained, whether inflation could be contained in what was certain to be a new boom economy. The voices blended together and he no longer heard words, merely noise. He reached into his side jacket pocket and removed a handkerchief. It was covered with dark, rust-colored stains. He unfolded it. Inside was a pair of sunglasses, mirror-tinted, cracked, stained in places with the same rust color that spotted the handkerchief. The correspondent shook his head. Such a strange man.

# ACKNOWLEDGMENTS

In any project that requires as much research and planning as this novel did, there will inevitably be more people to whom appreciation is due than it is possible to acknowledge individually. We hope that no one whose name is not listed here will feel that omission is a sign of ingratitude, but rather will understand that spacial limitations do not allow for complete justice. We are thankful for and do appreciate all help we have received from all sources.

Special aid and cooperation were shown us by the employees of the Federal Reserve Bank of the United States for the St. Louis District, Union Electric, Bell Telephone, Civic Memorial Airport in Alton, Illinois, Radio Stations WAKC, Normal, Illinois and WJBC, Bloomington, Illinois, Ryder Truck Rentals, Holiday Inn, the staff of the Illinois State University Library, Normal, Illinois and SIG Industrial Co., Neuhausen Rhine Falls, Switzerland.

Special thanks go to Walt and Sarah Ptasnick and Pat Doman for hospitality shown us when we were on research trips to the St. Louis area.

Very special appreciation is owed Dave Conklin, senior pilot for Eastern Airlines for time given us and information supplied for the money drop flight sequence.

Our profound gratitude and thanks go to the officers and men of the St. Louis Police Department. Their cooperation was frank, courteous, open. We especially wish to thank Information Officer Al Bartlett and the Senior Command Officers.

We wish to make particularly clear that no character in this novel is intended in any way as a portrait of an actual St. Louis Police Officer, and no scene or action is intended as a reflection on the character or abilities of any St. Louis Police Officer or the Department as a whole.

*Terrence Lore Smith*
*David Alan Doman*
*May, 1975–May, 1976*

# SHARKY'S MACHINE

WILLIAM DIEHL

### 1944

Three American soldiers, killed on a bizarre mission behind German lines, sprawl dead beside an Italian lake. At the bottom of the lake: four million dollars' worth of gold . . .

### 1976

Sharky, ace undercover cop busted to the Vice Squad for being too damn sharp, listens to some outrageous erotic tapes that catapult him into the murderous world of financial manipulation, top-level political intrigue and sexual corruption spawned by that wartime bloodbath.

Soon Sharky and the team he calls his 'machine' are headed for the storm centre of the most lethal conspiracy America has ever known . . .

*Sharky's Machine* sweeps from Nazi-occupied Europe to the deadly opulence of Hong Kong's brothels, from the steel-and-glass fortress that houses one of the world's mightiest financial empires to the depth of the criminal underworld and on to the most shattering climax in modern thriller fiction.

0 7221 2985 8    £1.50

ADVENTURE/THRILLER FICTION

# FIRE STORM

ROBERT L. DUNCAN

The Japanese 'Red Watch' are the new samurai of international left-wing terrorism: ruthless, blood-hungry young fanatics prepared to kill – and be killed – for the sake of their burning ideals of anarchy and revolution.

When the Red Watch attack one of the ships belonging to the company that troubleshooter Charles Corwin works for, he's under instructions to buy the guerrillas off quietly. Or so he thinks. Until he finds that the company has double-crossed him. Suddenly he's accused of a murder he didn't commit, sexually entangled with a beautiful girl bent on revenge, and running for his life from an international big-business conspiracy of horrifying dimensions.

And that's even before the Red Watch strike again. Hitting the huge oil installations at the port of Los Angeles in a Kamikaze mission calculated to set the world on fire. Literally . . .

0 7221 0519 3   £1.10

FICTION

And don't miss Robert L. Duncan's

DRAGONS AT THE GATE

TEMPLE DOGS

Also in Sphere Books

Book
Tokens

**Give them
the pleasure of choosing**

Book Tokens can be bought
and exchanged at most
bookshops.

# A selection of bestsellers from SPHERE